Three different couples—
three very different seasonal celebrations.
But they have one thing in common:
they're all cooking up trouble!
The harder they try to resist a Christmas courtship, the
faster they seem to head toward a mistletoe marriage!

CHRISTMAS
Treats

We've included three holiday recipes in this special
collection, as Harlequin's way of wishing you
a very merry Christmas

And season's greetings from

Penny Jordan

Day Leclaire

Lindsay Armstrong

PENNY JORDAN

New York Times bestselling author Penny Jordan has written more than 100 novels since she was first published in 1981. Internationally acclaimed, she has more than 50 million copies of her books in print, with translations in 26 languages. Born in Preston, England, she now lives with her husband in a beautiful fourteenth-century house in rural Cheshire. Penny continues to make her mark in the world of women's fiction.

"Jordan's record is phenomenal."—*The Bookseller*

"Women everywhere will find pieces of themselves in Jordan's characters."—*Publishers Weekly*

DAY LECLAIRE

American author Day Leclaire is a rising star. Her book, *Who's Holding the Baby?* was the winner of the *Romantic Times* award for best Harlequin Romance. Day has also been nominated for many other honors, including a Career Achievement Award for writing romantic comedy, and for creating the Most Gorgeous Hero! Her fresh, fun, emotional stories have earned her praise from readers and authors on both sides of the Atlantic.

"Day Leclaire writes wonderful romance stories that leave the reader with a smile and a warm heart."—Debbie Macomber

LINDSAY ARMSTRONG

Although born in South Africa, Lindsay Armstrong has lived for many years in Australia, with her New Zealand-born husband and five children, now grown up. Having moved around a lot and tried many occupations, they are now settled on the coast in Queensland. Lindsay's first romance was published in 1981, and she has now written more than forty books. In all her stories she has vividly conveyed the Australian setting and life-style, and she has peopled them with fascinating and emotionally intense characters.

"Lindsay Armstrong orchestrates great interplay between hero and heroine."—*Romantic Times*

CHRISTMAS
Treats

PENNY JORDAN
DAY LECLAIRE
LINDSAY ARMSTRONG

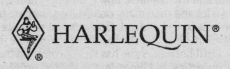

HARLEQUIN®

TORONTO • NEW YORK • LONDON
AMSTERDAM • PARIS • SYDNEY • HAMBURG
STOCKHOLM • ATHENS • TOKYO • MILAN • MADRID
PRAGUE • WARSAW • BUDAPEST • AUCKLAND

ISBN 0-373-83371-7

CHRISTMAS TREATS

Copyright © 1998 by Harlequin Books S.A.

The publisher acknowledges the copyright holders of the individual works as follows:

FIGGY PUDDING Copyright © 1997 by Penny Jordan

A MAN FOR ALL SEASONINGS Copyright © 1997 by Day Totten Smith

ALL THE TRIMMINGS Copyright © 1997 by Gillian Crowe

This edition published by arrangement with Harlequin Books S.A.

Printed in U.S.A.

CONTENTS

FIGGY PUDDING

Penny Jordan

Dear Reader,

To me, there is no more magical and traditional time of the year than Christmas—perhaps because, as a Sagittarian, a small part of me has always retained my childhood wonder in the specialness of Christmas: its bright shining warmth in the darkest time of the year, a time to celebrate the triumph of hope over adversity and of love over pain.

These are all emotions that are strongly expressed in this short story, with its heroine who is my favorite type of woman—strong, gutsy, determined to stand true to what she believes in and yet at the same time endearingly vulnerable. My hero in this story also embodies, I believe, the very best of traditional male values, "magicked" by a special sprinkling of that extra ingredient that makes a man *the man!*

Since my own home is old and traditional, a cozy cottage nestling in the countryside, it is the traditional things in life in which I tend to take most pleasure. The Figgy Pudding recipe on which this story is based is as traditional as Christmas itself—although my heroine, Heaven, has added her own special *extra* ingredients! In bygone centuries every member of the household would have taken a turn in stirring the rich fruity pudding mixture, uniting them all in its preparation. I hope that in reading this story you will share this special sense of Christmas as it unites us all in spirit and in love, no matter how much we may be divided in other ways.

Penny Jordan

PENNY JORDAN'S FIGGY PUDDING

(Makes two large puddings)

This is a traditional English recipe.

110g/1 cup chopped almonds
110g/³/₄ cup chopped figs
450g/3 cups raisins
225g/¹/₂ lb currants
225g/1¹/₂ cups sultanas
110g/³/₄ cup mixed peel
110g/³/₄ cup chopped glacé cherries
110g/³/₄ cup plain flour
2 tsp ground mixed spice
2 tsp ground cinnamon
1 tsp ground nutmeg
225g/1¹/₄ cups firmly packed brown sugar

225g/¹/₂ lb shredded suet or vegetarian suet
225g/4 cups fresh white breadcrumbs
225g/¹/₂ lb grated apple (about 2 medium apples)
1 large grated carrot
Juice and grated zest of 2 large lemons
2 tbsp molasses
4 large eggs, beaten
225 mL/1 cup Guinness or milk
4 tbsp rum or brandy

Combine the chopped almonds, figs, raisins, currants, sultanas, mixed peel and cherries. Add the sifted flour, spices, sugar, suet and breadcrumbs and mix thoroughly. Add the grated apple, carrot, lemon juice and zest and molasses and mix again. Stir in the beaten eggs, followed by the Guinness (or milk) and rum (or brandy). Spoon into two buttered casseroles (2 ¹/₂ pint capacity each) and cover with a double layer of waxed paper. Leave overnight to mature. Cover the casseroles with a double layer of foil, pleated down the center and tied securely with string. Steam for 8 hours, checking regularly to see that the pan hasn't boiled dry. Remove and set aside to cool. Cover with fresh waxed paper and foil, then store somewhere cool and dark, ideally for 4 to 6 weeks. When ready to be eaten, steam the puddings for an additional 3 hours before turning out into serving dishes. Warm a ladleful of brandy, set alight and pour over the puddings.

PROLOGUE

'Mmm…well, I suppose he's all right,' Christabel announced as she looked critically at her less than one-week-old cousin as he lay contentedly in his mother's arms.

In four weeks' time it would be Christmas and Heaven and Jon would be going up to the Scottish Borders to spend the Christmas season in their home there, but right now they were still in London where Jon was enjoying showing off his newborn son to his sister, her two daughters and their doting stepfather.

'What I *don't* understand, though,' young Christabel continued seriously, 'is *why* you've called him Figgy.'

Over the dark downy head of Charles Christopher Hugo, nicknamed 'Figgy', Heaven grinned at her husband.

'Well, it's a long story,' she began 'and let's just say that figgy pudding is a very special Christmas treat and "Figgy" here—'

'I think you'd better stop there,' Jon warned her ruefully, but his niece, picking up on the very interesting adult messages passing between her uncle and her new aunt, decided she wanted to hear more.

She had just reached the age where adult secrets,

adult conversations were beginning to make her curious.

'Tell me,' she demanded imperiously. 'I *like* stories…'

Heaven laughed into Jon's eyes. In his mother's arms Figgy continued to sleep despite his father's attempts to make him wake up.

'Well,' Heaven began importantly, 'just as figgy pudding is a pudding with a difference, so too is this a story with a difference, and it all began like this…'

CHAPTER ONE

'YOU'RE really going to go ahead and do it, then—*take* the job, despite…*everything?*'

Looking up from the pudding mixture she was stirring, Heaven Matthews grimaced at her best friend and nodded emphatically, confirming, 'Yep, Janet, I'm *really* going to go ahead and do it.'

'Well, I can understand why,' Janet Viners acknowledged. 'Anyone would, and after the way Harold Lewis treated you—after what he did to you—he certainly deserves to receive a taste of his own medicine!'

'Oh, he will,' Heaven said fervently, the stern look on her small, heart-shaped, vivacious face not really masking the pain Janet knew she was still suffering from the traumatic events which had so catastrophically affected her life. 'He quite definitely will,' Heaven averred, adding quietly, 'Revenge, so they say, is a dish best eaten cold. We shall see. In this instance the proof of the pudding will quite definitely be in the eating—his eating, not mine. He always was a greedy pig, and not just for food.'

The smile which had brought into prominence the pretty dimples on either side of her generously curved mouth had faded again and as she watched her Janet reflected sadly on how much the last months had sapped her friend's normal *joie de vivre* and how rarely she had heard the infectious happy laughter that had always been such a wonderful part of Heaven's personality. The fact that she was the kind of person—*woman*—who was loved and valued by all those who knew her only made what had happened to her seem all the more unbelievable, all the more unpalatable—if Janet was to follow Heaven's humorous habit of using food metaphors and clichés in a tongue-in-cheek fashion to illustrate her conversation and to underline and emphasise her passionate love of good food.

Not that you would ever know it from her enviably slender figure, Janet acknowledged wistfully as she contrasted her own much plumper frame with Heaven's delicate sylph-like figure.

Even when they had been at school together Heaven had been determined that one day when she was grown up she was going to be famous for her cooking.

Some months ago when Janet had reminded her of that childhood dream Heaven had given her a bitter smile and said painfully, 'Well, I was nearly right, wasn't I? Only instead of becoming famous what I've become is *infamous*…infamous, notorious and unemployable…' And her strikingly beautiful dark blue eyes had filled with painful tears which, true to character, she had dashed impatiently away. The last thing that Heaven was was the kind of person who wallowed in self-pity, despite the fact that right now she had every reason to feel sorry for herself, Janet acknowledged, reflecting on the events of the last eighteen months.

A promising career totally ruined, her life turned upside down by the media interest the whole affair had created, and as if that wasn't bad enough poor Heaven had also had to live with the fact that no matter how often she protested her innocence there would always be those who were going to disbelieve her.

'Who's going to want to employ *me* as a private cook now?' she had demanded bitterly some months earlier, when Janet had called round to find her friend busily trying to compose an ad for the classified pages of certain magazines.

'Even if my *name* wasn't recognised then sooner or later my face would be. I doubt there's a hostess in London who hasn't heard about the cook who tried to steal her employer's husband.'

'Are you really sure you're doing the right thing?' Janet tried now to counsel her friend gently. Perhaps because Heaven was so petite, too naively inclined to believe the best of everyone and she herself was so much taller, so much more wary, despite the fact that they were both the same age—twenty-three—Janet had always been inclined to be protective of Heaven.

They were standing in the kitchen of a pretty Georgian town house in Chelsea. Heaven's father had inherited it from his great-aunt who had in turn inherited it from her parents, so there was a good deal

of family history attached to it. Too much for the
house to be sold, and since there was no way that
Heaven's parents were going to uproot themselves
from the comfortable Shropshire village to which they
had retired her father had suggested that Heaven
should live there rent-free until she could restore some
sort of order to her shattered life.

'After all,' Janet continued, 'you're starting to build
up quite a nice little business for yourself and—'

'Selling puddings through the classified ads and at
country fairs,' Heaven interrupted her in self-con-
tempt. 'Janet, I'm a trained cordon bleu cook. Making home puddings…'

'It's a living,' Janet reminded her gently.

'It's an *existence,*' Heaven corrected her. 'If Dad
wasn't allowing me to live here rent-free…'

'Have you thought of looking for work abroad,
somewhere…?'

'Where no one knows me?' Heaven supplied
for her, shaking her head. 'Perhaps I should, but I
haven't. *This* is where I want to work, Janet. Here…
London…my home…the place where I *should* be able
to work, where I *would* be able to work if it wasn't
for that rat Harold.' Angry tears filled her eyes. Determinedly she blinked them away. 'I was just beginning
to make a proper name for myself. I *would* have made
a name for myself if that creep hadn't gone and destroyed everything I'd worked for and…'

Heaven put the mixing bowl to one side and gave

Janet a woeful look as she pushed her fingers into her already tousled dark curly hair.

'I'm sorry to be such a wet lettuce, Jan, but you know...'

'Yes, I know,' Janet agreed sympathetically.

'I just wish that Lloyd was earning enough for *us* to be able to employ you,' she added with a grin. 'He keeps complaining that he's getting sick of microwave cooking. I think, of course, he's using that as an excuse for getting me to go to his parents' for Christmas. Not that I mind. I get on really well with his family. Have *you* made any plans yet? After all, it's only next week...'

Heaven shook her head.

'Mum and Dad have offered to pay for me to fly out to Adelaide with them. They're off to spend Christmas and all of January with Hugh.'

Hugh, as Janet knew, was Heaven's married brother who lived in Australia with his wife and children.

'Why don't you go with them?' Janet urged her. 'Who knows? You might even find you like it so much that you decide to stay there.'

'Shipped off to Australia, like the family black sheep?' Heaven countered painfully. 'No...that isn't what I want, Jan, even if the days are long gone when someone in disgrace was sent away from home. I feel that if I run away now people will think I'm running because I'm guilty, because I was to blame for the break-up of Harold's marriage, because all those things he said…' She stopped and gulped in a steadying breath.

'I was not having an affair with him,' she told her friend fiercely. 'And even if he hadn't been the completely loathsome and reptilian thing that he is I *still* wouldn't have been tempted…not with another woman's man. That just isn't me, Jan… Mind you, some of it was my own fault,' Heaven admitted with what Janet privately considered was far too much generosity; she had her own opinion of Harold Lewis and it wasn't good—creep was far too kind a description of him, so far as she was concerned.

'I should have guessed what lay ahead when he pretended he didn't have enough cash to reimburse my travelling expenses when I went for the initial interview, but I was still green then and the job seemed such a good one. Residential, with summers with the family in Provence and the opportunity not just to cook for him and his wife and the two girls and do all their private entertaining, but also to cook for his business lunches and dinners as well…'

'I do understand how you must feel,' Janet consoled her. Heaven gave her a small smile.

'I'm sorry, I don't mean to rant and rave at you. It's just the unfairness of it all that gets to me still. He deliberately used me, set me up, *lied* about me by pretending that we were having an affair to Louisa, his wife, so that *she* would walk out on him, so that he could then divorce her and get away with keeping the house and hardly give her any proper settlement. *She's* the one I should be feeling sorry for…'

'Have you seen anything of her since?'

'Since I so publicly got the sack and my name and my supposed role in their divorce, not to mention his bed, got so much media attention?' Her pretty mouth twisted. 'No, not really. Oh, she did try to make amends; she apologised for the fact that I'd been dragged into things and she told me that she recognised with hindsight just how cleverly she'd been tricked into believing I *was* having an affair with her husband.

'Apparently he'd been dropping hints about "us" virtually even before I'd gone to work for them and had, in fact, insisted on employing me above her head; and he'd then gone on to deliberately arouse her suspicions and undermine her by letting her think that he was attracted to me.

'You'd never think he was virtually a millionaire, would you—not after the way he's been so mean with Louisa?'

'Sometimes the richer a man is the meaner he is,' Janet pointed out.

Heaven grimaced in distaste. 'If you ask me Louisa is well rid of him, and I suspect from what she hinted at that she has started to feel the same way since their divorce. She did say that she had tried to tell her friends that Harold had lied about me and about my role in the break-up of their marriage, but let's face it, no one is really going to believe her.'

As she saw the way Heaven's expressive eyes filled with sad tears, Janet felt her own eyes fill up in sympathy.

It wasn't just her job she had lost, Heaven reflected inwardly as she determinedly pulled the pudding mixture towards her and started to finish a fresh batch of puddings. The money she was earning from the small classified ad she had taken, offering 'Mrs Tiggywinkle's traditional figgy puddings by post', had brought her a much needed small income even if she was beginning to get sick of the sight and smell of her very saleable and mouthwatering puddings.

No, it wasn't just the job she had lost. Not even Janet knew about those delicate, fragile private hopes that had begun to grow after Louisa's brother had casually asked if she would like to take up a spare ticket he had for one of London's newest plays.

Jon Huntingdon, Louisa's brother, was an eminent financial consultant. Tall, dark-haired and suavely handsome. He had set Heaven's all too vulnerable heart beating just that little bit too fast the very first time she had been introduced to him by Louisa, several days after she had first taken up her new job. Unmarried and in his thirties, Jon Huntingdon was almost too swooningly male, too darkly handsome, with a heart-melting sense of humour betrayed by the twitch of his mouth as he gently teased Louisa's daughters, his nieces.

Heaven had prepared for their date in a fever of excitement; she had even cajoled an early birthday cheque out of her father in order to splash out on a new outfit. A Nicole Farhi dress and jacket, the dress a silver shimmer of thick matt jersey cut in a halter-neck style and supported simply by a thin silver collar.

She hadn't really needed to see the appreciative male gleam of sensual pleasure in Jon's eyes the evening he had picked her up to know that the dress looked good on her, but she had enjoyed seeing it there none the less.

After the play had ended he had taken her out for supper at a small French restaurant she had never even heard of, but when she had ordered and tested the French onion soup she had known that his taste in good food was as impeccable as his taste in well-made clothes.

After dinner he had driven her home, parking his silver-grey Jaguar discreetly in the drive of the Lewises' house and then switching off the lights.

Heaven, who had been awaiting this moment ever since he had made his casual invitation to take up his spare ticket, hadn't been sure if it was exhilarated excitement that was churning her stomach so nervously, or pure fear.

She had been out with good-looking men before, but she had never previously met anyone who'd affected her as quickly and overwhelmingly as Jon had done, and she had known even then, with that heart-deep instinct that all women possessed, that *he* was a man who could be something very special in her life…perhaps even be *the* man.

And then he had kissed her.

Briefly, decorously, unthreateningly…the first time!

After the world had stopped turning around her, after she had stopped feeling like one of those small figures in a child's toy snow storm, he had kissed her again.

And she had responded, totally unable to stop herself from letting her emotions show.

'I'm not used to this,' she told him shakily and plaintively when he eventually released her.

'Do you think I am?' he countered rawly before drawing her back into his arms. 'You smell of cinnamon and honey, and everything good that was ever created,' he told her huskily as he breathed in the scent of her with heart-rocking sensuality, 'and I could eat you—every tiny last bit of you.'

He didn't do that, but he certainly kissed her again, deeply, lingeringly, like someone relishing every mouthful of a delicious meal, parting her lips and tasting her mouth as though he were enjoying some sweet, juicy-fleshed fruit.

There wasn't anything else. He didn't make any attempt to touch her more intimately, and, despite the way he had aroused her, irrationally she was glad…glad of the fact that already he liked her enough, cared enough not to want to rush things, to gobble down the pleasure she knew instinctively the two of them could share.

'I have to go away tomorrow,' he whispered to her as he held her face and kissed her gently on the mouth a final time. 'Business in Europe. But once I get back I'll be in touch...'

But of course he hadn't been, she mused now. *She* hadn't been there for him to get in touch with. The storm had broken two days later, and she had gone to ground, with Louisa accusing her of having an affair with her husband and him having admitted it. Refusing to listen to Heaven's denials, Louisa had left her husband, taking their two children with her.

Although he had strenuously denied it Heaven had had a pretty shrewd suspicion that it had been Harold himself who had leaked the story to the press. The initial story had quickly turned into a nationally covered media debate on Heaven's supposed treachery in having an affair with Harold—a debate which had left her reputation in tatters and her self-esteem so low that she had been more than grateful to accept her parents' suggestion that she leave London and stay with them until the fuss had died down.

She had no idea just when Jon had returned from abroad but she had not been surprised when he had not got in touch with her, and, even though on a chance meeting in the street Louisa had apologised for not listening to her when she had originally tried to explain that Harold had been lying about the supposed relationship between them, no mention had been made of her brother and Heaven had not felt able to ask about him.

Over the last few months she had had the scales so well and truly ripped from her eyes where the male sex was concerned that she had few illusions left, and besides, right now she had far more important and immediate concerns to deal with.

Things like making sure that Harold Lewis paid for what he had done to her. Oh, not in money. No, something far more satisfactory… Something that would damage *his* reputation, *his* self-esteem, *his* standing in the eyes of the world, just as he had damaged hers.

'The proof of the pudding,' she reminded herself, muttering the words under her breath so that Janet shook her head slightly.

'I'm sorry.' She apologised again to her friend. 'It just makes me so mad, that's all. He gets away scot-free with what he's done and I'm left not just without a job but also without a reputation. What sane woman is going to employ me now when the whole world knows the risk she'd be taking? When everyone thinks I'm a cook from hell, the kind of employee who is more interested in making the man of the house than in making the dinner? Well, it's my turn now and fate has given me an opportunity to well and truly butter his bread for him. It's almost too good to be true…'

'Mmm…' Janet agreed doubtfully. 'Tell me in more detail what you plan to do.'

'Just let me get these puddings on,' Heaven said.

'I've got an order for fifty to fill and get sent off by tomorrow.'

'Fifty…' Janet groaned, watching as Heaven moved deftly around the kitchen.

'Right,' Heaven announced when she had finished. 'As you know I've been advertising in the classified ads as Mrs Tiggywinkle, selling figgy puddings, but saying that I can cater for private functions as well. Well, I got a phone call three days ago from someone who introduced herself to me as Tiffany Simons. She said that she was desperate to find someone to cook a special celebration pre-Christmas dinner for her fiancé who was returning from the States with a couple of important business clients who he wanted her to entertain along with some close friends and business associates. None of the agencies could supply her with a cook so close to Christmas and at such short notice—so she was literally ringing round every number she could find in the hope of getting a cook from somewhere.

'To add to her problems, as well as dropping this dinner on her it transpired that her fiancé had also left her with full responsibility for getting the work completed on a house he was having renovated for them both.

'We arranged to meet to have lunch and discuss everything. And that was when I knew…'

'When you knew what?' Janet questioned her.

'When I knew that she—Tiffany—must be engaged to Harold… She was wearing Louisa's old engagement ring,' Heaven told her simply. 'I recognised it straight away. Louisa threw it back at him the day she walked out. Later she told me that she'd never liked it and had always considered it too vulgar. It was a huge brilliant-cut solitaire. Very flashy.'

'Louisa's engagement ring and now this Tiffany's wearing it?' Janet gasped.

'Yes, but I doubt that she knows it was Louisa's. She's very young—I feel quite sorry for her. She's obviously terrified of doing anything to annoy or up-set Harold and it's typical of him that he should have sprung this dinner thing on her—and typical as well that the fee he's willing to pay the cook he's told her to hire is nowhere near enough—not for the type of meal he's ordered her to organise.

'She's panicking like mad that the guest bedrooms aren't going to be finished on time. She confided to me that Harold's refusing to pay the interim payments he promised the designers and suppliers unless they get everything ready ahead of schedule. I don't know who these people are he's so keen to impress but they must be pretty important to him...'

'More important than his new fiancée,' Janet suggested shrewdly.

'Oh, *much* more important,' Heaven agreed. 'I could tell from the way she was talking about him that she hardly knows him at all. There's some kind of distant business connection between Harold and her father, apparently, and that's how they met.

'Anyway, once she told me what was happening, I

realised that if I took on the job of cooking this dinner
for her it would give me the ideal opportunity to get
my own back on Harold. He always did have a sweet
tooth,' she added inconsequentially, a wide, cat-like
smile curling her mouth as her eyes danced.

'Heaven...' Janet said uncertainly. 'You're not
thinking of doing anything *too* over the top, are you?'

She was suddenly remembering the scrapes her
friend's irrepressible sense of humour had got them
into as schoolgirls and remembering too just how
much reason Heaven had to want to punish Harold
for the damage he had done to her.

'That depends,' Heaven answered soberly, but Janet
could see that her eyes were still gleaming with
amusement.

'On what?' she asked warily.

'On what one considers to be too over the top,'
Heaven replied promptly, but unsatisfactorily—at
least so far as Janet was concerned.

Janet tried again.

'What I meant was, you're not planning on doing
something illegal...?'

'Illegal?' Heaven's eyebrows rose. 'Certainly not,'
she denied emphatically. 'What *I* have in mind is designed quite simply to hurt Harold's pride, to damage
it just as he damaged mine. Poisoning him and ending
up in prison for it—if that's what that anxious mother-
hen look in your eyes means you're worrying about—
is the *last* thing I'd want to do, although...' A
thoughtful far-away look in her eyes made Janet's

anxiety increase. 'There are certain hallucinogenic mushrooms which I could—'

'No, no, you mustn't do anything like that,' Janet intervened quickly.

'No, I mustn't,' Heaven agreed, adding with mock primness, 'It would be quite unethical.

'No, what *I've* got in mind will teach Harold a much more salutary lesson than anything like that...'

'If he doesn't recognise you and throw you out,' Janet warned her.

'He won't recognise me,' Heaven assured her positively. 'For a start Tiffany only knows me by my new professional name of Mrs Tiggywinkle and she obviously hadn't a clue who I was when we met. She was at great pains and rather embarrassed to ask me if I would mind keeping a very low profile—apparently Harold wants his guests to think that *she* cooked their meal.

'He would, of course, since he's obviously being too mean to take them out to an expensive restaurant or pay the fees charged by the kind of frantically up-market caterers he'd enjoy boasting about hiring. He's decided it will give him more kudos to have his victims—sorry, his *guests*—believe that poor Tiffany has cooked their dinner, so I'm to lie low in the kitchen whilst she serves the meal.

'Knowing Harold as I do, I very much doubt he'll come anywhere near the kitchen—for a start he'd think he was demeaning himself and no doubt he'll try his best to get away with delaying paying me for as long as he can—I've asked to be paid cash on the night. No, Harold won't see me to recognise me.

'It won't matter, not so long as they eat their dinner—and they will.

'Revenge is sweet, so they say, and, as I've already told you, Harold has an extremely sweet tooth, so he shall have an extremely generous portion of revenge,' Heaven told her, giving Janet a kind smile when she saw that she was still looking anxious.

'I wish you weren't doing this,' Janet told her.

'I don't,' Heaven responded cheerfully. 'You can't imagine how much better I've felt these last few days knowing that at last Harold is going to get his comeuppance, or rather his just deserts! Do you know, I think I'm going to enjoy Christmas this year after all?' she added conversationally as the timer on her oven pinged and she went to attend to the puddings she had made earlier.

'All alone here?' Janet asked her doubtfully. 'I wish you would change your mind and come with us to Lloyd's parents'. I know they'd make you welcome.'

'No…I want to be alone… Next year is going to be *my* year and I want to be ready for it.'

'Those puddings smell marvellous,' Janet told her.

'Mmm…they do, don't they?' Heaven agreed with a small smile that made Janet's maternal heart beat even more anxiously.

CHAPTER TWO

'I HOPE you don't intend to allow him to get away with this.'

Louisa gave her brother an unhappy look as he put down the letter he had just been reading. She had received it from her ex-husband's solicitor only that morning and had telephoned Jon straight away to tell him what had happened.

'I don't want to. If he does insist on refusing to pay the girls' school fees they'll have to change school and Belle is already having a few problems following the divorce…but I don't know what I can do to stop him.'

'My God, when I think…' Jon began, and then stopped when he saw the unhappiness on his sister's face.

'I know what you're thinking, Jon,' she told him. 'I admit I have only myself to blame for the fact that Harold has made such a fool of me financially. If I hadn't walked out on him and insisted on an immediate divorce and if I hadn't been so desperate to let my pride rule my head I could have obtained a much better financial settlement from him.'

'The fact that he's depriving not just you but also his own children of the financial comfort you've all every reason to expect has nothing to do with your pride and everything to do with his greed,' Jon told her gently. 'I just wish I hadn't been working abroad and away so much when the divorce was going through. I'd give a lot to know just how he managed to convince the divorce judge that he didn't have the assets to give you what you were fully entitled to.'

'He manipulated me,' Louisa admitted grimly, 'by pretending that he was having an affair with Heaven. He tricked me into walking out on him. I should have stayed where I was. After all, it wasn't as though she was his first affair—not that they were having an affair, of course,' Louisa corrected herself hastily. '*She* was just as much a victim of his machinations as I was myself—even more of one, really, when I think what that poor girl suffered...'

'Have you seen her at all since?' Jon asked her casually, turning slightly to one side as he did so so that Louisa couldn't see his face.

'Only once,' she told him. 'Not unnaturally I don't think she really wanted anything to do with me but we literally bumped into one another in the street. At least I was able to apologise to her. Even now, you know, I've still got friends who quite plainly don't believe that she wasn't involved with Harold even though I've told them that it was all a mistake. Harold treated her almost as vindictively as he did me and I've wondered since if he did actually make a play for her and got turned down. That would explain the obvious pleasure he took in deliberately blackening her character…

'Jon, what am I going to do about this?' she asked her brother, returning to the original subject of her urgent phone call to him. 'If I accept this reduced level of maintenance and Harold's refusal to pay the girls' school fees, I just don't know what we're going to do.'

'I'm more than happy to cover the cost of the girls' education. After all, they are my nieces,' Jon told her firmly.

'Your *nieces,* yes, but one day you could well have children of your own, a wife of your own who might not look too kindly on you having to virtually support my children as well as your own.'

'Any woman who felt like that would never be my wife,' Jon told her truthfully, and Louisa hugged him.

'It says in this letter that the reason Harold is seeking to reduce his payments to you is the fact that he is planning to remarry and he and his new wife intend to have their own family…'

'Has he said anything to you about wanting to cut my maintenance payments?'

'No,' Jon told her, shaking his head. 'I have managed to convince him that I'm more interested in maintaining the friendship I've struck up with him than I am in whatever problems *you* might be facing, but as yet he still hasn't opened up to me as much as I'd hoped about how and where he's managed to conceal so much of his wealth. But I am still trying.

'He's invited me to a pre-Christmas dinner he's giving at the end of the week. He faxed me from New York to tell me about it. He's over there on business at the moment.'

'A pre-Christmas dinner?' Louisa questioned.

'Mmm...his new fiancée is arranging everything, apparently, and it's being held at the house he's been having renovated in Knightsbridge.'

'The house he bought with the profit he made on selling our house,' Louisa said fiercely.

'Yes,' Jon agreed grimly.

'That poor girl. I hope that, unlike me, she finds out what he's really like before they get married,' Louisa told her brother bitterly. 'Oh, Jon, what am I going to do?' she asked him plaintively. 'The parents have offered to help but they've already done more than enough, and so has Rory...'

Jon noticed the way his sister's skin changed colour slightly as she mentioned the old family friend who had done so much to support her both emotionally and practically since the break-up of her marriage. It was no secret to Jon that Rory Stevens loved his sister and Jon suspected that she was now beginning to return his feelings.

'Do you think Harold believes that you want his friendship and that you approve of what he's done?'

'He seems to,' Jon told her, 'but I must admit I had hoped by now to at least have some proof for you that he deliberately concealed the major part of his assets in order to pay you far less money than he should.'

'We already know that he did,' Louisa pointed out fiercely.

'We *know* it, yes, but we can't prove it,' Jon reminded her patiently.

Later, as he set off back to his own apartment—a set of traditional and old-fashioned rooms in Fulham which he owned along with a home in the Scottish Borders where he spent as much time as he could, and another large apartment in a renovated Belgian château which he used whenever he had business in Brussels—he was still thinking over his sister's financial problems.

It infuriated him that a man like Harold could use the law as he had done and he had to admit it was getting harder and harder to keep his real feelings about the man to himself whenever they were together.

He had no idea why Harold should be so keen to pursue their 'friendship', unless he felt that in doing so he was somehow or other getting one up on Louisa.

Well, Jon was damned if he was going to let Harold get away with cheating Louisa and more importantly their children out of their financial due a second time, especially when Harold could well afford to be far more generous with them than he had been. At the very least Louisa should have had the family home— would have had it if she hadn't been manipulated into walking out on him.

When he opened the door of his car Jon froze momentarily as a girl walked into his line of vision, thick dark curls bouncing softly on her shoulders as she hurried down the street wrapped up against the raw December wind in a coat which looked three or four sizes too big for her slender frame.

And then she turned her head and he saw her face. When was he going to stop doing this? When was he going to stop reacting blindly and ridiculously every single time he saw a woman who bore the slightest resemblance to Heaven?

Heaven. What a name…what a *woman*. He had been attracted to her the moment he saw her, attracted to her, enchanted by her, instinctively aware of the importance of not rushing her…not panicking her by coming on too strong too soon. He could still remember the way her lips had quivered so softly and tellingly under his, still see the way her eyes had opened and widened as she'd looked back at him, unable to conceal what she was feeling.

God knew where she was now, but wherever it was it was obvious that she wanted nothing to do with him. The man whose sister had been responsible for the destruction of her reputation, the man whose brother-in-law had dragged her name through the tabloids, publicly labelling her as his mistress—publicly and completely untruthfully. Jon had known *that* immediately and instinctively but by then it was too late. She had gone and no one had seemed able to tell him where.

Her parents, when he had approached them, had

been polite but pointedly determined. Their daughter had told them quite categorically that she wished to have no contact whatsoever with anyone connected with Harold—no matter who—and they'd been afraid that they could not tell him where she was or how to get in touch with her.

At one point he had actually thought of employing a private detective to find her for him but just in time he had come to his senses and recognised what an appalling intrusion of her privacy *that* would be—but that hadn't stopped him searching every even half-familiar face glimpsed in the street just in case…

Did she still have that irrepressible sense of humour, that impish smile? He hoped so. Had she got over the trauma of what had been inflicted on her? Did she ever think of him? Somehow he doubted it.

Grimly he climbed into his car and started the engine. It was pointless now cursing the fate that had led to him being out of the country when the whole nasty affair of Harold's manipulation of Louisa's vulnerable emotions had blown up, but of course that didn't stop him from doing so.

They had only shared one date…a few chaste kisses…and two far more memorable ones that had been anything but chaste…but that had been enough to have him comparing every woman he had been tempted to date since with Heaven and finding them wanting—and finding himself even more wanting for being so emotionally hung up on a woman he had known so briefly and so tenuously.

*   *   *

Thank goodness for that, Heaven puffed, heaving a sigh of relief that the last of the large batch of puddings she had received orders for had been passed over to the post-office clerk for onward despatch.

It was a fine if cold winter's day, the sky a pale smudgy blue over the steel-grey waters of the Thames as she walked back towards the house. As always the river fascinated her, causing her to stop and look at it.

Had her ancestors, her great-grandparents, who had lived in the house before her, been equally fascinated by the ebb and flow of its tides, the magnificence of it?

The weather forecasters had predicted a heavy frost for the next few days and idly Heaven wondered what it must have been like to be alive when the Thames had actually frozen over. She remembered reading that it had once frozen so deeply and so hard that a fair had actually been held on it complete with burning braziers to warm the skaters and provide the excited crowds who had flocked to enjoy the novel experience of actually walking on the solid surface of the river with tasty snacks. What exactly would they have served? she wondered dreamily.

Eel pie, whelks, whitebait, hot bread and buns, confectionery of all descriptions. She had a much treasured recipe book from the eighteenth century which had been a twenty first-birthday present from her parents and just reading the lists of some of the ingredients brought forcibly to her a mental image of the merchant vessels which had once thronged the Thames, bringing home their cargoes of exotic and expensive spices and sugar.

This afternoon she was due to meet with Tiffany Simons to go through the menu she had produced for her. With the dinner scheduled for the end of the week that wouldn't leave her very much time to do her shopping and she still had the kitchen to inspect and to check on.

Her thoughts firmly back in the present, she turned her back on the river and hurried home.

'Figgy pudding… What exactly is that?' Tiffany enquired, her forehead crinkling in a small frown.

She and Heaven were seated opposite one another at the table of the kitchen of the house she had explained to Heaven she was going to share with Harold once they were married.

'My parents are rather old-fashioned,' she had told Heaven with a small sigh. 'They wouldn't be happy about me moving in with anyone before we were married. Mummy didn't have me until she was forty. They had given up all hope of having a family when she became pregnant with me and so…' She had paused, but Heaven could guess just how precious she was to her parents and just how protective of her they were—but not apparently protective enough—not if they thought that Harold would make her a good husband.

'Figgy pudding,' she started to explain now in response to Tiffany's question, 'it is an old-fashioned, traditional and very rich pudding mixture. Men love it,' she added when she saw the doubt shadowing Tiffany's pretty soft brown eyes.

Instantly the other girl's expression cleared.

'Oh, do they? Well, in that case that's all right, then,' she declared ingenuously, adding, 'I'm afraid I'm not much of a cook. That's why Harold said I had to find someone to prepare this dinner.

'Apparently the people he's bringing back from New York are some very important new business contacts he's made. Harold owns his own software company,' she told Heaven importantly. 'These Americans want him to sell the business to them. Harold's brilliantly clever, though,' she went on, giving Heaven a proud smile, 'because if he does sell the company to them he's still going to keep a new software program he's been working on, although he won't be able to sell it in America, not at first; but Harold says there's a huge market for it in the Middle East and Taiwan.'

Heaven had to shade her eyes with her lashes to conceal her true thoughts as she listened to Tiffany's artless prattle. Knowing Harold as she did, Heaven suspected that the kind of deal he was hoping to pull off with the Americans would not only benefit him financially but would also involve him practising the same sort of deliberate manipulation he had used with his wife, to gain yet another financial victory just as underhandedly as he had Louisa's divorce settlement.

As she listened to Tiffany enthusing about Harold's supposed cleverness Heaven couldn't help but feel sorry for her. The girl really had no idea what Harold was about at all. Heaven, though, could well understand why Harold wanted to marry her. Her naivety would appeal to him almost as much as her undoubted prettiness.

'So you're quite happy with the menu we've decided on,' Heaven checked with Tiffany as she started to gather up the notes she had made, giving the kitchen a thorough professional visual inspection whilst she did so. She hadn't missed the nervous half-whispered telephone conversation Tiffany had had with the kitchen designer halfway through their own conversation, from which it had been obvious that the designers still had to be paid, not just for their own work but for the units and equipment as well. Well, that didn't really surprise Heaven, not knowing Harold as she did.

'Oh, yes, it's perfect,' Tiffany was assuring her now happily. 'especially the pudding. Harold adores sweet things.'

The menu Heaven had suggested was simple enough: a thick home-made winter soup followed by a fish course, a sorbet to clear the palate and then the main course, for which she had suggested a rich casserole of red meat with accompanying vegetables, filling but not so filling that Harold's guests wouldn't have room for her pièce de résistance—the figgy pudding on which as Mrs Tiggywinkle she had based her small new mail-order business.

'And you'll have everything ready here in the kitchen for me to carry through to the dining room?' Tiffany checked anxiously.

'Yes, everything will be ready,' Heaven told her, adding reassuringly, 'Don't worry, no one will ever know that you haven't cooked everything yourself.'

Quickly she stifled her own uncomfortable qualm at the thought of Harold blaming Tiffany for her wrongdoing—but of course Harold would know that Tiffany hadn't actually done the cooking. He simply didn't want to admit as much to his guests—he would, of course, try to discover who had cooked the meal but she would be safely hidden behind the anonymity of Mrs Tiggywinkle.

Tiffany blushed.

'I wouldn't normally be so…so deceitful, but Harold says it's vitally important that we make a good impression on these Americans and apparently there's nothing they like more than home-cooked food.'

'You said there'd be eight of you to cater for,' Heaven reminded her.

'Yes, that's right. Harold and me, the three businessmen who are coming back with him, his accountant and his wife and a friend of Harold's who's a business consultant.'

A business consultant and his accountant. Heaven might not know the former but she certainly knew Harold's accountant and his wife, an avaricious, acid-

tongued woman whom Heaven had overheard on
more than one occasion running Louisa and the children down to Harold. She had even tried to tell
Heaven herself how to do her job and had, Heaven
knew, been instrumental in spreading the completely
untrue rumours about her supposed affair with Harold.
She was a thoroughly unpleasant woman whom
Heaven had no qualms about allowing to share
Harold's fate. Harold obviously wasn't taking any
chance on letting the big fish he had landed slip away
from him, Heaven decided sardonically as she gave
Tiffany a small smile and stood up. She found herself
liking Tiffany. Somehow she would have to find some
way of ensuring that Tiffany herself didn't eat any of
the figgy pudding.

Not that there was anything wrong with her figgy
pudding—far from it—at least not when she made it
without the addition of the certain extra ingredients
she planned to put in the one for this dinner party!

CHAPTER THREE

NERVOUSLY Heaven smoothed her hands down over the crisp white apron she was wearing over the simple short-sleeved black dress she had picked up at a bargain price because of its small size.

It wasn't any worries about her cooking that were making her feel so jittery, her stomach muscles clenching every time she heard a noise on the other side of the very firmly closed kitchen door. Despite her stalwart assurances to Janet that she knew exactly what she was doing and that her plan was completely fireproof, it was still a fact, as Janet had pithily pointed out to her, that all it would take for her to be run out of the house in very short order would be for Harold to walk into the kitchen and see her.

'Harold won't walk into the kitchen,' Heaven had asserted. 'Harold is the kind of man who boasts about barely knowing how to find the fridge door—he wouldn't dream of visiting any kitchen but most especially not his own.'

But despite the fact that Tiffany had already inadvertently confirmed that view by explaining apologetically to Heaven that although Harold would actually be paying her fee for the evening Tiffany doubted that Heaven would actually see him she still felt nervous.

'This business deal is so very, very important to him, that I doubt he's even going to have time for me. He rang me three times yesterday just to check on how things were going. He says it's vitally important that he gets the Americans to sign the purchase contract for his business before the end of the year. Something to do with some patent he's taking out on this new software he's designed,' she had told Heaven vaguely.

Tiffany had in fact told Heaven rather a lot over the past couple of days, and Heaven couldn't help feeling sorry for her, quickly coming to realise how lonely and bereft of any real friends the other girl was and how, in many ways, she was much more naive and unworldly than one would have expected a young woman of twenty-one to be. Heaven herself at only two years older felt so much more mature.

The sound of the kitchen door being opened had her tensing and automatically turning her back towards it, but it was only Tiffany who came in.

'Harold has just rung from the airport,' she announced breathlessly. 'They will be here within the hour; he wants dinner to be served promptly at eight-thirty…'

'That will be fine,' Heaven assured her.

'It's eight o'clock now,' Tiffany jittered. 'I'd better go just in case anyone arrives early. Thank goodness all the bedrooms are finished at least…'

Heaven gave her an understanding smile. It would be interesting to say the least to discover Harold's reaction when he found out that the elegant *en suite* bathrooms which complemented every bedroom might *look* fully fitted and finished, with their impressive reproduction Victorian sanitary ware, but that look at them was all one could do because the owner of the firm who had supplied and installed them had been so incensed by Harold's refusal to pay him a single penny until after *he* had inspected everything that none of it had actually been connected up to the mains.

'You do know he's got guests staying, don't you?' Heaven had pointed out to the contractor who had poured out his grievances to her over a cup of coffee and a generous bowl of her delicious soup in the kitchen.

'Yup...they'll have to make do with the downstairs cloakroom; *that's* all in order,' he had told Heaven with a wink.

Perhaps *she* ought to have warned Tiffany about what the contractor had told her, Heaven acknowledged, but why add to the poor girl's problems?

A sharp thrill of fear-cum-excitement drilled through her as she heard the front doorbell ring.

Well it was too late for second thoughts now. Everything was ready. *Everything*...everything, just as she had planned.

She swallowed hard as she looked across at the hob where the pudding was still steaming gently.

Figgy pudding...

She glanced down at the handwritten recipe she had used, all of the ingredients delicious and sinfully rich, especially the almonds, cherries and mixed peel.

That was the basic recipe but because these puddings were going to be extra-special she had added three extra ingredients, ingredients which never in a lifetime would she actually commit to paper, and those ingredients were a generous pouring of liquid paraffin, an equally generous measure of cascara and, just to make sure no one could detect the suspicious taste of such strong laxatives, a large glass of very rich, full-bodied sherry.

A naughty smile curled her mouth as she contemplated the results of her inventive additions to the pudding.

Harold and his guests were going to find it a serious inconvenience that the contractor had omitted to connect all the plumbing. Oh, she hadn't added enough cascara or liquid paraffin to cause any real health risk, but there was certainly enough to cause anyone who had a generous portion of the pudding to be seriously embarrassed by its effect on their digestive system...very seriously embarrassed.

Harold would of course be furious and guess that *her* cooking was to blame but by then *she* would be long gone and anyway he would only know her as Mrs Tiggywinkle, whom he would never connect with her, Heaven! It would be well worth the fact that she had used some of her carefully hoarded income from the recent sales of her puddings in order to buy the ingredients for tonight's meal to know that Harold was finally having a taste of his own medicine.

She had to admit, though, that she had been extremely relieved when Tiffany had informed her that *she* would probably pass on the pudding.

'Harold doesn't want me to put on weight,' she had confided to Heaven. 'And this pudding sounds sinfully rich to me.'

Smiling reassuringly at Tiffany, Jon introduced himself. She reminded him of a timid fawn, all gauche movements and nervous eyes. There was no way she was any match for Harold and Jon couldn't help feeling sorry for her. In many ways she was almost more child than woman and so far as he was concerned, despite her obvious prettiness, not really his type at all.

'Am I the first to arrive?' he asked her as she dutifully took his coat.

'Yes. Harold should be here soon. The Concorde flight from New York was delayed by the weather,' she told him nervously.

'Mm...they've had heavy snowfalls in New York, and according to the forecasters, we're due for some soon. If they're right, we could have the first white Christmas for a long time.

'Harold's bringing some business colleagues back with him, I understand...'

'Yes...he is... They're the people he's hoping will

buy the company. Oh...' Tiffany blushed. 'I'm not supposed to talk to anyone about business things, but since you're his friend I'm sure it will be all right...'

'Of course it will,' Jon soothed her.

So Harold was intending to sell the business—a business which, according to the accounts he had produced at the time of the divorce, was heavily in debt and not making any money. It would be interesting to see just who would want to buy that kind of company—and why, he decided as Tiffany bustled away with his coat and then returned to ask him what he would like to drink as she invited him into the drawing room.

As he walked past the half-open dining-room door, Jon paused and then stiffened as he recognised the dining-room set which his parents had given Louisa.

Harold had refused to return the furniture to Louisa, claiming that it had been a joint gift to both of them and that she had forfeited her right to it when she had walked out of the house.

In desperation Louisa had actually gone to the expense of hiring a furniture van and going round to the house to reclaim her furniture when she knew that Harold would be away, but Harold had of course had all the locks changed and even though Louisa had eventually managed to gain admittance by persistently hammering on the door until the housekeeper had let her in, as she had told Jon afterwards, the furniture was no longer there and in its place had been a cheap ugly fifties table and chairs.

Through the kitchen door, which Tiffany had left open, Heaven could hear people arriving. She went to close the door and then stiffened as she just caught the sound of a warm deep male voice that sent a sharp volley of shocked emotion surging through her veins.

She must be hearing things, imagining things, her memory distorted by time and thrown into confusion by the fact that she was in some ways resurrecting the past.

It was inconceivable that the male voice she had so tantalisingly heard could possibly belong to Jon. He was, after all, Louisa's brother. Even so, she found that she was lingering by the still half-open door, her ears stretched, her stomach churning even more than it had already been doing.

It was just her own memory playing tricks on her, she told herself as she made herself walk away from the door, but beneath the buoyant determination which had made her so keen to see Harold get his just deserts, in both senses of the word, she was warily aware of a sudden sharp sense of nostalgia and loss, a foolish yearning for what might have been.

Stop daydreaming, she warned herself sternly. Remember why you're here.

Whilst Tiffany hovered uncertainly, obviously wondering why Jon was staring so intently into the dining room, the front doorbell pealed again.

The new arrivals were Harold's accountant and his wife, neither of whom Jon particularly liked although he always made a point of concealing the fact from them.

'Harold not here yet?' Jeremy Parton asked, rubbing his hands together as he went to stand in front of the fake log fir in the equally fake Regency fireplace.

'No, but he should arrive soon. I hope he does... He told me he wanted dinner served at eight-thirty and—' Tiffany fluttered.

'Who have you got in to do the catering?' Freda Parton interrupted Tiffany sharply. 'Some of the caterers are dreadfully over-priced and as for the *food* they serve...'

'Er—'

'Whoever it is, it won't be a certain deliciously sexy and mouthwateringly tasty little brown-haired nymphet of a cook,' Jeremy interrupted with what Jon privately considered to be totally inappropriate licentiousness.

What was it about the man's face that made him want to punch it—extremely hard? Jon wondered angrily. He certainly wasn't normally so easily provoked and physical expressions of anger just weren't his style at all.

'Jeremy,' Freda Parton warned her husband curtly.

'Oh, come on; it's no secret that old Harold had the hots for the girl, and who could blame him? I wouldn't have minded a little taste of what she had on offer myself.'

'Jeremy!' Freda Parton warned a second time even

more curtly, turning to explain to Tiffany, who looked both embarrassed and confused.

'Jeremy is just joking, my dear. He's referring to the young woman who was the cause of the break-up of Harold's first marriage. A most tenacious type of girl. She deliberately set out to trap Harold into having an affair with her...'

'He—he's never mentioned anything about that to me,' Tiffany stammered.

Freda Parton gave her husband another dire look and soothed, 'No, well, of course not. Although *Harold* had nothing to blame himself with, men being what they are, I'm sure quite naturally the whole subject is something he wants to put behind him, but then, of course, if Louisa had had her wits about her she would have realised what was going on sooner and— How is Louisa, Jon?' she asked Jon pointedly.

'She's fine,' Jon responded calmly. 'She and the children are spending Christmas with our parents.'

Still smiling, he turned to Tiffany and explained, 'Louisa, Harold's first wife, is my sister...'

Tiffany blushed hotly. 'Oh, I—I didn't know...' she started to stammer, but Jeremy ignored her discomfiture to challenge Jon.

'*Some* people might find it rather odd that you should have chosen to remain so close to Harold; after all, the divorce *was* pretty aggressive.'

'I'm a businessman,' Jon returned with a casual shrug. 'I don't allow my emotions to get in the way

of my judgement. Harold has put some very good
business my way...'

'And you're hoping for some more? Well, you
could be in luck; I expect the reason he's asked you
here tonight is to make sure this sale he's planning
for the business is all sound and watertight.'

For some reason the smile Jeremy was giving him
made the tiny hairs at the back of Jon's neck lift ata-
vistically but he had too much self-control to allow
his feelings to show as he responded calmly, 'Well, I
would certainly be pleased to advise Harold on whatever aspect of the proposed sale he chose to consult
me on. I take it he's planning to sell off the company
in its entirety...?'

'Lock, stock and barrel,' Jeremy agreed cheerfully,
breaking off as they saw the lights of the taxi that was
drawing up outside the house through the window.

'Oh here's Harold now,' Tiffany announced in relief. 'I'd better go and let them in.'

Twenty past eight. Heaven had heard Harold arriving,
recognising the familiar loud aggressiveness of his
voice; another ten minutes and Tiffany should arrive
to collect the soup plates and the soup.

Whilst Tiffany was serving it to their guests,
Heaven intended to finish off the second course—a
fish dish of which she was particularly proud.

'They loved the soup.'

'Good, then they'll love the fish even more,'

Heaven promised as she and Tiffany exchanged con-
spiratorial smiles some time later.

'Freda Parton keeps on asking who the caterers
are... I fibbed a little bit and said I'd just had some
help from a friend... Well, it isn't entirely untrue... I
do feel that we have become friends these last few
days.'

It amazed Heaven just how protective she was beginning to feel towards the other girl. How could she
have become involved with Harold? Louisa, too, must
have loved him once, but Heaven had sensed that Jon
had never really liked his brother-in-law. Jon—what
on earth was she doing thinking about Jon when she
ought to be concentrating on what she was doing, not
daydreaming over a man who was past history?

Only the sorbet and the main course to go before
they had their pudding. Heaven could feel the nervous
tension beginning to build up inside her stomach.

To keep herself occupied and out of habit she
started to clear away the used crockery and cutlery
Tiffany had returned to the kitchen.

She had just placed the last plate in the dishwasher
when Tiffany came back for the next course.

Jon frowned as he listened to the conversation taking
place between Harold and the Americans. On the face
of it, there was no reason why he should feel so instinctively suspicious that Harold was concealing
something, but then he knew Harold.

Tiffany, looking increasingly hot and bothered, was bringing in the pudding course.

Jon shook his head when she offered him some. He had never had much of a sweet tooth, unlike Harold who was greedily indicating that Tiffany give him an extra-generous helping of the pudding.

'Wow, that was some meal,' one of the Americans commented enthusiastically to Tiffany, gallantly insisting on helping her to remove the dirty dessert plates and carrying them out to the kitchen for her whilst Harold reminded Tiffany that he wanted the men's biscuits and cheese to be served in his study.

In the kitchen Heaven heaved a small sigh of relief. Only the cheese and biscuits and the coffee and petits fours left now and then she could leave, before the disastrous explosive effects of her special additions to her pudding recipe began to make themselves felt!

She stiffened as Tiffany came into the kitchen accompanied by a man. Fortunately it wasn't Harold.

'Hey now, *who* is this?' the American demanded.

'I've been helping Tiffany with the meal,' Heaven told him quickly before Tiffany herself could say anything.

'Say, isn't that the pudding we've just had?' the American demanded, his attention distracted away from Heaven towards the segment of pudding still left.

'You ought to try it,' he told Heaven. 'It's something else...' And then, to Heaven's horror, he reached for the bowl and, picking up a spoon, dug it into the pudding and then held out a spoonful towards her.

As she stepped back from him Heaven mentally prayed for help. There was *no* way, no way in this world she could eat that pudding but the American was very large, very determined and, she suspected, slightly drunk.

'Oh, dear,' she suddenly heard Tiffany cry anxiously. 'Mr Rosenbaum...Eddie... Please, we must get back.'

'Where the hell is Tiffany with that cheese?' Harold demanded angrily. 'Jon, be a good chap and see what's doing, will you?'

As he threw the command across the table at him, Jon had to grit his teeth to prevent himself from throwing it right back at him, but for Louisa's sake he couldn't afford to betray any of the antagonism he felt towards his ex-brother-in-law and so instead of telling him in no uncertain terms to go himself he stood up and pushed his chair back, heading for the kitchen, but not before he caught sight of the smirking smile that Jeremy Parton was giving him.

Grimly Jon pushed open the kitchen door and then came to an abrupt halt at the scene in front of him and the woman dominating it.

As Heaven looked up and saw him all the colour drained from her face. For a minute she thought she was actually going to faint. What on earth was Jon doing here?

'Oh, Jon, is everything all right?' she heard Tiffany twittering. 'Is Harold—?'

'Harold sent me to check up on what had happened to the cheese and biscuits,' Jon informed her, causing Tiffany to start scurrying frantically round the kitchen.

The American, sensing an ally, looked at him and announced, 'Say, she won't eat the pudding…'

'I can't. I'm allergic to nuts and it's got almonds in it,' Heaven garbled. Oh, God, what on earth was she going to do *now?* There was no doubt whatsoever that Jon had recognised her, and no doubt either, she suspected from the thoughtful way he looked first at the pudding and then at her, that her refusal to touch it was arousing his suspicions.

As he reached past the American, for a moment Heaven thought he was actually going to force-feed the pudding to her. The thought made her feel quite giddily sick but to her relief he simply relieved the American of the bowl and spoon and told him firmly, 'Harold wants to talk with you…'

Her relief was short-lived, though, because instead of following the American as he scuttled quickly towards the door Jon simply stood watching her.

'Heaven?' Tiffany started to panic, looking uncertainly from Heaven to the trolley.

'Harold is waiting, Tiffany,' Jon reminded her, and whilst Heaven watched in helpless dismay Tiffany gave her an apologetic look and then followed the American through the kitchen door, letting it swing closed after her, leaving Heaven completely alone with Jon, enclosing her in the now far too small space of the kitchen with a man whose presence had once filled her with excitement but which now filled her with apprehensive dread.

In a voice that warned her he wasn't prepared to play any games, Jon demanded. 'What have you done to the pudding, Heaven?'

'The pudding?' Heaven hedged instinctively. 'Nothing...why should you think I might have done anything?'

Oh, God, if only she had had time to get away before he had come into the kitchen. Desperately she tried to glance at the clock to check the time without him seeing what she was doing. How long before the extras she had added to the pudding started to make their existence felt?

That depended very much on the individual person's digestive system, but at a guess...Heaven's heart started to beat nervously fast. She *had* to get away before the consequences of her retaliatory actions came to light. As she had good cause to remember, Harold had a nasty temper; she had never actually seen him physically abuse another person but she had sensed that he had the temperament to do so if pushed too hard—he was that kind of man; you could see it in his face...in his eyes...especially now that he was approaching forty and the slightly florid good looks she had seen in photographs of him as a younger man could no longer mask his real personality.

'*You* were refusing to eat it,' Jon reminded her dryly.

'I told you…I'm allergic to nuts,' Heaven fibbed, hoping he would put the betraying tide of colour warming her throat and face down to nervousness and not guilt.

'You weren't allergic to them the night I took you out,' he told her softly. 'I distinctly remember that the pudding you ordered and ate on that occasion contained them.'

Heaven's eyes widened. He could remember *that? She* could certainly remember what they had ordered to eat, but then she could remember every single small detail of that evening, and the hopes it had brought her.

'Er, how much pudding did you have?' Heaven asked him warily.

'None,' Jon returned promptly. 'I wasn't very hungry and I don't particularly enjoy sticky puddings.'

'None.' Heaven couldn't manage to keep the relief out of her voice. 'You really mean that?' she checked. 'You didn't have *any* at all?'

'I didn't have any at all,' Jon confirmed, grimly adding. 'So, I'll ask you once again. What have you done to the pudding, Heaven?'

Heaven hung her head. She knew he wouldn't let her escape until he had got the truth out of her.

'I put cascara in it…cascara and liquid paraffin,' she told him, dry-mouthed.

For a moment Jon simply looked at her in silence and then, when he managed to find his voice, he demanded, 'You did *what?*'

'I put cascara and liquid paraffin in it,' Heaven repeated. Then, taking a deep breath, she added challengingly, 'And you may as well know that although it had nothing to do with me Harold hasn't paid the contractors so they haven't connected the plumbing upstairs and—'

'Oh my God…'

Heaven could hear someone walking towards the kitchen and immediately she started to panic.

'Jon…' She froze as she recognised the voice of Harold's accountant, knowing that he would recognise her.

Jon obviously realised it too from the look he was giving her, but, to her amazement, as the other man pushed open the door Jon reached for her, wrapping his arms tightly around her and pushing her face against his shoulder so that it was virtually concealed by his body and her own hair.

'What—?' she began indignantly, but Jon quickly silenced her, bending his head to cover her open mouth with his own and then proceeding to kiss her slowly and thoroughly— *very* slowly and very thoroughly, Heaven acknowledged as her head began to reel with shock and her body literally melted against him with the devastating immediacy of hot chocolate sauce poured over ice cream.

'What the hell is going on in here?' Heaven tensed as she heard Harold's voice and realised that he must have come looking for the other two men. 'And who in hell's name is this?' he demanded, no doubt referring to her, Heaven recognised as she trembled in Jon's arms, instinctively cuddling closer to him as she allowed him to tuck her face back into the protective and concealing curve of his shoulder.

'My girlfriend, Harold. I rang her and asked her to come and pick me up; I don't want to risk losing my licence...' she heard Jon responding smoothly.

'Your girlfriend, great,' she heard Harold snarling. 'Well right now you've got more important things to do than practising for the sexual olympics on my kitchen table, and—'

Harold stopped speaking abruptly, his hands going to his stomach.

'Oh my God...God...' Heaven heard him cry as he clutched his body in desperation and started to run towards the doorway.

In the hallway total pandemonium seemed to have broken out, with everyone—but more especially the men—groaning and clutching their stomachs as they complained of the griping pains gripping them.

'Come on,' Heaven heard Jon saying as he started to release her, but instead of freeing her completely as she had expected he kept hold of her arm, hustling her towards the back door. When she balked at this treatment and tried to break free he shook her arm and warned her, 'If I were you I'd leave whilst I still could. Once Harold—'

'That was exactly what I was trying to do before *you* interfered,' Heaven informed him indignantly, 'and if you'd just let go of my arm...'

'Tiffany, where the hell's the cook?' Heaven heard Harold screaming above the cacophony of noise in the hall.

Grimly Jon smiled at her.

'I want to talk to you,' he told her, 'so make up your mind, Heaven. Either you stay here and face Harold or you leave now with me.'

He wanted to talk to her. What about? Heaven wondered nervously as, without waiting for her decision he pulled open the back door and half pushed and half dragged her through it.

'Tiffany...' Harold was still bellowing.

Heaven winced.

'It won't be just Harold you'll have to answer to,' he warned her as he marshalled her towards his car and, still holding her captive with one hand, unlocked the driver's side with the other. 'Those Americans aren't going to feel too happy with you. You do carry professional insurance against being sued, I take it...?'

Heaven's expression, mercilessly revealed by the interior light of the car, gave away her shocked consternation.

'Ah, I see—you *don't* carry that kind of insurance.'

Jon answered his own question. 'Rather foolish of you, I would have thought.

'Get in, Heaven,' he commanded, holding open the passenger door for her.

Reluctantly Heaven did as he instructed. After all, what alternative did she have? She had planned to be well away from the scene of her retribution before the effects of her innovative recipe additions took hold and she shuddered inwardly as she contemplated what might happen to her if Jon chose to turn her over to Harold now.

She still couldn't believe that he was actually working for Harold, but what other reason did he have for being one of Harold's dinner guests?

Which meant that Jon could not possibly be the man she had once thought him to be. And that discovery should surely have meant that her heart could have no possible reason to bounce crazily against her ribs just because she was seated next to him and just because she could still smell the warm, sexy male scent of him, still feel the sensual erotic pressure of his mouth against her own.

'Why did you kiss me?'

As soon as she had blurted out the words, Heaven regretted them. She had quite obviously been spending too much time with Tiffany, she derided herself, because that was the kind of naive, gauche remark more acceptable from someone like Tiffany than from a streetwise life-wary woman like herself.

'Why do you think?' Jon challenged her back as he

set the car in motion and activated the central locking system. 'If I hadn't, Jeremy Parton could well have recognised you and Harold most certainly would…'

'Why should *you* want to protect me from them?' Heaven demanded aggressively. 'After all, you're Harold's business advisor and you're just as—'

Abruptly she stopped, biting down hard on her bottom lip.

'Go on, I'm just as what? Just as dishonest—is that what you were about to say?'

Heaven lifted her head.

'Well, it's the truth, isn't it?' she challenged him. 'Harold is dishonest, morally if not legally, and I'm surprised that you, knowing what he did to Louisa, how he cheated your own sister, should have anything to do with him. Tiffany told me all about the American deal,' she added assertively. 'I know that although Harold is planning to sell the business to them, he's also planning to withhold from them the patent for the new software he's originated.'

'What?'

They had just joined the mainstream of traffic on the road outside the house but, instead of accelerating, much to her shock, Jon actually braked.

'Run that by me again, will you?' he demanded as he took his foot off the brake and the powerful Jaguar started to glide forward again.

'You heard me the first time,' Heaven told him bravely. '*I* know that Harold is planning to sell the business to the Americans letting them believe that

they've got sole rights to all the software but in reality
he's come up with a new program that supersedes the
ones they're buying and he's planning to fix it so that
the patent takes effect from immediately after the sale.
Tiffany told me.'

'He might be planning to do that but the Americans
aren't stupid. They're putting certain clauses into the
contract which prevent Harold from rewriting *any* of
the programs they're buying or selling any new program within a prescribed area...'

'But that area doesn't include the Far and Middle
East, at least not according to Tiffany and that's where
Harold Lewis intends to sell it,' Heaven pronounced
triumphantly.

As he quickly assimilated the information Heaven
had just given him, Jon recognised that she had unwittingly given him the very tool he needed to pressure Harold into giving his sister a much fairer financial settlement; he also recognised that Harold had
perhaps guessed all along just why he, Jon had publicly appeared to take his side.

No mention of Harold's plans to withhold the new
patent, or even a whisper of their existence, had been
included in the information Jon had been given about
the deal, which would have meant that had he even
the smallest part in helping to draw up any kind of
sale contract his reputation would have been destroyed in much the same way and just as effectively
as Heaven's had been once the Americans discovered
how Harold had cheated them.

But also, and right now far more importantly, once Harold realised who his cook for the evening had been, and if he discovered just how much Tiffany had told her about his business affairs, Heaven herself could be in grave danger.

Quickly he came to a decision. As luck had it he had called at the petrol station on his way out and filled the car up, so he had enough fuel to get most of the way to the Borders before having to stop...

Now that she was over the initial shock of having him walk into Harold's kitchen, and her fear that Harold might discover her presence there, Heaven was growing tense, increasingly aware of the danger of her remaining in Jon's presence for a single second longer than necessary. That kiss he had given her in the kitchen had proved more than well enough to her, thank you very much, just how femininely vulnerable she still was to him.

'You can drop me here,' she announced determinedly, reaching for the door handle as Jon stopped for the lights and then frowning as she discovered that the door was locked.

'Jon,' she started to protest as the lights changed and the car moved away, her initial irritation giving way to disbelief as Jon swiftly changed lanes and she saw the road sign up ahead of them indicating the distance to the M25.

'Jon,' she protested this time more forcefully. 'I want to get out...'

'You can't,' he told her promptly, adding dryly, 'Not in the middle of the traffic.'

'Then pull over to the side,' Heaven insisted irritably. 'I—'

But instead of obeying her Jon changed gear and the car picked up speed as the traffic opened up ahead of them and they started to leave the congested heart of the city behind them.

'I want to go home,' Heaven told him angrily, 'and I—'

'Really…? It won't take long for Harold to track you down, you know,' he warned her grimly.

'Harold doesn't know it was *me*,' Heaven shot back. 'Tiffany found me in the classified ads: ''Mrs Tiggywinkle's figgy puddings''…'

'Maybe she did, Mrs Tiggywinkle, but I noticed she referred to you as Heaven and it isn't the most common of Christian names, is it?'

Heaven bit her lip. She had forgotten about that, deeming it unimportant in the heat of her determination to pay Harold back for the damage he had inflicted on her.

'No doubt you gave Tiffany your telephone number, where she could reach you even if you didn't give her your actual address,' Jon continued remorsefully. 'As I said, it won't take a man like Harold long to track you down, Heaven, and when he does…'

'He won't be in any state to think about tracking me down for at least twenty-four hours.' Heaven retaliated spiritedly, but in truth Jon's warning had made her stomach muscles clench in nervous fear.

'I'll bet you haven't even given a thought to the outcome of your little piece of culinary engineering, have you?' Jon demanded scornfully. 'Harold isn't the kind of man to grin and bear it, Heaven; you should know that already,' Jon reminded her.

'In view of the fact that you have such a low opinion of him I'm surprised that you're working for him,' Heaven shot back, determined not to let him get the better of her, too engrossed in her argument with him to realise that they were now on the M25 and heading north, the large Jaguar picking up speed under Jon's expert touch.

Jon was aware of it, though. Hopefully he could keep her occupied...talking...arguing...until they were far enough away from the city for her to accept what he was planning to do...

The car's speedometer crept upwards and he thanked the fates that the road was relatively quiet and empty of other traffic.

'The reason I'm *working* for him, as you put it, has nothing to do with any fellow feeling for him,' he told her grimly. 'Far from it.'

'No? You're just earning your living, is that it?' Heaven demanded scathingly. 'What about your sister? What about Louisa?'

'It's *because* of Louisa that I'm doing this,' Jon returned curtly. 'Heaven...'

'I don't want to hear any more. In fact, what I want

right now is for you to stop this car and let me out…
At once… Immediately!'

'Heaven, listen to me…'

'No. I don't want to hear another word,' Heaven
told him fiercely, lifting her hands to cover her ears.

'Heaven, this is important dammit,' Jon told her
grittily. 'I've spent months trying to get Harold's confidence so that I can find out how he managed to
conceal his financial assets and persuade the divorce
judge that he couldn't afford to give Louisa and the
girls a decent settlement. *Months*…' he stressed as
Heaven slowly uncovered her ears and looked uncertainly at him.

'Why should I believe you?' she asked him flatly.
'You might just be trying… You're Harold's business
advisor; Tiffany told me so.'

'I *was*, you mean,' Jon told her grimly. 'Once
Harold realises that you were the one who fed them
that appalling concoction—and he will find out—and
he realises that I concealed the fact—and you—from
him, I doubt he's going to have a lot of faith left in
my loyalty, don't you?'

'So why did you do it?' Heaven asked him slowly.
'Why did you protect me from him?'

'I'm going to have to claim the fifth amendment on
that one,' Jon told her forthrightly. 'At least for the
time being.

'Heaven, you said something earlier about some
new software Harold is planning—'

He broke off as Heaven's eyes suddenly widened

as she caught sight of the motorway sign ahead of them. She turned furiously towards him, demanding, 'That said "North". North where? Where are you taking me, Jon?'

'To the Borders,' he told her quietly.

'The Borders? What Borders?'

'The Scottish Borders. I've got a property up there and I—'

'You can't be serious,' Heaven interrupted him again. 'I just don't believe this. Pull over and stop this car immediately, otherwise I'll...'

'You'll what?' he asked her dryly. 'You can't get out. I've activated the central locking system.'

'I don't believe this... This is...this is kidnap,' Heaven told him wildly. 'This is...'

'The safest precautionary measure I could come up with,' Jon intervened grimly.

Precautionary measure... Heaven's throat had suddenly gone very tight. Her lips felt dry. She touched them nervously with the tip of her tongue and then wished she hadn't as she saw a sudden certain male gleam flicker in Jon's eyes.

'Yes...precautionary measure,' Jon repeated, 'for both of us. Once Harold discovers that you and Tiffany talked about far more than recipes—and, again, he will—you are going to be in very grave danger. *Anyone* who has the kind of information you have is going to be in danger, at least until after he's got those contracts safely signed.

'I've no doubt that Harold thought he was being

extremely clever, planning to get the contracts signed before Christmas and then having the new patent come into effect with the new year, but what he hadn't bargained for was you and the fact that your figgy pudding will mean that the Americans aren't going to be in any fit state to sign *anything* for several days. It's probably too late now for him to stop that patent going through and until he gets those contracts signed he's going to be in a very, very vulnerable position. The first thing he's going to want to do is to make sure *you* can't use the information that Tiffany has given you.'

Despite the heat inside the car Heaven had started to shiver.

'I know that you are deliberately trying to frighten me,' she warned him. 'You're just exaggerating…Harold wouldn't—

Abruptly she stopped.

'Harold *would*,' he told her softly, and as she looked across at him Heaven knew that the knowledge that what he had just said was true showed in her eyes, and with it her growing apprehension.

'Perhaps what I've done is rather dramatic,' Jon acknowledged, 'but it seemed the best solution for both of us, given the short time I had in which to make a decision.

'Harold's possibly forgotten that I own property in the north and being there will provide *you* with a safe haven and give *me* the chance to use the information you've given me to force Harold into giving Louisa the money she's entitled to…'

'Aren't you afraid he might try to retaliate? To…?' She stopped and shivered again.

'To what?' Jon asked her softly. 'To ruin my reputation the way he did yours? Well, I suspect he was intending to do that anyway, but thanks to you that won't now be possible. I *know* that taking you off like this must seem a trifle dramatic, but believe me, Heaven, I am *not* in any way overdramatising when I say that you will be much safer somewhere where Harold can't find you.

'Is there any problem about you being away from home?' he asked her carefully. 'A friend…a lover who might—?'

Quickly Heaven shook her head.

'No. There's nothing…no one like that. My parents are in Australia with my brother and—'

'You were going to be on your own over Christmas?'

Heaven's vulnerable heart gave a small treacherous leap at that past tense 'were'.

'I…I was invited to join a friend and her family but…' She took a deep breath. 'What about you? Was Louisa…? Were you…?'

'Louisa is taking the children to stay with our parents,' Jon told her, shaking his head as he added, 'I did have the option of joining a party of friends who are going skiing but a telephone call is all it will take to notify them that I shan't be going.'

'But surely all this will be over by Christmas?' Heaven pointed out, suddenly panicking at the thought of having to spend several days with him.

'Perhaps, but not necessarily, and you have to remember that it's going to be quite some time before Harold forgets the part *you've* played in ruining his plans to cheat the Americans. Although, with a bit of luck, he should have rather more on his mind than pursuing you.'

'Quite some time... How...how long?' Heaven asked him dry-mouthed.

'It's hard to say,' Jon told her seriously, but inwardly he was feeling far more light-hearted than he looked and than the situation warranted because, if anything, he had played down rather than over-emphasised the danger they were both potentially in.

'What about Tiffany?' Heaven queried, suddenly remembering the other girl. 'Won't Harold...?'

'Harold won't be able to do anything to harm or hurt Tiffany. I happen to know that her mummy and daddy are very protective of their precious little chick and none too happy about losing her to Harold.'

'But I can't stay with you...I...I don't have any clothes...'

For the first time since their journey had started Heaven saw Jon smile.

'No! What a pity,' he drawled teasingly. 'That means...'

The look he gave her made Heaven turn crimson from the tips of her ears all the way down to her toes.

Toes which curled up in her shoes with something that was very, very different from the self-conscious embarrassment burning her skin.

'Well, I'm sure we can remedy that. We're not far from the nearest town.'

'But I can't go out and buy a new wardrobe just like that,' Heaven protested. 'For a start I haven't—'

She stopped, closing her lips over the admission she had been about to make. But Jon had obviously guessed what she had been about to say as he finished her sentence for her by saying, 'You can't afford it. Did Harold pay you for the dinner?'

'No.' Heaven shook her head.

'Well, then as his business advisor I strongly suggest that you write to him in strong terms demanding payment, and in the meantime I will be more than happy to make you a small loan against that payment.'

Heaven was not so easily gulled.

'He won't pay me,' she told Jon positively.

Jon was equally positive back.

'Oh, yes, he will,' he told her softly. 'I shall make sure of that! I've spent months searching for a way to force him to make a decent settlement on Louisa and the girls but he's kept on claiming that the business is losing money even though it's been perfectly obvious that he's lying, that that sleazy accountant he employs has no doubt siphoned off all the assets to some dubious off-shore tax haven. He's even threatening to stop paying the girls' school fees.'

'What makes a person like that? So mean and...and

horrid,' Heaven wondered out loud, adding, 'He's even kept the dining-room furniture that Louisa was given by your parents.'

'Yes, I know,' Jon agreed, his mouth growing grim. 'And thank you for reminding me of that, Heaven. That's something else to put on the list.'

'What will you do?' Heaven asked him uncertainly. 'You're not going to let him cheat the Americans, are you? I mean…'

'Oh—' Jon shook his head '—the *most* he can expect from that is I keep quiet about the potential fraud he was planning to enact; the price for my keeping quiet will be Louisa's settlement and the sale of the company with *all* its software.

'We have very strong fraud laws in this country and so do the Americans. If what he was planning to do becomes public it won't just be his reputation he'll lose and somehow I can't see Harold settling happily into prison life.'

'Prison…' Heaven's eyes widened.

'*Now* you see why I'm so concerned for your safety,' Jon pointed out to her.

'What about yours?' Heaven challenged.

'Oh, I shall be safe enough,' he assured her.

'The Borders,' Heaven murmured sleepily, smothering a yawn as the events of the evening began to catch up on her. 'That sounds so romantic…'

Her eyes were already starting to close so she didn't see the look that Jon gave her, but she did hear the softly sensual note in his voice as he told her, 'Then we shall have to see if we can't make them live up to your image, shan't we?'

CHAPTER FOUR

SLEEPILY Heaven struggled to sit up. Outside the car everything was pitch-black.

'Where are we?' she asked Jon groggily.

'Nearly home,' he told her.

Nearly home. Heaven could feel her heart start to beat just a little bit too fast.

'Look, it's starting to snow,' he told her urgently as small fine white flakes started to drift across the car windscreen.

'Snow!' Heaven peered out of the window as excitedly as a small child, whilst Jon watched her and laughed.

'You look about sixteen,' he teased her, 'with your hair all ruffled and your make-up...'

When his glance drifted to her mouth Heaven discovered that she was colouring up again as she remembered how she'd come to be denuded of her lipstick. Self-consciously she touched her lips with her fingertips and then tensed as Jon told her softly, 'Don't do that...'

'Why not?' Heaven whispered back to him, her eyes soft and huge in her small face as she turned uncertainly to look at him.

The road was empty; it was three o'clock in the

morning. Swiftly Jon brought the car to a halt and reached for her, gathering her into his arms as he whispered against her mouth, 'Because it makes me want to kiss you.'

Heaven tried to protest as logic and common sense dictated that she must, but happily the very fact that Jon's mouth was already covering hers, caressing hers, meant that her protest never got further than an 'Oh'—and for some reason instead of recognising this for what it was Jon seemed to think that the soft parting of her lips wasn't so much representative of a womanly objection to his kiss-stealing actions but in fact a very feminine invitation to make the kiss even more intimate and devastating to Heaven's vulnerable self-control.

Mmm… Outside the car it might be cold enough to be snowing but *inside* the temperature was quite definitely rising. The sexual chemistry and magnetism between them were positively making the air sizzle, Heaven recognised dreamily as she snuggled closer to Jon, her hands automatically sliding beneath his jacket to hold him closer.

The deep sound of satisfaction he made in response to her own softer but very recognisable sensual response made Heaven feel as though she was melting, slowly, deliciously, languorously, and as inevitably as a dish of ice cream in the warm summer sun. Jon made her feel all soft and sensual and deliciously, dangerously wanton, as though…as though…

'What happened to you? We should have done this

months ago,' she heard Jon groaning as he drew her even closer.

Months ago he had left on a flight to goodness knew where after one brief date, whilst she…

The shudder of remembered revulsion and shame which had begun to tense her body turned to a shivery muscle reaction of a very different type as Jon's hand slid upwards over her body towards her breast. She could hear her own heartbeat picking up speed, feel her whole body starting to react to the urgent pressure of his hand against her breast.

'Oh-h-h…' Heaven couldn't stop herself from giving a small betraying gasp of pleasure as Jon's thumb circled her nipple, causing it to harden and beg unashamedly and very provocatively for even more of his touch.

'You're making me feel…react…more like a teenager than a grown man,' she heard him whispering, groaning in her ear as he started to drag a passionate line of kisses along her jaw and over her throat.

'Jon…' Heaven could hear the passion in her own voice as she arched her neck, her instinctive response throwing the profile of her body into clear relief, revealing her tightly erect nipples.

Totally lost in what she was feeling, she was unaware of Jon's momentary tension and hesitation, and of the fact that he was muttering something very male and urgent below his breath, but the sudden sensation of his mouth against her body as his hands cupped her breasts sent a thrill of sharp, dizzying feminine pleasure hurtling through her.

In his urgency to taste the delicious nubs of flesh that were being so innocently and irresistibly offered to him, Jon couldn't wait to unzip Heaven's dress, hungrily pulling the fabric down and quickly laying bare one soft round breast.

Heaven felt the shudder that went through him as he studied the feminine softness of her avidly for a heartbeat of time, gently rubbing her bare nipple with his thumb before guiding it into his mouth.

The sensation of his lips closing round her flesh, of him suckling on her bare flesh—carefully at first and then with far more urgency as his reaction to the taste of her overwhelmed him—made Heaven's whole body contort with delicious pleasure. Willingly she gave herself up to the erotic sensation of Jon's mouth tugging on one breast whilst his hand caressed the other.

Yearningly Heaven reached out to touch him, an erotic image of his naked body dancing behind her closed eyelids, her imagination tantalising and arousing her. Her fingertips found the buttons on his shirt and impetuously tugged at them.

The shudder that racked Jon's body as she touched him had nothing to do with the cold beyond the passionate heat they had generated inside the car—and nor had the low male groan of need he gave as the hand that had been caressing her breast captured her wrist, pressing her palm flat against the soft, silky dark hair that arrowed downwards from his chest.

'Lower,' Heaven heard him growl pleadingly. 'Lower, Heaven—touch me here,' he begged rawly, moving her hand down towards his waistband as his mouth released her breast to whisper the tormented words against her lips.

All at once Heaven started to panic. She was behaving as though she and Jon had known one another for ever, as though it was the most natural thing in the world for them to be together like this, as though the intimacy they were sharing was so natural and preordained that to deny or obstruct it would be like denying one another air to breathe.

But their relationship *wasn't* like that. She knew him, yes, had been attracted to him, yes, and yes, all right, had felt perhaps even more than mere attraction for him—had, if she was honest, hoped, even *felt* that he had shared the feelings she had experienced the evening he had taken her out. But *this—this* explosion of passion and intensity between them, this sense of coming home, of being completely at one with him— these were surely far too dangerous emotions for her to put any trust in.

She had, she reminded herself, already been on an adrenalin- and tension-induced high even before she had realised that Jon was one of Harold's guests, and events since she had realised it had done nothing to help her come down from that high—far from it.

'What's wrong?' she heard Jon ask her softly as he felt her tension.

'Nothing...' Heaven denied, and then added shakily, 'This wasn't meant to happen. I didn't want...'

'To be dragged off into the night and driven half the length of the country? Or to be made love to by me?' he asked her wryly. 'Which?'

'Neither,' Heaven lied primly, taking advantage of the fact that he had released her to hurriedly straighten her dress and turn her head slightly away from him so that he couldn't see her face properly.

'I'm sorry,' she heard him apologising. 'It wasn't my intention to. You're a very special woman, Heaven,' he added in an even softer and very deep voice. '*So* special in fact that...'

He was starting the engine as he spoke, and set the car back in motion without finishing his sentence, but, even though she was desperately curious to know what he had been about to say, Heaven didn't trust herself to ask him—nor him to answer her.

Along with the intense passion and sensuality of the lovemaking they had just shared there had also been a heart-tugging skein of sweetness and tenderness. Or was she just imagining it? Would the spell he had woven around her by reigning in the urgency of his passion be broken if she forced him to put what he was thinking and feeling into words and then discovered that he was not sharing her thoughts and feelings after all?

So much had happened so quickly—too much and

too quickly, perhaps, Heaven rationalised as they rounded a bend in the road and she could see the lights of what looked like a small village ahead of them.

'Not much further,' Jon told her as they drove through the village, which was picturesquely sheltered by the surrounding hills of the Borders, its stone cottages hugging the winding road, the narrowness of the humpback bridge crossing the river that Jon drove over making Heaven breathe in automatically.

Ahead of them lay what was obviously the village's main street, its bare trees currently adorned with Christmas lights.

It had stopped snowing, the sky clearing to reveal the stars, and Heaven couldn't stop herself from exclaiming out loud, 'Oh, Jon, it's so pretty! So Christmassy.'

'It may look pretty now,' he responded, 'but it has a rather bloody history. The actual border with Scotland isn't very far from here and this village was the home of border reivers from the English side of the border and the target from those from the Scots side. When a truce was finally declared it was decreed that it would be celebrated and remembered annually at Christmas time, which means that Christmas for the villagers is a doubly special time of joy and celebration. It's a tradition that everyone attends a special thanksgiving supper. *We* could go to it if you'd like?'

'Could we…?' Heaven began, her eyes shining, and then abruptly she stopped, reminding herself of

just why she was here with Jon in the first place, the
excitement dying out of her face as she asked him
anxiously, 'But Christmas is a week away and I
can't...'

'You can't stay...' Jon finished quietly for her.

Heaven bit her lip and turned to look out of the car
window. They had left the village behind and were
starting to climb now, the road winding upwards
through the hills. The snow lay more thickly on the
road here, but not too thickly for Jon's car, thank
goodness.

Heaven could feel her eyes starting to close as
waves of tiredness washed down over her. Sleepily
she snuggled deeper into her comfortable seat and
then, as Jon swung the car off the road and down a
gravel drive, she sat up abruptly and asked him, 'What
on *earth* is that?'

'Home,' Jon responded, laughing, obviously enjoying her surprise.

'Home?' Heaven stared in bemusement at the ancient tall square slit-windowed tower looming in front
of her. 'You live *here?*'

'Yes,' Jon confirmed with a smile, bringing the car
to a halt on the gravel and causing the building's security lights to come on, further illuminating the
building and the soft warm stone from which it was
built.

'But what *is* it?' Heaven asked in fascination as she
studied the tower's unfamiliar shape, height and its

narrow, almost slit-like windows. That it was very old was obvious.

'A peel tower,' Jon told her promptly, and then explained, 'They were fortified homes built by those who lived on the border, very often, I'm afraid to say, using stone they "acquired" from Hadrian's wall. The tower acted as a protective place of retreat for the family should they come under attack, and it has to be said that it was equally used as a means of holding captive goods and even people they themselves had purloined on their own reiving trips across the border.

'Originally there would have been a collection of wooden shelters at the base of the tower to hold their livestock, with the family accommodation at the top of the tower where it was deemed to be safer. Because of their height the towers also served as good lookout points. On a clear day from here you can see right across the border for miles. Of course this particular tower was renovated and modernised quite some time ago—before I bought it in fact.

'I was staying in the village some years ago and heard that it was up for sale. I've always loved the Borders and buying it was certainly a hell of a lot less expensive than going for a Cotswold cottage.'

'Just imagine the stories it could tell,' Heaven breathed.

'Mmm...' Jon agreed. 'It's said locally that one misty November night a long time ago—ideal weather for stealing your neighbour's sheep—the then owner of this tower decided to break the truce which existed between him and his neighbour and set off to reive his cattle. When he reached the farm he discovered that the only person there was the seventeen-year-old niece of the farmer who was visiting from Edinburgh, so as well as taking his cattle he also took his neighbour's niece. However, apparently she was so beautiful and so good that our border reiver fell completely in love with her, and, much more unlikely, she with him, and rather than leading to another bloody feud his abduction of her led instead to a wedding.'

'They lived happily ever after,' Heaven laughed.

'Can you doubt it?' Jon laughed back as he opened his car door and went round to open Heaven's door for her.

As she followed him towards the tower, Heaven found herself instinctively moving a little closer to him. It wasn't that she was afraid of anything—no, of course not—but she still jumped and gave a small startled gasp as something rustled in the ivy that clothed the front wall of the tower.

'It's all right; it's just an owl,' Jon comforted her as he pushed open the door and switched on the lights, but he still took her hand in his, holding it comfortingly, and Heaven didn't make any real attempt to pull away from him as they walked into the tower together.

As she stood with him in the hallway Heaven blinked in surprise.

'Oh, but this is lovely,' she enthused as she studied

the plain soft cream plaster walls and the rustic iron wall sconces that held the lights. Plain coir matting covered the floor and the three doors which opened off the hallway were all of dark polished wood, like the stairs which led upwards.

'That door leads into the kitchen,' Jon informed her, indicating the door immediately in front of them. 'The other two rooms are my study and a rather small, cold sitting room; the main living room is on the next floor. Come up and I'll show you it and the bedrooms on the floor above that.'

The living room was huge.

'This must take up the whole of this floor,' Heaven guessed.

'It does,' Jon agreed. 'The main drawback of this place so far as I'm concerned is having the kitchen and this room on separate floors, but it's a drawback which is more than made up for by the panoramic views you get of the countryside from here. On a clear day you can virtually see as far as the coast.'

Heaven nodded sleepily as she tried and failed to stifle a yawn.

Like the hallway the living room was furnished simply with coir matting and three huge sofas covered in natural creamy white linen.

Heaven yawned again and immediately Jon frowned, exclaiming, 'You're tired! Come on; I'll take you up and show you your room.'

As he guided her towards the stairs, Heaven reflected that just once in a while it felt surprisingly good to relax and let someone else take charge.

Two doors opened off the upper landing and Jon pushed open the right-hand one for her, switching on the light inside the room and then ushering her inside.

'Both bedrooms have their own *en suite* bathroom,' he told her as she blinked sleepily around the room, but it was the large and oh, so comfortable-looking bed with its traditional brass bedstead and its heavenly plain bedlinen that her gaze kept on returning to.

'Look, why don't I leave you to get ready for bed,' Jon suggested gently, 'whilst I go down and make us both a hot drink? You'll find plenty of towels in the cupboard in your bathroom, along with a spare toothbrush and all the usual necessities. Mrs Frazer from the village, who comes in to go over the house for me and keep an eye on things, believes in being equipped for all emergencies.'

As soon as she heard the door close behind him Heaven walked over to the bed. She only intended to touch it, to test it, just to see if it was as deliciously comfortable as it looked, but for some inexplicable reason touching it became sitting on it, and sitting on it became lying on it, so that when Jon returned he found her curled up fast asleep on the edge of the bed still fully dressed.

Very gently he tried to wake her but when he realised how deeply asleep she was he hesitated for a moment, wondering whether to simply cover her with a spare duvet and leave her as she was. But he knew enough about women to recognise that when she woke up in the morning and discovered that she had slept in the only clothes she had to wear she would not be very happy and so, still frowning, he bent down and started to remove her shoes.

The bedroom light was still on, and he wasn't sure if it was for her benefit or his own that he stopped what he was doing and went and switched it off before returning to complete his self-appointed task in the semi-darkness, which, if he was honest, did little to conceal the feminine beauty and desirability of her naked body from him. In fact he could see far too much, arousing the urgency and intensity of his own male hunger and desire for her.

The temptation to remove his own clothes, to slide beneath the bedclothes with her, to hold her in his arms was so strong, so intense, so demanding that he felt himself literally grinding his teeth together as he fought to control it, bending instead to scoop up the clothes he'd removed, but as he straightened up his resolve wavered. She looked so adorable, so... kissable...so...so *Heaven*, lying there with only her face and her soft hair visible above the bedclothes, that he just had to bend down and kiss her very gently on the mouth.

In her sleep, Heaven smiled against his lips and her own clung softly, to him—softly, temptingly... Sternly Jon made himself withdraw from her.

If he couldn't share the intimacy of her bed with her then at least his clothes could share the intimacy of the washing machine and dryer with hers, he told himself ruefully as he closed the door behind himself and went to strip off his own things before taking them down to the kitchen to put them in the washing machine.

At least she could have clean clothes in the morning even if they were the same ones she had worn the previous day. After he'd pushed everything into the machine and selected a suitable washing cycle he paused to scoop up the single small item which had fallen onto the floor, quickly picking up the tiny pair of pretty lacy knickers and pushing them hastily into the machine before closing the door on them and on his own tantalising erotic thoughts.

Eighteen months ago when he had first set eyes on Heaven he had been attracted to her. The evening he had taken her out he had known that that attraction was deepening into something more, something much stronger, and by the end of the evening he had known...sensed... But then had come all the trauma and tragedy of Harold's cruel manipulation of her situation and he had forced himself to acknowledge that he was the last person Heaven would want in her life.

But now fate had thrown them together again and it hadn't taken that intoxicating interlude in his car earlier on to make him realise that far from lessening his feelings towards her the intervening months had only strengthened them.

But what about *her* feelings for *him?* She had certainly been responsive to him earlier this evening; he knew she was not the kind of woman to indulge in casual sexual intimacy with anyone and the sexual and emotional chemistry they had generated between them certainly argued well for the future he hoped they would have together.

The *future*. The smile which had begun to curl his mouth suddenly disappeared. Before he could invite her to think about sharing that future with him there was the present to be dealt with—the present and his unpleasant ex-brother-in-law.

His mouth compressing grimly, Jon mentally reviewed the information Heaven had given him.

As he walked out into the hallway he glanced ruefully towards the stairs leading up to Heaven's bedroom, to Heaven, both literally and metaphorically, he acknowledged. He fought the temptation to ignore his responsibility towards his sister, sternly admonishing himself for the highly erotic and passionately emotional nature of his thoughts as he turned away from the stairs and headed instead for his study.

Once inside he firmly closed the door and then sat down at his desk and switched on his computer.

He had begun to think he would never find a lever with which to manoeuvre his ex-brother-in-law into giving his sister and their children a fairer financial settlement, but now, thanks to Heaven, he suspected that at last he had. And what a lever. A grim smile curled his mouth as he set to work.

CHAPTER FIVE

HEAVEN stretched sleepily and luxuriously and then opened her eyes. Abruptly she sat bolt upright in her bed—no, not *her* bed at all, she recognised as she snatched up the duvet which had fallen away from her body to cover her naked breasts and warily glanced around her unfamiliar surroundings.

She was not at home in London any more, she was in Scotland, in an ancient border fortress which had once been the home of wild border reivers, and which was now the home of Jon.

Jon. Just thinking about him made her toes start to curl and her tummy flutter in a way that had nothing to do with nervousness or apprehension.

If she sat right up in the high bed she could see through the window to the hills that lay beyond it— white with snow beneath a blue sky from which shone a brilliantly sharp winter sun.

In London it would no doubt be dull and grey and damp; in London she would have been waking up in her admittedly very warm and cosy Chelsea home, her haven—but how long would it have remained her haven once Harold had discovered her identity and tracked her down? And in London there would have been no Jon.

A rosy blush suffused her face. She only had a very vague memory of their arrival the previous evening, but one thing she was very clear about and that was that she had most certainly not undressed herself. Which meant…which meant…

Jon stretched his taut muscles under the sharp, hot sting of the shower. He had finally gone to bed at six o'clock in the morning, very pleased with what he had done. He smiled broadly to himself as he contemplated Harold's reaction to the discovery of just how much Jon knew about his underhand, not to mention virtually fraudulent business dealings.

Of course he had already been aware of Harold's dishonesty—after all, he had spent a large part of the last year investigating his affairs—but knowing it and proving it were two very different things, and now, thanks to Heaven, he was well on the way to having that proof. He knew about the trickery Harold had used to carefully conceal the money he had made via a complex network of interlinking off-shore companies—carefully, but not carefully enough, Jon acknowledged jubilantly.

Soon he would have written evidence of just where Harold's assets were, evidence his sister could put before a judge, but Jon cynically acknowledged that once Harold knew just what they had discovered he would never allow Louisa's maintenance petition to get to court. If he did then the whole of his business empire could be destroyed.

No, Louisa should find that she got a much fairer divorce settlement from her ex-husband now, and with it the return of her family furniture, Jon decided grimly as he reached for a towel and quickly dried off his body before pulling on a towelling robe.

Was Heaven awake yet? There was only one way to find out...

Jon! Where had *he* slept last night after he had undressed her? This bed, *her* bed, was certainly big enough for both of them. Heaven wriggled uncertainly beneath the duvet. *Had* they spent the night together? Had Jon...? She gave a small gasp as the bedroom door was pushed open and the subject of her wantonly sensual thoughts came in carrying a tray with two mugs of tea, and her clothes.

'I put these in the washer for you last night,' he began prosaically as he put her clothes down on a chair several yards away from the bed.

'My clothes...?'

Hard though she tried to suppress it, Heaven could feel her blush starting to deepen, and then, unable to keep the suspicion to herself any longer, burst out, 'Last night did we...did you...?'

The hot-faced look she cast in the direction of the opposite side of the double bed made Jon want to smile as he realised what was going through her mind.

She thought he might have done more than remove her clothing, did she? Well, in some respects he almost wished he had, although if he had...

'Don't you know…can't you remember?' he teased her, watching with enjoyment as her eyes rounded with uncertainty. In her consternation Heaven forgot to hang onto the duvet, which started to slither away from her body immediately she released it, causing Jon, who was just in the act of placing her mug of tea on the table at her side of the bed, to react swiftly and with gentlemanly concern to retrieve the errant duvet for her.

It was mere misfortune, of course, that he should fail in his mission to spare Heaven's blushes and protect her modesty, missing the recalcitrant duvet by millimetres—so few millimetres, in fact, that the tips of his fingers actually brushed against the soft warmth of Heaven's breast.

It was the effect of the cool air against her body that was causing her nipples to pout so provocatively, Heaven tried to reassure herself, and their wanton stiffness had nothing whatsoever—*could* have nothing whatsoever—to do with Jon's proximity, nor his touch.

'You can't remember, can you?' she heard him accusing her as he sat down on the bed next to her.

Heaven gave a small gulp, not so much because of her near-nakedness, or even because the towelling robe he was wearing was, so it seemed to her, very precariously tied at the waist—so precariously in fact that she suspected that all it would take for it to fall open completely would be for…

Hastily she averted her eyes and her hot face from

the interesting darkly shadowed area just below his firmly flat belly. No, it was neither of those two things that was responsible for her agitation. What *was* causing it was her awareness that she could not remember whether or not she and Jon had spent the night together. What she did know, though, was that she did not find the idea that they might have unbelievable— or unappealing.

'So you think I might have taken advantage of your sleeping state and spent the night here in bed with you, do you?' he was asking her.

Heaven rallied enough to remind him, 'You took my clothes off.'

'Mmm... A purely altruistic action, I can assure you, and done merely so that you could have clean clothes to wear this morning.'

'Oh...'

Jon cocked an eyebrow and smiled encouragingly at her.

'Could that have been an ''Oh'' of apology...or even one of disappointment?' he asked her teasingly.

Heaven gave him a wrathful look but before she could denounce him with the words clamouring for utterance on her tongue he neatly cut the ground away from her by telling her softly, 'Not that I wasn't tempted...very tempted. You've got a very sexy body... And a delicious little mole just here,' he told her, finding with dismaying accuracy despite the duvet the spot on her hip bone where she did indeed have a small mole.

'A very kissable mole,' he whispered, leaning closer to her.

Heaven couldn't help it. Instinctively, as he moved closer to her she moved closer to him. With his lips only a breath away from hers Jon told her huskily, 'No, I didn't sleep with you, and if I had... If I had, you may be sure that you most certainly would have remembered it...'

'Remembered...' Heaven whispered shakily.

'Mmm...' Jon agreed. 'You would. Because I would have made love to you so thoroughly, so...so sensually...starting like this...'

Heaven had been about to speak but it was too late; Jon was already cupping her face with both hands, pressing slow, mouthwateringly delicious kisses against her mouth. The kind of kisses that made her reach out and wrap her own arms around him to hold him closer.

'Mmm...and then what would you have done?' Heaven asked him dizzily.

'Then I would have done this, and you'd certainly have remembered it,' he told her, sweeping her hair to one side and stringing a line of toe-curling little nibbles all the way down her throat and along her shoulder, bringing her whole body out in a rash of responsive goosebumps as he did so.

Heaven gave a small moan of sheer delight, unwittingly digging her nails into the flesh of his arms, but he didn't mind the pain.

'Oh-h-h...' she gasped as he trailed a row of kisses

all the way down the inside of her arm to her wrist, planting one in her palm before he closed her fingers over it and carried that hand to his own body, placing it right where his heart was thumping with heavy irregularity.

'And then…what would you have done?' Heaven pressed him, opening eyes heavy with desire and arousal to focus on him.

Jon felt his heart skip a full half a dozen beats. Just that look in her eyes alone, never mind the softer tempting fullness of her naked breasts, was enough to make him want…

'Then I'd have told you that this isn't a game and I want you so much that I ache like hell for you,' he told her rawly, the emotion in his voice and in his eyes making Heaven catch her breath…

'I want you too,' she admitted bravely as she held out her arms to him.

Very gently he reached out and cupped her breasts and then equally gently leaned forward and started to kiss her.

Heaven gave a soft moan low in her throat as she felt Jon rubbing the pads of his thumbs over and over her sensitive nipples, her whole body writhing in sensual pleasure as she opened her mouth to the deep, pulsing thrust of his tongue.

When he released her mouth to capture one of her nipples and draw it tenderly into his mouth she could feel the soft sensuality of his body hair and the sleek hardness of the muscles that lay beneath his skin.

She wanted to explore every inch of him, to touch and taste all of him, but she hadn't realised she had said so out loud until Jon buried his face between her breasts and groaned, 'Oh, God, Heaven, have you any idea just what you're doing to me?'

'I know what *you're* doing to *me,*' Heaven responded bravely.

His robe had fallen completely open. Fascinated, torn between her natural feminine shyness and her equally instinctive female awe and curiosity, she studied him, unable to resist the temptation to reach out and run her fingertips down the hard length of his erection.

'Heaven,' she heard him protest in a satisfactorily guttural moan of mingled torment and pleasure.

'What's wrong?' she teased him. 'Don't you like me doing that?'

'Don't I *like* it?' Jon groaned, and closed his eyes. 'You wait,' he warned her. 'I'll get my own back.

'You can't know how often I've thought about you,' he told her more seriously as he shrugged off the robe and took her back into his arms, kissing her mouth gently at first and then with increasing passion as he felt her respond to him.

'When you never got in touch with me after...after everything, I thought that you mustn't have been interested,' Heaven admitted hesitantly.

Jon immediately shook his head.

'I couldn't get in touch because no one knew where to find you. I contacted your parents but they refused to tell me where you were. Then I thought about it and reasoned that anyone connected with...with what had happened would be the last person you'd want to see...'

'I did feel a bit like that,' Heaven admitted, ducking her head so that he couldn't see the anxiety in her eyes as she added, 'And I felt...well, people do say there's no smoke without a fire and—'

'Stop right there,' Jon warned her sternly. '*Other* people may have made the mistake of believing Harold's lies, but *I* never did,' he announced grimly. 'I never did, Heaven,' he repeated, cupping her face and holding it so that she was forced to meet the look in his eyes. 'I never did and I never could...'

Heaven couldn't hide it. His words made her eyes fill with emotional tears which she couldn't disguise from him. Gently he wiped them away and then bent his head and licked the last traces of moisture from her skin. The erotic sensation of his tongue moving against her damp skin sent a tell-tale shudder of re-action jolting through Heaven's body.

'Jon,' she whispered shakily as she clung to him, no longer shy of letting him see the effect he was having on her or her need for him.

'I know,' he whispered back. 'I know.'

And then he was laying her down on the bed and removing the duvet, caressing every inch of her skin, kissing the small mole on her hip as he had intimated he had wanted to do, but Heaven wasn't sure if it was the sensation of his mouth against her mole or the fact that as he kissed it his hand was resting on her belly, covering her sex, that was making her tremble so wildly.

'What's wrong?' he teased her huskily as his hand slid between her legs and he started to caress her with the same gentle explorative intimacy with which she had touched him earlier. 'Don't *you* like it?'

But Heaven didn't need to make any response; Jon already knew what her answer was and his own body, his own arousal, his own emotions were reacting chaotically to the feel and warmth of her.

He bent his head and Heaven gave a shocked gasp of pleasure as she felt his mouth caressing the most intimate part of her, his tongue stroking, seeking, questing.

Unable to bear the erotic sensuality of the sensation he was giving her, she called out protestingly to him, her sharp, high cry smothered by the fierce pressure of his mouth on hers, instinctively sensing and satisfying her need for that intimacy, and just as instinctively satisfying her need for the powerful, sensually fulfilling thrust of his body within her own.

It was like poetry, a perfect dawn and even more perfect sunset, every good sensation and feeling you could ever experience or imagine experiencing, to feel the harmony that their bodies were creating together, to share the upward gravity-free surge towards the ecstatic moment of release, to lie dazed and replete in one another's arms.

'That was *heaven*,' Jon whispered gruffly to her.

Heaven started to giggle and then Jon, realising what he had said, joined in.

'Heaven…' he began, but she suddenly tensed.

'I can hear a car outside,' she told him anxiously. 'You don't think…?'

'Wait here,' he cautioned her, reaching for his robe and pulling it on as he walked towards the door.

Whoever it was who'd arrived was ringing noisily on the doorbell, and Heaven shivered as she listened to the piercing, demanding sound.

'Wait here,' Jon had told her, but if they had been pursued by Harold there was no way she was going to be discovered huddled vulnerably in bed.

Picking up the clean clothes Jon had brought her, she headed for the bathroom, firmly locking the door behind her once she was inside. At least the brisk sound of the shower drowned out whatever might be happening downstairs. The women of the family who had originally built and lived in the peel tower would not have been so fortunate, she acknowledged, unable to stop herself wondering how many times they had huddled together in silent terror at the top of the tower whilst downstairs their menfolk repelled the border reivers who had come to attack them and steal away their cattle.

It had been a very thoughtful gesture on Jon's part to wash and dry her clothes for her, Heaven reflected as she quickly dried herself and then pulled on her clean clothes. By the looks of it, he had even had an attempt at ironing her dress.

She flushed a little as she slipped on her lacy briefs. They were a pair that Janet had given her as part of a surprise 'cheer you up' present and as such rather more skimpy and provocative than the ones she normally wore, hardly large enough to cover the palm of Jon's hand, never mind...

Hastily she reached for her dress. Her mind might be overrun with anxious fears, but her body was still clinging to the faintly languorous feeling of voluptuous satisfaction and completion that Jon's lovemaking had given it.

Jon. A delicious little tremor of pleasure ran delicately across her skin. There could be no doubts from the way he had made love to her and responded to her just how much he had wanted her, desired her, but wanting and loving were not necessarily the same thing, she reminded herself starkly as she unlocked the bathroom door and paused uncertainly, trying to gauge the silence. Had whoever it was gone...or...?

Heaven tensed as the bedroom door opened, but to her relief it was only Jon.

'Has he...? Was it...?' Heaven paused and moistened her dry lips.

Jon started to shake his head, but Heaven had guessed the truth from the severity of his expression.

'It was someone after me, wasn't it?' she insisted.

When Jon nodded, she bit her lip nervously, before asking, 'Was it Harold...?' He shook his head, a small smile starting to curl his mouth as he told her, 'No, Harold wasn't on the doorstep. Apparently he isn't feeling very well. It's all right, Heaven,' he reassured her, walking over to her and taking her in his arms, tucking her head under his chin as he wrapped his arms tightly round her.

'There were two men looking for you, yes—contacts of Harold's who work in Glasgow and whom he'd asked to try and locate you, but fortunately, seem to have convinced them that I came up here alone. Harold had told them that you'd left the house with me and they wanted to know if I knew where you were…'

'Couldn't Harold have asked you that over the telephone?' Heaven asked him uneasily. 'Why send people to your home?'

'I think Harold decided that a personal visit might help to reinforce the urgency of his need to discover your whereabouts,' Jon told her gravely, choosing not to add to her anxiety by revealing to her the warning he had been given about the potential consequences if he had been tempted to either help or conceal her.

'What…what did you tell them about…about me?' Heaven asked him quietly.

'I told them that from what you'd said to me I rather suspected that you might have decided to fly out to Australia to join your family for Christmas,' he told her.

Heaven's eyes widened in admiration as she tilted her head back to look at him.

'Did they believe you?'

'For the time being, but Harold's bound to check,'

he warned her, 'which means that there's no way it would be safe for you to return to London, not until— well, not for the next few days.'

'Not until what?' Heaven pressed him.

Jon released her and walked over to the bedroom window. He was very fortunate in that the situation of the peel tower meant that it was impossible for anyone to conceal either a man or a car close enough at hand to be able to spy on the house. He felt sure that his unwanted visitors had accepted his story that he had no real idea where Heaven was, but sooner or later Harold would discover that she hadn't flown out to Australia and that neither had she returned home, and once he did, but hopefully before then, Jon would have gathered together all the information he needed to force his ex-brother-in-law's hand.

He looked out of the window, briefly studying the peaceful snow-covered hills and the clear winter blue of the cloudless sky. So very different from the storm clouds looming on the horizon of his life and the lives of those closest to him. The acrimony of his sister's divorce had affected his parents as well as Louisa herself, and his two nieces had also suffered, although thankfully their father had played a very distant role in their short lives. And as for what Harold had done to Heaven…

He looked back across the room and walked towards her, taking both her hands in his, holding them in a close and protective warm clasp as he told her what he had already found out and what he planned to do.

'You're going to do that... Will it work? Is it safe?' Heaven said nervously.

'I *am* going to do it, yes, it will work, and no, it probably isn't the safest thing I've ever done,' Jon admitted wryly. 'But I have to do it—for Louisa's sake; I'm just sorry that you had to be dragged into it. But without you I doubt that I would ever have got that vitally important bit of information about Harold's plans to cheat the Americans.'

'Tiffany might have told you,' Heaven demurred, but Jon shook his head decisively.

'No, I doubt it; you have the gift of bringing people close to you. Your natural warmth, your ability to give love encourages them to feel safe with you, to confide in you...'

He paused as Heaven's face clouded.

'What is it?' he asked gently.

'I'm worried about Tiffany. If Harold discovers what she's told me...'

'Tiffany will be fine,' Jon assured her.

Heaven bit her lip. 'You can't *know* that,' she protested.

'Oh, yes, I can,' he argued, then went on quietly, 'Right about now I suspect that Tiffany's parents will be driving into London to collect their lamb and remove her from Harold's presence—and his life. I sent them a fax warning them that Harold was not the man for their daughter and urging them to dig a little deeper into his background and past history. After all, how could a man who had already deserted two children be relied on to support their daughter and any children she might have?'

'Harold could trace the fax back to you,' Heaven responded fearfully.

'Not a chance,' he assured her. 'When the occasion calls for it, I can be just as devious as him. By the time Harold has unravelled the tangled skein of communication I've knotted around my fax, it will all be too late.'

'You make it all sound so simple and…easy, Jon, but I'm frightened,' Heaven admitted. 'If Harold's prepared to go to the lengths of sending someone here to look for me…'

'It's simply his outraged male pride that's caused him to do that,' Jon soothed her. 'After all, you did make him look very foolish in front of the Americans.

'It could be that the men he's sent here to check me out will keep tabs on me for the next day or so and then I expect they'll get bored and give up and go home. It will mean, of course, that you've got to stick to the tower and its close environs for the next couple of days,' he warned her, gently touching her arm as he added, 'No clothes shopping, I'm afraid, although… Hang on a minute,' he told her, releasing her and striding across the bedroom to open a door in the bank of wardrobes set against one wall.

'Ah…I thought so,' Heaven heard him announcing triumphantly as he pushed open the adjacent door and indicated the half dozen or so items of women's clothing hanging there.

'I don't know if any of these will fit but you're more than welcome to give them a try,' he assured her, giving her a warm smile. But Heaven was already turning away from him, her body set like stone, her head down so that he wouldn't see the wounded pain in her eyes.

How could she have been so foolish as to start weaving fanciful, happy daydreams around the pair of them when it was plain just what kind of light *he* viewed their intimacy in if he could so casually and carelessly offer her the use of clothes which quite patently must have belonged to a previous incumbent of this room—and no doubt of his bed?

'What's wrong?' he asked with true male confusion when he saw the way she was responding to what he had imagined would be a very well-received suggestion.

'I couldn't possibly wear another woman's clothes,' Heaven told him freezingly.

'Another *woman...*' Jon began, puzzled, and then enlightenment dawned. 'I'm sure Louisa won't mind,' he told Heaven gently.

'Louisa...your sister? They're Louisa's clothes?' Heaven asked him, not just her voice but her whole body reflecting her relief.

'They're Louisa's,' Jon confirmed. 'And although I know she's nothing like as petite as you there may be something you could wear. *And,* for your information,' he added mock sternly, 'apart from Louisa and the girls, *you* are the only woman I've... Damn,' he cursed under his breath as the telephone started to ring down below them.

'I'd better answer that. I'm expecting several calls in response to the proceedings I've set in motion...'

He was gone before Heaven could ask him what he had been about to say. Was it that she was the only woman apart from his sister and nieces whom he had invited to his border retreat, or was it that she was the only woman apart from them he'd *wanted* to invite?

'Stop it,' she warned herself firmly. 'Stop trying to read more into things than there might be. More than Jon himself might want there to be.' But not more than she knew she wanted there to be, she acknowledged.

The attraction she had felt for him when they had originally met might have gone to ground, suppressed by the sheer immediacy and shock of everything else that had overtaken her, but as last night—and this morning—had proved it had never really died and had in fact simply been waiting for the right moment to show its true strength.

All those slow, gentle weeks of gradually getting to know him, of talking with him, of seeing the loving way he reacted to his sister and his nieces, of gradually falling in love with him, had shown their true effect on her in his arms. What she felt for him *wasn't* just something born of the urgent, adrenalin-fuelled trauma of the moment; her love for him wasn't merely some kind of dangerous viral infection—a winter madness brought on by proximity and physical arousal. It was a forever, once-in-a-lifetime love, the kind of love that went with waking up with him every morning, bearing his children, sharing his whole life. But did he feel the same way about *her?*

'I'm sorry about this,' Jon apologised to Heaven as he walked into the living room where she was busily engaged looking for the final edge piece of a jigsaw she had discovered tucked away in a cupboard. The subject of the puzzle was a real Victorian family Christmas, complete with a dozen or so assorted aunts, uncles and elderly relatives, a mass of small, excited children, a tree, presents and even a small side table groaning with a mouthwatering selection of fruits and sweets. In effect the kind of Christmas that everyone, in a small corner of their heart, had a sentimental place for, whether or not they chose to acknowledge it.

'Why, are you bored? Never mind, we're nearly there. By this time tomorrow with any luck we'll have Harold exactly where we want him.'

'No, I'm not bored,' Heaven assured him, giving him a warm smile and then crowing with triumph as she pounced on the final edge piece of the jigsaw. She grinned up at Jon as she told him, 'This is definitely a figgy pudding sort of family, don't you think?' She made room on the sofa for him as he dutifully peered at the picture on the lid of the box.

'Oh, definitely,' he agreed, and then, unable to keep his face straight, teased her, 'But minus *your* special extra ingredients, I trust…'

They were both still laughing when they heard the phone ring.

'Keep your fingers crossed,' Jon told her. 'Hopefully this will be the call—the confirmation—that will prove incontrovertibly just what Harold's been up to.'

CHAPTER SIX

FOUR days after their arrival in the Borders Jon walked into the living room in relief.

'So everything is finally settled? You've got Harold's written and witnessed legal agreement to a proper divorce settlement for Louisa and the girls?'

'Yes, thanks in no small part to you,' he agreed warmly. 'Louisa's solicitor has just confirmed by fax that all the legal papers have been signed and Louisa's bank is in receipt of a very large cheque from Harold. The threat of having his underhand business dealings made public and possibly having to face a full-scale fraud investigation were more than enough to make Harold agree that he could be far more generous than he had been to Louisa and the girls.'

'And Tiffany...?'

'Tiffany is safely at home with her parents,' Jon assured her, adding wryly, 'And before you ask, I suspect that Harold's American buyers may very well be, if not having second thoughts about purchasing the business, then at least putting several more legal restraints on his future activities where they might affect their potential profits.'

'So all's well that ends well,' Heaven said slightly hollowly, getting up from the sofa where she had been sitting to walk across to the window and look at the still snow-covered landscape. 'And it's safe for me to go home?'

'Yes, it is,' Jon agreed tersely. 'It seems that Harold has decided to spend Christmas in the Caribbean—somewhere where I doubt that figgy pudding or anything like it will be on the menu.'

Heaven tried to smile but for some reason her facial muscles were refusing to co-operate. For *some* reason! She knew perfectly well what the reason was.

Although she and Jon had been living as closely together as any two people who were not true lovers could, not once in the four days which had elapsed since the morning he had made love to her had he shown any inclination, either physical or verbal, to repeat the intimacy.

Why? Because he regretted ever having made love to her? Because he was afraid that she might have read too much into what had happened...? Too damn right she had. Far *too* much.

'If I left this afternoon, I could be home for Christmas Eve,' she told Jon numbly.

'I'll make the arrangements for you if that's what you want,' he said abruptly.

What was she supposed to say? That what she wanted was to stay with *him;* that what she wanted was to be with him, to be loved by him?

She dipped her head.

'Please, if you wouldn't mind,' she confirmed formally.

Jon had switched on the television to catch the morning news and suddenly the room was filled with the sweet sound of a youthful choir singing Christmas carols.

To Heaven's consternation, she felt her eyes start to fill with tears in response to the emotional effect of the sound. She had always been a sucker for the sentimentality of Christmas and couldn't so much as pass a high-street store decorated with a Christmas crib without being flooded with a warm feeling of goodwill towards her fellow men.

But right now, when she was feeling so emotionally vulnerable, so heart-achingly aware of all that she felt for Jon and all that it seemed he did not feel for her, the last thing she needed was any additional pressure on her frail emotional self-control. She tried to force back the tears, but it was too late—Jon had already seen them.

'Heaven, what is it…what's wrong?'

He was at her side, reaching for her, before she could push him away. The sleeves of the overlong sweater that she had 'borrowed' from Louisa unravelled, impeding her efforts to free herself from him as he took hold of her, one hand soothingly stroking her sweater-clad arm, whilst the other…

Heaven gulped as she felt him brush away her tears.

'Why?' he asked her quietly. 'What is it? If you're worrying about Harold…afraid…'

'I'm not afraid of Harold; you've seen to it that he'll not be suing me for my foolhardy revenge on him,' Heaven replied. 'It's...' She tried to lift her hand to her mouth to stem her betraying words, but the sweater sleeve got in the way and to her dismay she could only shake her head.

'I should be the one doing this—not you,' she heard Jon telling her huskily as he touched her tear-damp face.

'You?' Heaven stared up at him. 'Why?'

'Because I don't *want* you to leave... I don't *want* to lose you again, Heaven. Because I want to keep you here with me for ever...'

'You *want* me to stay?' Heaven couldn't quite hide her disbelief. 'How can you say that when for the last four days you've behaved as though...?' She stopped and bit her lip.

'Go on... When for the last four days I've behaved as though what?' Jon pressed her.

'As though you don't want me,' Heaven told him bleakly.

'Not want you...?'

The raw passion in his voice made Heaven's stomach muscles quiver. Urgently Jon cupped her face and forced her to look up at him.

'Of *course* I want you... I more than merely want you, Heaven, I love you, and there's nothing I've wanted more these last few days than to be in a position to tell you so, but first I had to get this whole sorry mess of Louisa's divorce settlement out of the way, not just because the very nature of the information you gave me about Harold meant I had to act quickly, but, even more importantly, because I wanted you and I to have time together that nothing else, *no one* else, could intrude on.

'Eighteen months ago when we first met I knew you were someone special, very special—that the way I felt about you was very, very real and permanent; but then…well, you disappeared and I felt that anyone connected with Harold, no matter how distantly, would be the last person you'd want in your life, to remind you of what he'd put you through. But then fate decreed that we should meet again and when we did…'

The look he gave her as he carefully brushed a stray strand of hair off her face made Heaven's heart turn over with awed joy. Never even in her most vivid imaginings had she ever imagined she would have the power to make a man look at her the way Jon was looking at her right now—as though she was his whole world, his whole reason, his whole being.

'Nothing's changed, Heaven,' Jon whispered passionately to her. 'My love for you is very, very real and very, very permanent. I love you and if you want to make my Christmas wish come true you—'

'You really love me?' Heaven interrupted him, unable to keep silent any longer, her eyes starry with emotion.

'I love you,' Jon confirmed. 'I really love you. I love you and my Christmas wish is for you to return my love…for you to be my wife…'

Behind them the TV choir launched into a triumphant burst of praise but Heaven barely heard them, her own heart singing too loudly with joy, and besides, Jon was kissing her so passionately that she was blind, deaf and dumb to everything, everyone but him.

'Promise me one thing,' he begged her when he finally, reluctantly released her mouth.

'What?' Heaven asked him, giddy with joy and love.

'That you'll never, ever make me your special version of figgy pudding,' he told her fervently.

Heaven was still laughing as he swept her up into his arms and headed for the stairs, and the bedroom.

EPILOGUE

'Is THAT it—the end?'

Jon looked lovingly at his wife.

'No, not the end; this story will never end,' he told his niece. 'This is just the beginning, and like our love it will last for ever,' he told Heaven in a voice low enough for only her to hear as he leaned across to kiss her.

'Oh, grown-ups—yuck!' Christabel exclaimed. 'You're just like Mum and Dad—they're always hugging and kissing too. I'm *never* going to get married…'

'You'll change your mind, you wait and see,' Jon warned her with a smile. 'The proof of the pudding's always in the eating—you ask Heaven.'

'Oh, always,' Heaven agreed, laughing.

Grown-ups, Christabel decided crossly, were a complete mystery to her. First of all that silly kissing and now they were laughing for absolutely no reason at all that she could see!

A MAN FOR ALL SEASONINGS
Day Leclaire

Dear Reader,

I have a confession to make. I can't cook. Well…that isn't quite true. I cook a little better than my heroine, Maddie. But not much. You see, with a mother and two sisters, there were always plenty of able bodies to prepare meals when I was growing up, so we'd all take turns in the kitchen. Except me.

Christmastime wasn't much different. My older sister would prepare a coffee cake wreath. My younger sister would do a wonderful crab dip. My mother had an assortment of casseroles she'd whip up (with one hand tied behind her back!). My grandmother cooked a gorgeous turkey. I'd wash dishes. I did try, though.

One year I decided to bake Christmas cookies—that wouldn't be too tough, right? Unfortunately, I used a margarine substitute instead of butter or lard. The dense black smoke was my first clue that all was not going well. When I whipped open the oven door and pulled out the tray, I discovered…cookie ooze! The dough had slopped over the edge of the tray and burned interesting cookie rivers all over the inside of my oven. Now, most people would have just trashed this experiment gone awry. Not me. Hey—I'd gone to all that trouble; I couldn't just throw it away! So that Christmas we started a new tradition—cookie ooze. (I have it on expert authority that great chefs are born of mothers who don't cook: are you listening, Matthew?) Anyway…

I'd like to wish all of you a joyous holiday season—health, happiness and prosperity. I'd also like to offer a special thank-you to Chef Robyn Fennessy, who was of such immense help. I literally couldn't have written this book without her. A very merry Christmas to you all!

Day Leclaire

DAY LECLAIRE'S
CHRISTMAS MOUSSE

(Serves six)

Mousse

110g/½ cup sugar
55mL/¼ cup water
4 large egg whites
450g/1 lb grated white
  chocolate
450 mL/2 cups chilled whipping cream
Shaved slivers of white chocolate to decorate

Raspberry Sauce

2 pints raspberries
2 tbsp crème de cassis
Pinch of salt
1 tbsp sugar

For the mousse, combine the sugar and water in a saucepan and bring to the boil. Shake the pan as the sugar dissolves and watch carefully until syrup reaches 225° F. (124° C.). Set aside when correct temperature is reached.

Whip the egg whites until stiff (soft peak consistency) and then slowly add the sugar syrup. Beat in the grated chocolate a little at a time. It will partially melt as it mixes with the egg whites and syrup. Set aside to cool.

In a separate bowl, whip the cream until it forms peaks. Using a metal spoon, fold the whipped cream carefully into the mousse mixture. Chill for 2-6 hours in the refrigerator.

Meanwhile, make the raspberry sauce. Purée the raspberries. Add the sugar, salt and crème de cassis, mix well and chill for one hour.

Spoon a small amount of raspberry sauce in the bottom of six dessert glasses. Add the mousse, then spoon raspberry sauce over the top. Garnish with shaved white chocolate slivers. Serve and enjoy!

CHAPTER ONE

Il Ristorante…

or

Single in Seattle

'DID YOU say Joe Milano?' Maddie's co-worker questioned in disbelief. 'He's the "cook" you won as a Christmas wish?'

Maddie glanced up at Joy. 'Do you know him?'

'Are you sure we're talking about the same guy? House Milano, Joe Milano? That sexy stud who does those special cooking segments on *Seattle at Sunrise?* That Joe Milano?'

'I'm not sure. All I know for certain is that he's a cook.' Maddie glanced down at the paper she'd been given. On it was Joe's name, his address and a handwritten reminder to approach him in person instead of by phone. 'I've never seen his show. Have you?'

'Where have you been, girl?' Joy sank into the seat across from Maddie's desk and stared in amazement. 'There isn't anyone in all of Seattle who hasn't either seen that show or been to his restaurant or read about his latest affairs in the society pages.'

Affairs? As in romantic affairs? Maddie wondered.

'Well, I haven't eaten at House Milano or seen his show.' She frowned. Nor had she read about those affairs.

'Yeah, well, at a guess there's maybe two people in the entire northwest unfamiliar with him,' Joy informed her caustically. 'You and possibly some guy with his head buried under a rock. That's about it, I guarantee. Joe Milano's famous!'

Maddie didn't like the sound of this. 'You're exaggerating.'

'I am *not* exaggerating.' Joy groaned. 'I can't believe this. You won him? You actually won him?'

'No,' Maddie corrected pedantically. 'I bought him. And he didn't come cheap, either.'

'Guys like that never do.' Joy sighed. 'What I wouldn't give to have Joe Milano cook Christmas Eve dinner for me.'

'*I'm* going to cook Christmas Eve dinner. He's just going to teach me how.'

Joy wrinkled her snub nose. 'What a waste. If I'd bought him, I'd say the hell with cooking. *He* can be my Christmas dinner.'

'Well, that's not why I bought him,' Maddie insisted. 'I have other plans in mind.' And she did, too.

Whether he knew it yet or not, Joe Milano had a Christmas wish to fulfill.

The instant Joe threw open his front door and saw the angelic creature hovering on his doorstep he knew his days of carefree carousing were at an end. There wasn't a single doubt in his mind. He'd been waiting all his life for this woman and she'd finally arrived— delivered right to his door, no less.

He'd always assumed the eventual loss of his freedom would make him mad as hell.

Instead, he gave a broad grin.

Her response came just as promptly. Taking a quick step backward, she threw a nervous glance over her shoulder at the deserted Seattle street.

'Yes?' he prompted gently. 'May I help you?'

Reluctantly, she returned her attention to him, gazing upward with serious bluish-gray eyes. 'Are you Joe Milano?' she asked doubtfully, glancing at the slip of paper she held. The biting December wind tugged coffee-brown curls free of the knot at the nape of her neck and tossed them with carefree abandon about her face. Apparently, she didn't care for carefree abandon, for she forced them back into place with a gloved hand. 'Mr. Joe Milano?'

'You've found him, *cara,*' he confirmed, hoping like hell she wasn't one of the mindless groupies that hung around the television studio whenever he taped a cooking show. He'd like the future Mrs. Milano to have more common sense than that. Fortunately, she struck him as too self-contained for a groupie, too intelligent and purposeful. Still... One never knew. 'What can I do for you?'

'Mathias Blackstone sent me.'

'How kind of him.' Another smile cut across Joe's face, one of satisfaction this time. Mathias, a modern day Santa Claus, wouldn't have given out his home address if she hadn't been thoroughly investigated—and in need of help. Interesting that she'd dropped by without prior warning. That had to be Mathias's idea. He must be up to something. 'Remind me to thank him for his thoughtfulness.'

'You don't understand—'

'Then why don't you come inside and explain it to me?' He caught her elbow before she could retreat from him again and drew her across the threshold. 'Please, *cara.* It's starting to rain. I'd feel badly if you got wet.'

'No, I'd really rather not come—'

The door closed behind her, cutting off the rest of her comment, and she drew a quick breath, her eyes apprehensive beneath a fringe of bangs.

Dio! He made her nervous, he realized in astonishment. How the hell could that be? He never made women nervous. Far from it. Rather, he could be counted on to tease a laugh from them. More often than that, he ignited their passion. And always he'd succeeded in uncovering the soft spot in even the most prickly woman. But never, in all his thirty-seven years, had he ever filled a woman with dread.

A frown creased his brow. This was definitely not the sort of reaction he'd hoped to inspire in his wife-to-be.

'Mathias sent you?' Joe prompted, pitching his voice to a soothing level. To his utter astonishment it only served to make her more skittish. Her eyes widened as if she'd just spotted a snake hiding beneath her bed, and she took a hasty step away from him. Not giving her time to flee, he slipped the coat from her shoulders and hung it on the mahogany rack by the door, searching for a way to ease her fears. 'Mathias and I are very good friends. Do you know him well?'

'No, I don't know Mr. Blackstone well at all.' She gazed longingly at her coat, as though more than anything she wanted to snatch it back and make a quick escape. Then a light of determination brightened her eyes and she tilted her chin to a more aggressive angle. 'The truth is, I just met him recently.'

'And after meeting him he sent you to me?' Joe encouraged her.

'He thought you could help.' Doubt colored her tones.

'But of course. It would be my pleasure.'

On impulse, he seized her hands and slipped off first one leather glove, then the other. She wanted to protest, he could tell. But instead she stood stiffly before him, her gaze glued to the family photos on the wall behind him. Her hands were lovely, he noted, smooth and long-fingered, yet capable. They were also ringless. Perfect. Finished with the small chore, he released her, tucking the gloves into the pocket of her coat.

'Why did you do that?' she demanded.

He knew without asking that she referred to the gloves. 'Curiosity,' he admitted with a shrug.

'Is your curiosity satisfied now?'

He met her gaze steadily. 'Not yet. But it will be.' After all, this woman was his destiny, and his curiosity wouldn't be satisfied until he knew everything about her. He wanted to discover what brought her joy, what caused her pain, what her hopes and dreams were and how he could help fulfill them. But most of all he wanted to find out why she looked at him with such deep-rooted suspicion.

He gestured toward the door leading to the den. 'Come sit by the fire and tell me what I can do for you.'

Her gaze flickered toward the doorway and she drew a deep breath. He had the annoying impression that she was steeling herself to be closeted in a room alone with him.

'I'm here on business,' she announced. 'Is there somewhere we can discuss that?'

'But of course.' He touched her elbow and indicated the den again. 'We can discuss business in here.'

For the first time, a smile flitted across her mouth. 'By the fire,' she murmured.

He inclined his head. 'By the fire.' He led the way, motioning toward one of the two wing-backed chairs in front of the hearth. Then he crossed to the wet bar. 'Have a seat. Did you drive here or take a cab?'

'I came by bus. Why?'

He poured wine into two lead-crystal glasses. 'I wouldn't offer you anything to drink if you'd driven.'

He joined her, placing one of the goblets at her elbow. 'It's a '72 Château Suidurant. Tell me what you think.'

She hesitated, and in that moment he understood why she regarded him with such mistrust. He lifted his glass to hide his amusement. Mathias must have filled her head with tales of his past—as a warning, no doubt. Helping her with her coat and gloves, offering her a drink—hell, just smiling at her—had undoubtedly roused her suspicions. Joe made a mental note to have a long, private chat with his good friend Mathias and explain the facts to him. He didn't want any unnecessary complications during his pursuit of this woman.

Taking a sip of wine, she glanced up with a hint of surprise. 'This is wonderful. What is that I'm tasting? Mint? Chocolate?'

'Very good,' Joe approved, settling into the chair next to her. 'It's a bit on the sweet side, yet crisp. Don't you think?'

Her gaze touched briefly on his face before focusing on the fire. 'I'm not much of an expert.'

'Do you like it?'

'It's delicious.'

'Then that's all that matters.'

She deliberately returned her glass to the side table, and folded her hands in her lap. 'I suppose we should get down to business.'

'That sounds like a good idea.' He cocked his head to one side. 'Why don't you start by telling me your name? After that, you can explain why Mathias sent you.'

She froze for an instant, and then turned sharply to look at him. 'I didn't introduce myself?'

He shook his head. 'I've controlled my curiosity very well, don't you think?'

A smile trembled on her mouth and then she began to laugh. 'I'm so sorry. Perhaps we should start over.'

Her amusement gave him immense pleasure. It would have worried him if she hadn't displayed a sense of humor. Life's problems were much easier to deal with when confronted with laughter. The fire flared as it tackled a fresh log, casting her features in a rosy glow. She wasn't the most beautiful woman he'd ever known, he acknowledged. But she was quite lovely, exuding a quiet warmth that held infinite appeal. Her dark brown hair flattered a creamy complexion. Her nose was straight, her cheekbones high and angled, her chin suggesting a certain obstinacy of character. And her mouth was a perfect shape for kissing.

But he liked her eyes best of all. Calm, serene, hinting at a closely guarded vulnerability, they reminded him of a blue Seattle sky fighting to free itself from a layer of misty clouds.

Whether she knew it yet or not, she was his, just as he had become hers. He'd known the inevitability of their joining from the moment he'd first seen her. Once he'd convinced her that he wasn't a threat, their relationship would progress with due speed. He rubbed his hands together. With luck, he'd have a ring on her finger by Christmas and a bride in his bed by the start of the New Year.

He took another swallow of wine. Perfect. Everything was absolutely perfect.

Maddie lifted her glass and took a quick sip of wine. This whole situation was terrible. Absolutely terrible. She never should have come—no matter how desperate her need. Unfortunately, she didn't have a choice if she wanted Joe's help.

'Perhaps we should start over,' she said again, this time infusing the words with a businesslike crispness. 'I'm Maddie Wallace.'

'Maddie,' he repeated. The faintest of Italian accents lent her name a unique flavor, and she had the oddest sensation that he could actually taste the syllables as they rolled across his tongue. 'And why have you come to me, Maddie Wallace?'

She drained the glass of wine in an effort to muster her courage. She'd been warned that Joe might not be entirely receptive to her request. 'Break it to him gently,' Mathias had advised. 'Don't give him any more information than necessary. And, no matter what, wait until he's agreed to help before you hit him with the whole truth.'

She peeked at Joe over the rim of her empty glass, striving to determine the best way to approach him. He sat quietly beneath her scrutiny, his posture one of both elegance and contained power. If only he weren't so good-looking, came the helpless thought. Good-looking men couldn't be trusted. She'd learned that at a painfully early age. And with deep brown eyes shot with gold, a forcefully squared jaw and thick dark hair, this man had to be the most magnificent she'd ever had the misfortune to meet.

'Is this business of yours so difficult to discuss?' he questioned quietly. 'Is it personal, by any chance?'

It was now or never. If she didn't tell him what she wanted and get it over with, she'd leave and never come back. Which meant that she'd fail to achieve the goal she'd set for herself at the tender age of five. 'It's just...' She took a deep breath and announced bluntly, 'You're my Christmas wish.'

To her utter amazement, a gleam of satisfaction sparked deep in Joe's eyes and he smiled in the same manner as he had when he'd first found her on his doorstep—offering a nerve-racking, predatory sort of grin. The urge for flight had never been stronger, and it took every scrap of self-control for Maddie to remain seated.

'How nice,' he commented gently. 'I always wanted to be someone's Christmas wish.'

'I don't think you understand.'

'You're right, *cara*. I don't understand.' He finished off his wine and carefully placed the delicate crystal on the table beside him. Then he stood and took an unhurried step toward her chair. Planting his hands on each of the high-backed wings, he leaned toward her. 'Why don't you explain it to me?'

She pressed her spine as deep into the cushions as they'd allow, staring at him with huge, apprehensive eyes. 'Mathias said you owed him a favor. So he...he gave you to me.'

'As a Christmas wish?'

She nodded, feeling her hair slipping free of its knot as it brushed against the back of the chair. 'I have it in writing. You're all mine until Christmas.'

'All yours.' He reached out to capture a loosened lock of hair, trailing it through his fingers. 'I like that.'

'I hope you'll still like it once I explain what I want,' she retorted in a tight voice.

'Hmm. Good point.' He released her hair and tucked it back into place. She found the gesture unbearably intimate, the type of service a husband or lover would perform—the type of service she needed to prevent him from ever performing again. 'What's that expression? "Your wish is my command"? Is that what you're hoping I'll say?' he asked.

'Yes.'

It had become impossible to breathe. Frustrated anger drove soft color into her cheeks. He must know the effect he had on her. Men like Joe Milano came equipped with a special radar that alerted them to a woman's reaction. Maybe they even put out some sort of vibes that caused normally intelligent, logical and responsible women to lose all rational thought.

'In that case... Your wish is my command.' His gaze locked with hers, holding her with damning ease. 'Name this wish, Maddie Wallace. What can I give you? Or is it a dream I can help fulfill? Tell me, *cara*. How do I please you?'

Please her? Oh, no. Not a chance. 'It…it's not that sort of wish!' she insisted, horrified.

Husky laughter broke from him. 'Then what sort is it?'

'Just not *that* sort,' she managed to say.

'What a shame. I think I would have liked satisfying *that* sort.' He lifted an eyebrow. 'You're certain?'

Good heavens, he had to be the most gorgeous man she'd ever seen. She'd thought so when she'd first set eyes on him. But, up close and personal, he was absolutely devastating. Lean and broad-shouldered, he'd been endowed with the sort of classic good looks that drove women to make complete and utter fools of themselves. Fortunately, devastating men were on her list of forbidden pursuits—fortunate, that was, assuming she could resist such sweet temptation.

'I'm positive. My wish—it isn't personal.' She moistened her lips. 'I told you, remember? It's business.'

'In that case, I think I'm going to enjoy doing business with you.' His gaze fastened on her mouth and for an insane second she thought he meant to kiss her. Or did she merely *hope* he'd kiss her? 'Tell me this wish and, if it's within my powers to grant it, it's yours.'

Elation gripped her. 'Anything? You'll give me anything I request?'

'Anything.'

She inched her hand into the pocket of her skirt and freed a thin packet of papers. Unfolding the glossy pages, she carefully smoothed the tattered corners before holding them out. 'These are recipes I clipped from a magazine a few years ago. I want you to teach me how to prepare the meal that's described here. And I need to have you do it by Christmas.'

He straightened abruptly, his expression switching from sensuous to downright forbidding. He glared at the magazine article she'd extended as though she were offering him a handful of poison. 'Excuse me? You want me to do what?'

So much for giving her anything she asked, Maddie thought. Mathias had been right. She should have approached her request with more care. 'I'm having a family gathering for Christmas Eve dinner,' she explained, striving to keep her voice level and devoid of anxiety. 'I want to cook a particular meal they describe in this magazine article. And…and I'd like you to teach me how.'

'Teach you,' he repeated.

'You're a cook, aren't you?' she asked with a twinge of uncertainty. 'Mathias said you were.'

Joe's eyes narrowed. 'Fast food restaurants hire cooks. I am a cordon bleu-trained chef.'

'I see.' She'd clearly insulted him, although it hadn't been deliberate. Chef…cook… Was there that big a difference? One just had a fancier job description, right? 'It's a rather elaborate meal. I guess that's why Mathias thought of you. It's a bit beyond my capabilities.' An understatement, if ever there was one.

He stood by the fireplace, his forearm resting on the mantel. All hint of gold had vanished from his eyes, and he studied her with a brooding darkness that bothered her far more than she cared to admit.

'Why don't you hire a caterer?' he questioned at last.

'It's vital that I do this myself.'

'Why?'

'To prove I can.'

'You must prove this to your family?' His brows drew together. 'What sort of people are they to expect such a thing?'

She shook her head. It wasn't *her* family, she almost admitted, but then thought better of giving him too much information. She'd already made that mistake once. Besides, she didn't know him well enough for those sort of confidences. 'I need to prove to myself that I'm capable of handling an occasion like this.'

'It's that important to you?'

She didn't hesitate. 'Yes.' Not sure whether she'd convinced him, she used what little leverage she had. 'Mr. Blackstone promised you'd help. He said you owed him.'

He took a moment to digest her comment, then asked, 'Tell me how you met Mathias.'

'We were introduced at a charity benefit last week-end. I gather he's some sort of middleman. He finds items that others can't.'

'He prefers the term "procurer". But, yes. He's basically a middleman.'

'Oh. Well, I was told that he donates his time each December to fulfilling special requests.'

Joe inclined his head. 'He calls them Christmas wishes. Just out of curiosity—what convinced him to give you one of his wishes?'

'He didn't give it to me. When I learned what Mr. Blackstone did, I purchased one at the benefit. They had an auction to raise money and I put in the winning bid.' It had cost her a fortune, but she didn't resent a single penny. Or she wouldn't if Joe taught her all she needed to know.

He gave her an odd look. 'Mathias would have granted any wish you requested and this is the one you chose?'

Maddie nodded. 'I chose you.'

'Why?' he asked again.

'I told you. It's important to me.'

'Why?'

She stirred uneasily. 'Look… Could we discuss this another time? It's late and I really should be going.' Not giving him time to argue, she added, 'You promised to fulfill my Christmas wish no matter what. I need to know…. Do you plan to keep your word, or not? Will you grant it or do I have to go elsewhere?'

'There's no need to go elsewhere. I'll grant it.'

Her relief was so great that it took a minute to

gather her composure enough to respond. 'I can't thank you enough,' she murmured, standing.

'Save your thanks until you have your wish.'

Sound advice. 'When would it be possible to get together again?' she asked. 'There isn't a lot of time.'

'First we need to discuss the menu. Are you free tomorrow night?'

'Tomorrow would be fine. Should I come here? Or—?'

'Stop by my restaurant around ten. It's called House Milano. Do you know it? It's downtown on top of King Tower.'

He'd confirmed Maddie's worst fears. She'd hoped Joy would be wrong, that he wasn't the infamous society page chef. She should have known better, especially after meeting him. 'I've heard of your restaurant,' she murmured, suddenly aware that he was waiting for her response.

'But you've never been there?'

She bit down on her lip and shook her head. 'A coworker recognized your name and made the connection.'

'Then you haven't seen my cooking show, either?' he questioned curiously.

'I'm afraid not. I don't watch a lot of television. But I've always wanted to dine at your restaurant.' She glanced at him to see how he reacted to her confession. To her relief he didn't seem insulted. If anything he appeared amused.

'In that case, meet me tomorrow evening and we'll

discuss how to proceed.' He took her empty wineglass to the wet bar and refilled it. 'Why don't you drink this and enjoy the fire while I call a cab?'

'Please, don't bother. I can catch the bus.'

'I insist.'

She decided not to argue. After all, she'd achieved her main objective. Joe had agreed to teach her how to prepare Christmas Eve dinner. She could afford to be gracious in return.

When the cab arrived ten minutes later, Joe walked her to the curb and waited while she gave the driver her address.

'*Cara,* you never told me why this dinner is so important to you,' he said, leaning through the window to pay the fare.

Maddie fastened her seat belt, deciding she wouldn't get a better opportunity to set the tone for their future meetings. 'It's important because that's the night Tupper is going to propose to me,' she informed him calmly.

Joe's brows crashed together. 'Tupper? Who's this Tupper?'

She folded her hands in her lap and fixed her gaze on the back of the cabbie's head. 'Tupper Reed. The man I'm going to marry.'

Joe stood watching in stunned disbelief as the cab pulled away from the sidewalk and disappeared into the rain-filled night. *The man she was going to marry!*

No. Not a chance. Maddie Wallace wanted *him*. He'd seen her reaction. No woman who stared with such huge, wistful eyes, who smiled with such passionate warmth, whose breath quickened whenever he leaned near, could be in love with a Tupper Reed. Joe's hands balled into fists as he considered the ramifications of her statement. Damn it all! He could lose this woman before he ever had the chance to win her.

Then he shook his head, determination setting in. No way. It wouldn't happen. No matter what it took, he'd convince Maddie they belonged together. Because no one—*no one*—was going to steal his woman!

Not even her fiancé-to-be.

Maddie leaned back against the seat cushions and released her breath in a long sigh. There. That would take care of any further problems with Joe Milano. Now that he knew about Tupper, he'd stop flirting with her. He'd turn off those powerful vibes of his and leave her alone. And maybe, just maybe, it would end those odd reactions she'd experienced every time he happened to glance her way.

She had to remember where she'd come from—and where she was headed. She wouldn't allow anything—or any*one* to interfere with her goal.

Especially not a sexy Italian cordon bleu-trained chef.

CHAPTER TWO

Carta Dei Vini...

or

Cooking Up Trouble!

MADDIE stepped off the elevator at the top of King Tower and into the lobby of House Milano, and found herself standing at the edge of a starlit paradise. It was stunning; she didn't hesitate to acknowledge that. Gracious, elegant, sophisticated—Joe's restaurant blended old world charm with a contemporary flair.

Beneath her feet lay a pathway of diamond-shaped pink and ivory marble that led to an imposing glass reservation desk. An elderly gentleman dressed in a black tux with a white rose pinned to his lapel stood behind the large podium. Clearly the *maître d'*, he gave a courtly bow as she approached.

'Good evening, Ms. Wallace,' he said, before she had a chance to speak. 'I'm Giorgio. Welcome to House Milano.'

'Thank you, Giorgio. It's a pleasure to be here,' Maddie replied, secretly impressed that he knew her identity. Joe must have alerted his staff that she'd be dropping by. Still, it gave her a warm feeling to be greeted by name. 'I have an appointment with Mr. Milano. Is he available?'

'He's expecting you. If you'll follow me?'

He led the way into the almost empty restaurant. Tables dotted a huge open area and were angled toward the dance floor. A small combo played a jazzy Nat King Cole classic for the few diners who remained. Past the tables, a wall of tinted glass gave an impressive view of the Seattle skyline.

'Have you been to House Milano before?' Giorgio enquired.

'I'm sorry to say I haven't,' she confessed. 'It's quite lovely.'

He beamed with pleasure. 'We're very proud of our establishment. It's a wonderful place to spend the evening. A leisurely meal, a glass of wine, some dancing.' Far from acting the part of the imperious *maître d'*, Giorgio smiled encouragingly. 'You must join us for dinner one night soon. I'll keep a table available for you. Would you like that?'

'Very much. Thank you.'

At the far end of the dance floor stood a three-quarter wall divided by a gated archway. Giorgio opened the gate and gestured for her to enter a second dining area.

This section provided a much more intimate setting. There were fewer tables here, their placement commanding an unparalleled view of Puget Sound. Low walls overflowing with plants insured the privacy of the diners. Maddie could still hear the music, though it was softer, less intrusive.

'We reserve these tables for those in the mood for romance,' Giorgio explained in an undertone. 'They may visit our dance floor if they so desire or stay here and enjoy each other's company while they watch the lights from the ferries.'

He escorted her to the far end of the room and up a short staircase. Joe sat at a table—unquestionably the best in the restaurant—working his way through a stack of papers. He still wore his chef's uniform, one side of the white jacket unbuttoned to expose the bronzed column of his throat. Thick black hair fell in a heavy wave across his brow as he leaned forward to slash a form with a bright red marking pen. Giorgio gave her a fatherly wink and then made a point of clearing his throat.

'Yes, Giorgio, what is it?' Joe asked absently.

'Ms. Wallace is here.'

Instantly, Joe looked up and tossed his pen aside, offering the sexy little grin that had followed her all the way home the previous night before climbing into bed with her. She'd dreamt of that smile, waking every hour on the hour to curse him for daring to invade her dreams. Not that it had done any good. The Joe in her dreams had been as obstinately determined as the real-life version.

'I'm pleased you could make it.' He stood, crossing to greet her. Before she had time to protest, he caught her hands in his and leaned down to plant a lingering

kiss on each cheek. As he did so, she caught the unmistakable aroma of sandalwood combined with the
faintest suggestion of cedar. 'So how do you like my
restaurant?' he asked.

'It's beautiful,' she replied, impulsively drawing
the seductive scent deeper into her lungs. The moment
she realized what she'd done, she hastened to slip
from his embrace. The further she stayed from him
the better. That way he wouldn't have a chance to use
any of that potent charm he had in such abundance.
To her annoyance, a trace of his scent clung to her,
stirring an unmistakable response. 'Now that I know
how beautiful it is, I'll make a point of dining here.'

'With your fiancé-to-be, no doubt,' he retorted
blandly.

She lifted her chin. 'It's the perfect place to celebrate our engagement, don't you think?'

His eyes narrowed, the rich chocolate brown con-
suming every speck of gold. 'Trust me, *cara*,' he murmured. 'You don't want to know what I think of that
idea.' Raising his voice, he addressed Giorgio. 'If
Cindy's free, ask her to bring coffee. And if you'll
handle any problems that crop up?'

Giorgio inclined his head. 'I'll see to it that you're
not disturbed.'

'Why don't we use the couch?' Joe suggested to
Maddie, gesturing toward a small sitting area close to
the windows. 'I'm afraid the table is too cluttered for
comfort.'

'I didn't realize being a chef involved so much paperwork,' she commented as Joe took her coat and tossed it over the arm of a nearby chair.

He gave a wry laugh. 'Some days it seems that's all I do.' He joined her on the silk-covered sofa and, although he settled at the opposite end, only a narrow gap separated them.

'You run this place and have your own cooking show?' she asked. 'Where do you find the time?'

'It's not my show. I make guest appearances once or twice a month on the morning program here in Seattle. They've asked me to do a weekly segment, but so far I've resisted.'

'Why?'

'I like being with my family whenever possible. If I did more shows, it would interfere with that.'

'You're married?' Maddie demanded, struggling to conceal her shock and failing miserably. 'You have children?'

He laughed, the sound warm and intimate, and darkly masculine. 'No, *cara*. I'm not the sort of man to flirt with one woman while married to another.'

'But you'll flirt with a woman who's engaged to someone else?'

'Not at all. I'll flirt with a woman who's thinking of becoming engaged,' he corrected. 'If her affections are sincere, it won't harm anything. And if they aren't...' He shrugged, leaving her to figure out the rest—something she preferred to avoid at all costs.

'I believe we were talking about your family,'

Maddie reminded him in a blatant attempt to divert the direction of their conversation.

'Were we?' His laughter held a gently mocking quality, but to her relief he didn't argue. 'I have a comfortably sized family—three brothers and their wives, a mother, a father and quite a few nieces and nephews. But I've learned that if I put in more hours at work than I do currently, I don't have anything left over for them. So I make sure that doesn't happen.'

'You're close to your family?' Did he hear the wistful note in her voice? she wondered uneasily. She hoped not.

'Very. You see, I only came to this country six years ago. The rest of the Milanos have been here for more than twenty-five. I'm still trying to make up for lost time.'

'They left you in Italy?' she questioned in disbelief. 'But you couldn't have been more than a boy.'

'I was twelve—nearly a man.' Obviously, he thought that would reassure her. When he realized it hadn't, he added, 'I was the oldest. And since my grandparents chose not to emigrate it was my responsibility to care for them.'

'Which meant remaining behind?'

'Of course.' He reached out and gave her hand a quick, reassuring squeeze. He had a strong grip, yet she sensed the underlying control, instinctively realizing that he would never hurt her with that strength. 'Don't look so sad. I came to Seattle for periodic visits during those years. And I adored my grandparents.

I miss them very much. Fortunately I now have the other members of my family to help make up for their loss.' He tilted his head to one side, fixing her with a questioning look. 'Your turn.'

'I don't think—' she began. He distracted her by running a hand through his hair and wincing. She frowned in concern. 'What's wrong?'

'It's nothing. Just a minor burn.'

She couldn't conceal her alarm. 'A burn? How did that happen?'

'A slight accident in the kitchen while breaking in a new crewman. It's nothing serious.'

'Burns *are* serious.' Two decades worth of habit took over. She leaned closer and ever so gently pushed his hair back from his forehead. 'Oh, Joe. That looks painful.'

A crooked grin creased his face. 'Would you believe it's feeling better already?'

'No, I wouldn't. Hang on. I have something that should help.' She reached for her purse and rummaged through the contents, pulling out a small amber bottle filled with vitamin E capsules. 'Do me a favor and lift your hair out of the way.'

'Do you always carry a supply of vitamin E with you?' he asked in surprise.

'Always.' Very carefully she pinched off one end of the gelatin capsule and squeezed the contents onto her finger. She glanced at Joe. 'I'll try and be gentle.'

'I trust you.' He sat quietly as she knelt on the

couch close to his side. 'Do you play nurse very often?'

'I used to.' She was vividly aware of him—aware of how close his mouth was to hers, aware of how carefully he watched her, aware of the thick, dark lashes framing his gold-tinted eyes. 'When I was younger, I always seemed to be patching up someone or other.'

'You must come from a large family. Did you grow up in Seattle?'

She ignored his question and very carefully dabbed the ointment on his burn. 'I think you're going to need a second capsule. I know it stings right now, but in about fifteen to twenty minutes it'll stop. I promise.'

'All right. So you don't want to talk about your family. How about work? What do you do with yourself when you're not buying wishes at auctions?'

She broke open a second capsule. 'I'm an accountant for a local firm.'

For some reason, he found that humorous. 'An accountant? And this Tupper Reed…does he own the firm by any chance?'

'Yes,' she replied briefly. 'Okay. I'm all done. You should feel better soon.'

'Thanks. That was kind of you.'

'It was nothing.' She returned to her side of the couch just as Cindy arrived. Determined to take full advantage of the interruption, Maddie dropped the vitamins into her purse and removed the recipes.

'Shall we get started? I brought the menu so we could discuss the various dishes.'

'If you wish,' he said, handing her a cup of coffee. He studied her, his gaze calm and direct. 'But eventually you're going to answer my questions. All of them.'

The certainty in his voice alarmed her. 'Only if I choose to.'

'You will—once you learn to trust me.' Leaving her to digest that distressing observation, he asked, 'So, this dinner is to celebrate both Christmas and your engagement, is that right? You weren't too clear last night.'

Maddie forced herself to focus. It wouldn't do any good to worry about what Joe might or might not attempt at some point in the future. He couldn't very well force a confidence from her that she was unwilling to give. And now—finally—he'd turned the conversation to business. If she was smart, she'd follow his lead.

'So far it's just a Christmas Eve dinner,' she confessed. As much as she'd have liked to tell him it was more than that, she couldn't bring herself to lie. 'I'm hoping Tupper will ask me to marry him then.'

That snagged his interest. 'You hope? There's some doubt?'

'No, of course not,' she instantly denied, busily adding cream and sugar to her coffee. She didn't dare look at him. 'We've discussed taking this step for a while.'

Joe appeared astounded. 'You've discussed it? What's there to discuss? He asks and you answer. Unless...' His eyes narrowed. 'Unless there's some question as to your feelings for each other.'

'There's no question at all.'

'This Tupper...' Normally the faintest of Italian accents gave Joe's words a melodic quality. But there was nothing in the least melodious about the way he said this particular name. Instead, it grated on his tongue. 'You love him?'

'I wouldn't agree to marry him if I didn't.'

'But do you love him?'

She shot him an annoyed look. 'I just said I did.'

Joe cocked his head to one side. 'No, *cara*. You didn't. You said you wouldn't agree to marry him without love. There's a difference.'

She took a sip of coffee, fighting for control. Why did he keep questioning her? Why did he keep forcing her to address issues she preferred to avoid? Very carefully, she returned her cup to the saucer and forced a cool, remote smile. 'Yes, I love him. Tupper Reed is everything I've always wanted in a man. Are you satisfied now, Mr. Milano?'

Apparently he wasn't. 'And what exactly is it that you want?' he persisted.

She didn't even have to think. 'Security. Stability. Dependability.' Being certain he'd never leave her. 'He should be a good man—kind.'

'And loving?' Joe inserted gently. 'You forgot to mention love.'

She fixed her attention on the twinkling lights that marked the few boats still plying the sound at this hour. 'That's a given.'

'For your sake I hope so.' Finishing his coffee, he gestured toward the magazine pages. 'Let me see what you have.'

Returning her cup to the saucer, Maddie picked up the magazine article. The aged paper crackled between her clenched fingers. Immediately she eased her grip and smoothed the deep creases with a gentle hand. The first page was her favorite—a gorgeous, soft-focus photo of a family sitting around a beautifully decorated table, clearly enjoying Christmas dinner. The subsequent pages listed the recipes, and offered close-up pictures of each of the individual dishes. She held the packet out to Joe.

'I'd like to recreate this meal—exactly.'

He turned his attention to the recipes, flipping rapidly through them. 'Have you attempted any of these yet?'

'One or two,' she replied cautiously. She still hadn't explained all the problems he would encounter helping to fulfill her Christmas wish. And she wouldn't enlighten him until she didn't have any other choice. 'I can't seem to get them right.'

'How many people will be attending your dinner party?'

'Not many. Tupper, one of his sisters and her husband, and, of course, his parents.'

'Six. That's a good number. Enough to make a

pleasant get-together without so many to make it a chore.' He flipped through the pages a second time, frowning as he studied them. 'There's a few of these dishes that you might wish to change or omit. I suggest you avoid anything that has to be prepared last minute or you won't be able to enjoy your company.'

'No,' Maddie said with an adamant shake of her head. 'I want to replicate the dinner they describe in every detail.'

'*Cara,*' he began. 'Be reasonable—'

'I'm serious, Joe. I want everything exactly the same.'

He glared in exasperation. 'Have you even tasted any of these dishes?'

'They sound delicious.'

'I assume that's a no.'

'All right, no. I haven't. But—'

'Then first we'll try each one and make sure you like it.'

She blinked in surprise. 'Oh. I thought you were going to tell me which ones I wouldn't like.'

'How can you know you don't like something unless you try it?' he asked reasonably.

She suspected they weren't discussing food anymore. 'We can taste-test the recipes as we go along.'

He shook his head. 'There's no point in learning to cook something you find unappetizing,' he retorted. 'I'll tell you what. We're closed this next Sunday night. I'll have my brother, Renzo, come in and prepare the entire meal. You sample each dish and decide whether you still want it. Would that be acceptable?'

'He'll use these recipes?' she questioned anxiously. 'He'll do it the way it's described here?'

Laughter sparked in Joe's gaze. 'If I force him, he'll follow the recipe. But you understand that chefs don't normally operate that way. Our creations are not so…by the book.'

'No, I didn't realize,' she admitted. 'I'm afraid I don't know a lot about how a chef works.'

Joe inclined his head. 'Then it will be my pleasure to teach you.'

She scanned his expression for any hint of double meaning, then decided he was serious. 'When do you want to start practicing the menu?'

He shrugged. 'We can decide that Sunday night.' Indicating the magazine article, he asked, 'Do you mind if I keep this? I'd like to give it to Renzo.'

'Go ahead. You can return it when he's through.' She stood and gathered up her purse and coat.

Joe stood as well. 'May I give you a lift home?'

'No, thank you. That's not necessary.' She hesitated, feeling unexpectedly self-conscious. How ridiculous to react like an awkward schoolgirl at the ripe age of twenty-eight, she thought in amusement. 'I guess that's it, then. I'll see you Sunday.'

He stopped her before she could make good her escape—stopped her with a single word. *'Cara.'*

Slowly she turned to face him, afraid of what she would see. Sure enough, his gaze was filled with sharp desire, as well as a need so clear and deep and certain that, instinctively, she took a step backward. And yet the temptation to respond to that look was almost more than she could stand. 'Joe, please,' she whispered. 'Don't do this.'

His mouth twisted into a smile and he reached for her. 'I wouldn't do anything to hurt you. If it's Tupper you want, it's Tupper you'll have.' He cupped the side of her face with a gentle hand while his thumb traced a scorching path the length of her jaw. Then he dipped his head, his breath brushing her lips like a whisper-soft kiss. 'But I don't think you want him.'

Almost she accepted what he offered. Almost she closed the scant inch between them to take his mouth with hers. At the last instant, sanity prevailed. With an inarticulate murmur she ducked free of his embrace. 'You're mistaken,' she said unsteadily. 'And now, if you don't mind, I'd better go.'

He stepped back, giving her some much needed breathing space. 'If you must. I'll see you Sunday.' He lifted an eyebrow. 'Is seven convenient?'

'I—' She closed her eyes in defeat. What choice did she have? If she wanted to host Christmas Eve dinner for Tupper's family, she needed Joe's help— badly. 'Thank you. Seven will be fine.'

Not giving him an opportunity to tempt her again, she turned and walked steadily away.

'Have you lost your mind?' Renzo snapped. 'You want me to cook this meal using someone else's recipes? Forget it. I don't work that way.'

'You owe me.' Joe's tone grew steely. 'And you owe me a hell of a lot more than one simple dinner.'

'It's not the dinner I object to, and you know it. It's having to use her menu.' Renzo gave it a moment's thought, then brightened. 'I'll tell you what. Invite your lady friend to my restaurant and I'll fix a meal you'll both remember for years to come.'

'I appreciate the offer, but it won't solve my problem.' Joe held out the magazine article and accompanying menu. 'I need this prepared exactly as it's written.'

Renzo folded his arms across his chest, pointedly refusing to accept the papers. 'If it's so important to you, fix the meal yourself.'

'Since I'll be dining with the lady in question, that's not an option. Come on, Renzo,' Joe argued, his patience fast giving out. 'This woman's important to me.'

His brother made a dismissive gesture. 'They're all important to you.'

'Then you won't help?' Joe demanded. 'You're going to turn down your future sister-in-law's one request?'

'Yes, I'm going to—' Renzo's mouth fell open. 'Wait a minute. Who said anything about—?'

'Of course, she hasn't agreed, yet. I still have to win her cooperation.'

Renzo shook his head in disbelief. 'You mean this woman hasn't already fallen for you? Incredible.'

Dona Milano bustled into the room just then. 'What's this?' she demanded. 'Did I hear someone mention marriage and Giuseppe's name in the same sentence?'

Joe gave his mother a loving hug. 'You have the most amazing hearing of any woman I know. Especially considering that neither marriage nor my name were mentioned at all.'

'You said you were giving Renzo a sister-in-law,' she argued. 'That's all I needed to hear.'

'Okay, yes. I've found the woman I intend to marry.' He pinched her cheek. 'Does that make you happy?'

'You're finally getting married?' Sheer joy spread across her handsome features. 'You aren't just teasing me?'

'I wouldn't do that to you,' Joe said gently. 'I'm quite serious.'

Renzo's eyes gleamed with amusement. 'Oh, *he's* serious, all right. It's the lady he wants to marry who isn't. It seems she doesn't return Joe's affections.'

Dona's eyes widened as she looked at her eldest son. 'No! That can't be. All women are crazy about you.'

Joe shrugged. 'Not only is she refusing to admit to the attraction, she still hopes to marry her boss—an accountant named Tupper Reed.'

'You're kidding.' Renzo's eyes widened in amazement. 'She wants some guy named Tupper when she could have you?'

Joe's reply was short and rude, but it succeeded in silencing his younger brother. 'She's confused. She doesn't want this other man. She just thinks she does.'

'And you plan to straighten out this confusion of hers?' Dona Milano questioned mildly. 'How generous of you.'

Joe winked at his mother. 'Yes. I thought so.'

'Giuseppe,' she began in a warning voice.

He planted a quick kiss on her cheek. '*Now* I'm teasing you. I wouldn't cause any trouble with this fiancé-to-be if it weren't for one minor detail.'

Dona eyed him with resignation. 'And what detail is that?'

'The lady loves me. She just hasn't realized it yet.' There was no mistaking his conviction. 'But she will. And by Christmas, too.'

'So soon?' Dona asked in amazement.

'But of course.' He gave his family a cheerful grin. 'How else can we marry by New Year's?'

'So, spill it! What's he like?'

Maddie avoided Joy's gaze and shrugged. 'You've seen his show.'

'Everyone's seen his show,' her co-worker retorted in exasperation. 'But what's he like in real life? I want details, girl.'

The memory of that almost-kiss flashed through Maddie's thoughts and she winced. Joy didn't need those sort of details. *Definitely* too much information. 'He's charming, of course.'

'I knew it. I just knew it.' Joy groaned. 'I'm so jealous. Tell me everything. Did he put the moves on you?'

'Joy!'

'Well, you said he was charming,' she claimed defensively. 'You can't blame me for wondering... Just *how* charming?'

'Not *that* charming. Besides, I want Tupper.'

'Yeah, I know.' Joy nibbled on her lip, casting Maddie a hesitant glance. 'Are you...are you positive you still want Tupper? Not that there's anything wrong with him,' she hastened to add. 'He's a sweet guy. Nice, successful, friendly. And real cute. But he's nothing like Joe Milano.'

'I'm aware of that.' The door leading to Tupper's office opened, and Maddie murmured, 'In fact, I'm counting on it.'

Tupper glanced her way. 'Maddie? Could I see you for a moment?'

Relieved to escape Joy's inquisition, Maddie hastened into his office. The minute the door closed, she slipped her arms around his waist and gave him a quick hug. Six months ago, when their relationship had turned personal, they'd agreed to keep the romance outside of the workplace. But she needed to touch him, to remind herself that this was the man she'd chosen to share her life with. This was the man she loved. There weren't any doubts.

There couldn't be.

'You okay?' Tupper questioned in concern.

His voice was a comforting tenor, without the least trace of Mediterranean lilt. She pulled back slightly, realizing that she only needed to lift her gaze a fraction of an inch to meet his kind blue eyes. How nice that she'd never have to worry about him towering over her like one man of recent acquaintance. Nor would she need to worry that he would attempt to seduce her with the scent of sandalwood and cedar. Or that he'd try and steal a kiss which she absolutely, positively, wouldn't be charmed into giving—unless forced to.

'I just needed a hug,' she explained. She brushed a lock of fine blond hair from his brow. So his hair wasn't thick and black and wavy, nor did it feel like silk sifting between her fingers. Tupper had more important qualities. After all, he'd always give her stability, dependability and security. And that was what she wanted more than anything, right? 'I'm going to miss you these next two weeks.'

'You know I'd rather take you to Spokane for these meetings than Joy,' he replied. 'Are you certain you have to use your vacation time now?'

'I'm afraid so.' She offered a bright smile. 'But once you're back it'll only be about a week until Christmas Eve.'

'True enough.' He kissed the tip of her nose before releasing her. 'Thank you again for agreeing to have my relatives for dinner. They'll only be in town that one week, and—'

'No thanks necessary. It's my pleasure.'

'I've told them what a wonderful cook you are. Mom always says—'

'I know,' Maddie cut in with a frown. 'Marry a woman who knows her way around a kitchen and the marriage will last forever.' She'd never figured out the correlation between the two, but she knew better than to say as much to Tupper.

'Obviously, you won't have to worry about that. You always seem able to whip up the most impressive creations at a moment's notice.'

She shifted uneasily, avoiding his gaze. 'You'd be shocked to know how I did it.'

'Not at all,' he instantly claimed. 'You're just a wonderful cook.'

'Listen, there's something you should know. I have to explain—'

'No, no. Don't tell me how you do it. Some things are better kept a secret.'

'Are you sure this is one of them?'

'Positive. Now we'd better get to work before people start gossiping.'

'Yes, of course,' she murmured. 'We wouldn't want that.'

'She wants what?' Dona asked in disbelief.

'Security, stability and dependability,' Joe repeated. 'Interesting, yes?'

'Most women want these things,' his mother replied dismissively, though a troubled frown continued to line her brow. 'Ask any of your sisters-in-law. They'll all agree.'

Joe lifted an eyebrow. 'They'll agree those things are more important than love? Would you have married for security alone?'

Dona sighed. 'You know I wouldn't have.'

'Neither should Maddie.'

'You're certain she's attracted to you?' Dona questioned in concern. 'It's not just wishful thinking on your part?'

He thought again of that kiss they'd almost exchanged. 'Trust me. I know when a woman's interested.' And Maddie Wallace was more than interested. He'd seen the wistful longing in her eyes—just as he'd seen the fear.

'Then there's only one option,' Dona said briskly. 'You must determine why these qualities are important to her. And then you must prove that you can give her these things, too—and do a better job of it than this Tupper Reed fellow.'

'Of course I can provide her with security,' Joe retorted, stung. 'I'm also very dependable.'

'She doesn't know that—especially if she reads the gossip about you in the newspapers. All she'll see is your reputation.' Dona folded her arms across her chest and eyed him grimly. 'You must admit, there've been quite a few women in your life.'

Joe shot her an innocent look. 'How else could I have found the perfect one?'

Dona clicked her tongue in exasperation. 'You listen to me, Giuseppe. If you hurt this girl, I'll never forgive you. You make sure she really wants you and that it isn't just wishful thinking on your part.'

His expression turned fiercely determined. 'She's mine, just as much as I'm hers. Any doubts she may have are from one thing—fear.'

'Fear can cause people to make foolish decisions,' Dona warned gently. 'Even marry the wrong man for all the wrong reasons.'

'Then I have until Christmas to relieve her fears and prove I'm the right man for her.' He set his jaw. 'And I'll do it, too. You have my promise. I've waited too long for the right woman to risk losing her now. I swear to you, by New Year's you will have a new daughter-in-law.'

CHAPTER THREE

Antipasto Milano...

or

A Tasty Dish!

'GOOD evening, Ms. Wallace,' Giorgio greeted Maddie the moment she stepped off the elevator. 'Welcome once again to House Milano. We're delighted to have you back so soon.'

'I thought the restaurant was closed today,' she replied with a concerned frown. 'Don't tell me Joe made you work tonight?'

'Most of us work on Sunday. We offer a champagne brunch during the day, and every once in a while we stay open into the evening for a special occasion,' the *maître d'* explained. 'I always remain on duty when that happens.'

'But tonight isn't special at all,' Maddie protested. 'Joe and his brother are just preparing a few recipes for me to sample.'

Giorgio gave a formal little bow. 'It will be my great pleasure to serve you these recipes.'

'You don't mind?' she asked uncertainly.

'Not at all,' he reassured her. 'Allow me to take your coat and then I'll show you to your table.'

Maddie slowly unbuttoned her coat as she considered Giorgio's comments. A special occasion...? House Milano's *maître d'* staying after hours to serve them...? What in the world could Joe be thinking? She'd assumed this would be a casual evening, that they would taste the various dishes she'd chosen for Christmas Eve dinner to make sure they were acceptable. But instead the evening felt like a—

Her eyes widened in alarm. It felt like a date.

No. It couldn't be. She must be mistaken, reading far too much into Giorgio's presence. Slipping her coat from her shoulders, she allowed the *maître d'* to dispose of the heavy wool garment. Thank heaven she'd dressed appropriately. She'd planned to wear trousers, but had changed her mind at the last minute, settling on a rich ruby-toned skirt and matching silk blouse.

As before, Giorgio led the way through the restaurant. Most of the lights were off in the large outer area, but overhead spotlights illuminated the small stage. The jazz combo had been replaced by a string quartet, performing a Viennese waltz.

'Does Joe always hire musicians to play to an empty restaurant?' she questioned drily.

Giorgio allowed a faint smile to crease his face. 'Ah, but the restaurant isn't empty, is it?'

'Well, then, is hiring musicians to play to an *almost*

empty restaurant standard procedure at House Milano?'

'I wouldn't know,' he retorted blandly, opening the gate that led to the private sector. 'I leave those sort of decisions to Mr. Milano.'

She shot him an admiring look. 'Nice comeback. I guess in your line of work you have to know what to say to impertinent customers.'

He hid his amusement well, only a faint glitter in his eyes giving him away. 'Thank you, Ms. Wallace. I strive to do my best.' He paused at the bottom of the stairs leading to Joe's table and gestured for her to continue. 'Please go on up. Mr. Milano is waiting for you.'

Not quite certain what to expect, Maddie climbed the steps, overwhelmed by the sight that greeted her at the top.

The entire area lay in peaceful darkness with one exception—Joe's table. There, candlelight cast a velvety glow over the intimate scene, the soft illumination quenched by shadows just as it reached her. She took a helpless step forward, drawn to the circle of warmth. Someone had taken great care with the setting. Champagne waited in a bucket of ice beside frosted flutes. Snowy damask napkins were pleated into fanciful swans and sat nestled atop gold-banded Limoges plates. Fine crystal and silver gleamed among shallow bowls overflowing with strands of miniature ivy, holly and creamy white gardenia blossoms. Thoroughly enchanted, Maddie drifted closer, enticed by the seductive scent of the flowers.

And then it struck her—struck with stunning impact. The table was set exactly as it had been in the magazine photos. Not only was Joe recreating the meal, but the setting as well. Why had he gone to such trouble? she wondered helplessly. He couldn't know how much those pictures meant to her, anymore than he could know how long she'd anticipated preparing a Christmas Eve dinner like this.

She froze, pausing just outside the pool of candlelight. *Joe*. She'd been so captivated by the table, she'd forgotten all about her host.

Glancing around the shadowed room, she finally spotted him. He'd taken a stance near the windows with his back to her. He stood, his legs braced apart and his arms folded across his chest. Instead of his chef's uniform, he wore a dark suit, crisp white shirt and tie. Apparently he hadn't heard her, for he didn't turn around.

Maddie couldn't resist taking a moment to study him. If she'd found Joe Milano devastating before, it couldn't compare to how he looked now. His suit jacket caressed the powerful breadth of his shoulders as he gazed out into the night, while his trousers hugged lean hips and sculpted the taut line of his thighs. If Tupper lifted weights for a full year, he wouldn't come close to matching Joe's physique, Maddie reluctantly conceded. Nor could he match Joe's innate grace and style.

The window closest to him acted like a mirror, reflecting features that would have been too perfect if it weren't for the aggressive tilt of his jaw and the slight crook to his nose. His mouth had a sensuous curve, and she shivered. What would it be like to kiss him? came the insidious thought. She'd almost found out on her last visit. Perhaps this time— Forcibly she dragged her gaze from his mouth, focusing instead on his eyes. And it was then she realized that, far from being unaware of her presence, he'd been watching her the entire time.

For a long, silent moment they stood motionless, staring at each other.

'The table is stunning,' she murmured at last, desperate to break the intensity gathering between them. 'Thank you.'

'My pleasure.' He turned and approached, and Maddie found she couldn't move...didn't want to move. Stopping directly in front of her, he reached out and ran his fingers through the length of her hair. 'You left it down. It looks beautiful.'

She shrugged. 'I left it down because it's Sunday.'

That won a smile from him. 'Do you always wear your hair down on Sunday?'

'Saturday and Sunday. And sometimes Friday night.'

He tilted his head to one side, clearly intrigued. 'And the rest of the week you wear it up?'

'Always.'

'No exceptions?'

'No exceptions,' she confirmed solemnly.

'Perhaps I can tempt you to change your mind. Do you think I could convince you to wear it down for me one Tuesday or Wednesday?'

'Not a chance. You see, I like order. It's...dependable.'

Burnished gold glittered within the rich darkness of his eyes. 'And dependability is important to you?'

'Very.'

'I'm dependable.'

'Flirts are never dependable.'

'I'm not a flirt.'

The slightest frown touched her brow. How she wished that were true. Perhaps she would be more inclined to trust him if it weren't for her father. Like Joe, Profit Wallace had been so damned beautiful and so damned sincere, *honestly believing* every word he uttered was the absolute truth. For a short while life with Joe would be wonderful, full of laughter and joy and excitement. Then, as abruptly as it had begun, their time together would end. Reality would come crashing down and his version of the truth would change as rapidly as a fickle breeze. A woman would catch his eye—just as someone more attractive or smarter or flashier than her mother had caught Profit's—and the chase for true love would begin all over again.

And she would be left on the sidelines. Forgotten.

Maddie closed her eyes, aware that the similarities between the two men were too great to ignore.

Joe cupped her chin. 'You don't believe me, do you?' he demanded, tilting her face upward so she was forced to meet his gaze. 'You think I'm playing games with you.'

She prayed he wouldn't sense her reaction, wouldn't realize how she longed to press her cheek into the warmth of his palm. In that instant, every self-protective instinct she possessed flared to life. She had to stop this before the situation got any further out of control.

'What I think is that we should give those recipes a try,' she suggested gently, slipping from his grasp. 'That's why we're here, remember?'

He acknowledged her retreat with an amused look. 'No, *cara*. That's why *you're* here.'

She rounded on him. 'Really? And what's your reason?'

'I'm your Christmas wish, remember?'

He left her standing there, scrambling for a reply. Crossing to the table, he pulled out her chair and waited until she'd taken a seat. 'The appetizers should arrive any minute. Why don't I pour us some champagne? I realize it's not on the menu you gave me, but I hope you're willing to make this one small exception.'

'I'd enjoy a glass,' she said, deliberately adding, 'Tupper and I don't often indulge. But, now that you mention it, perhaps I should serve wine with Christmas Eve dinner.'

'Excellent idea. After all, you'll want to toast your engagement. Assuming that's still the plan.'

She leveled a cool look in his direction. 'Of course it is. Why wouldn't it be?'

'Ah. Now that's an interesting question.' His eyes reflected the rich golden highlights of the champagne. 'One we can more fully discuss over the next few weeks.'

'I don't think—'

Giorgio arrived just then, preventing her from saying more. He removed the two appetizers from his tray and aligned them in the center of the table. 'Lemon salmon and Pâté Americano,' he announced. 'Your soup will be out shortly. Enjoy your meal.' He didn't linger, his departure as swift and silent as his arrival.

'Are you certain two appetizers are necessary?' Joe questioned. 'Considering the number of courses this dinner involves, I suggest you choose the one you like best and go with that.'

She didn't want to change a single item on the menu, and suspected he knew it. This meal called for both appetizers and that's what she intended to serve. At the same time, she was forced to concede that her culinary skills probably couldn't handle one appetizer, let alone two.

'Why don't we try them before making that decision?' she temporized. Helping herself to a generous serving from the nearest platter, she popped it into her mouth.

She instantly regretted her impulsiveness. Whatever spices they'd used in the lemon salmon, it tasted horrible—blistering hot and regrettably pungent. Her eyes widened, filling with pepper-induced tears. It was absolutely, positively, without any question or doubt, the most loathsome food she'd ever had the misfortune to put into her mouth. She forced herself to swallow.

Joe struggled to retain his composure and failed. A broad grin spread across his mouth. 'Something wrong, *cara?*'

'I… It's…' She shuddered, cutting the taste with half a glass of iced water. 'It's hot.' She grossly understated the case.

'But of course. Didn't you read the recipe? It called for chili peppers. A *lot* of chili peppers, if I remember correctly. And you did request that it be made exactly as written.'

'I guess I missed that part.' She glared at the innocuous-looking mound of salmon. 'And your brother forgot to cook it.'

'He didn't forget. It's seviche.'

'What's that?' she demanded suspiciously.

'Raw fish marinated in lemon juice, spices, oil—and, in this case, a generous portion of peppers. You see, the acid from the lemon juice 'cooks' the salmon.' He scooped up a large helping and tried it. To her disgust, he didn't even flinch. Instead he shrugged sympathetically. 'Perhaps it's an acquired taste.'

She took a quick sip of champagne, praying it would erase the unpleasant flavor. 'I'll take your word for it.'

'And your fiancé-to-be? Will he have acquired a taste for it, do you think?'

Reluctantly she shook her head. 'I doubt it. Maybe we should leave this one off the menu.'

'It's a good thing we're sampling the dishes first, isn't it?' he asked with a far-from-innocent smile.

She hated to consider what would have happened if she'd have served this to Tupper and his family. Her evening would have been over before it had begun. 'It was a very good idea,' she acknowledged. 'I'm glad you thought of it.'

'I'm delighted to be of service. Try the pâté. I think you'll find that more to your liking.' He frowned in consideration. 'Slightly bland, but palatable. I'm sure we can work on it.'

Taking a tiny amount this time, Maddie was pleasantly surprised. 'No changes,' she stated firmly. 'I want the recipes prepared exactly as they're written.'

He cocked an eyebrow. 'Why? The pâté isn't bad, but with some bacon and almonds, perhaps a few shiitake mushrooms, the taste can be improved. So why not go with the better recipe?'

'I've planned this dinner for a long time. And I want it just the way I've always pictured it—just as it's described in the article.'

He sighed. 'You're a stubborn woman, Maddie Wallace.'

'I'm just sure of what I want.'

'I disagree. You *think* you're sure.'

Her eyes darkened to a misty gray. 'Let me guess. You know better, right?'

'I know food better,' he stated. 'The pâté can be improved and that's a fact. As far as you're concerned…' He frowned in consideration. 'I don't know you quite as well. But I hope to in the near future.'

She shook her head. 'That's not our arrangement. You're supposed to teach me how to prepare this meal and that's it.'

'I've promised to give you your Christmas wish and I will. You have my personal guarantee.'

She didn't like the look in his eyes one little bit. 'Why am I not reassured?'

'I can't imagine.'

Her lips twitched at such a blatant and unrepentant lie. 'You're impossible,' she muttered.

The tension between them eased as he chuckled. 'Troublesome when crossed, but not impossible, I hope.' He leaned back as Giorgio approached with the soup course. 'Two appetizers *and* two soups? Might I suggest—?'

'I know,' she interrupted. 'Pick one. Right?'

'A wise decision, *cara,*' he teased. 'I'm glad you agree.'

'Actually, I do agree. We'll try them both and decide which wc prefer.'

It didn't take much discussion. The seafood bisque proved far too spicy for a holiday meal. But the

Meatball Surprise won them both over. 'And it doesn't look too difficult to put together,' she commented in relief.

'Not difficult at all.' He studied her curiously. 'Why did you think you'd have problems with it?'

There was absolutely no way she intended to answer with anything approaching the truth. 'I guess the description made it sound complicated.' Her gaze clung to him, betraying her trepidation. 'But it won't be a problem, right?'

'This dinner is that important?'

'It's that important.'

'Then consider me your insurance. We can always simplify if necessary.' As though anticipating an argument, he hastened to ask, 'How many salads are there?'

She laughed. 'You're in luck. Only one.'

But that one worried her, especially when Giorgio brought it out on a cart that also held a portable gas stove. 'Our salad this evening is called Flaming Spinach,' he announced, lighting the burner with a flourish. 'And it's very similar to one of our house specialities.' As he spoke, he emptied bowls of ingredients into a saucepan.

'How do I do this at home?' Maddie asked Joe nervously.

He caught her hand in his. 'Relax. It's simple. You heat the ingredients in the kitchen like Giorgio is doing here, and then add the warmed brandy. Next you can transfer everything to your dining room and ignite it in front of your guests. It'll only take a little practice to get the hang of it.'

'You won't have any problem, Ms. Wallace,' Giorgio added. 'Watch how easy it is.' He lit the brandy mixture and poured the flaming dressing on top of the spinach. The instant the flames were extinguished, he tossed the salad and served it. 'Anything else, Mr. Milano?'

'We're fine, Giorgio. Thank you.'

With a nod, the *maître d'* collected his utensils and wheeled the cart from the room. The salad delighted Maddie on every level—it had been impressive to watch Giorgio prepare and, even better, it tasted delicious. If Joe could teach her how to prepare the flaming portion without burning down the house, it would unquestionably impress Tupper and his family.

'I read through the recipes, by the way,' Joe commented, refilling their champagne flutes. 'I also examined the photos that accompanied the article.'

Something in the tenor of his voice made her unaccountably wary. 'And?'

'And the recipes appear to be quite old.'

She shrugged. 'They are old. I think I cut them out of the magazine when I was ten.'

He stared in amazement. 'You've kept them all this time? Why?'

'Because...' She hesitated, searching for the right words. 'Because it looked like the perfect Christmas dinner. I've always wanted to have one identical to it.'

'Your family never had dinners like this?' he asked gently.

She shook her head, unable to verbalize a response.

His accent deepened ever so slightly. 'Your family—they'll be able to attend this one, perhaps?'

Again she shook her head. Taking a restorative sip of champagne, she managed to say, 'The dinner's for Tupper's family.'

Joe released his breath in a gusty sigh. 'My apologies, *cara*. I don't mean to pester you with uncomfortable questions. I was just trying to understand why you've kept the recipes all these years. What is it about this particular dinner that appeals so much?'

'I'm not sure.' Her words sounded evasive even to her ears.

Sure enough, he regarded her intently. 'You've never tried the various dishes, so it can't be that.'

'They sounded wonderful,' she insisted. 'And the pictures made them look so good.'

'No doubt it helped to photograph them with such an attractive table setting.' He leaned back in his chair and picked up his glass, swirling the champagne slowly around the delicate crystal flute. 'Was it by any chance the family in the picture that attracted you to this menu?'

'Don't be ridiculous.'

'Why is it ridiculous? It made for a charming picture, don't you think? Especially for a ten-year-old. The handsome husband dressed in a tux… The Madonna-like wife wearing a demure Victorian gown... Four sweet, tow-headed children dressed in velvet and lace...'

'It's just a photo,' she protested. 'I know it's just a photo.'

'But it inspired hopes and dreams, didn't it?' He plucked a gardenia from one of the bowls and dried the stem with his napkin. Leaning forward, he slipped it behind her ear, his hand caressing the curve of her cheek. The delicious scent slipped beneath her defenses. 'You said your family never shared a Christmas like the one in the photograph. Why not?'

She closed her eyes. If only he would stop touching her. 'No reason. We just didn't.'

'Why?' he repeated, more urgently. 'Tell me, *cara*. Why were you denied such a Christmas?'

'Joe, don't.'

'Talk to me, Maddie. Tell me why that picture fills you with such longing.'

She didn't intend to tell him; she really didn't. But something in his eyes—the gentle expression she saw there, or perhaps the light of caring—drew the words of their own volition. 'I want to have the sort of dinner I never experienced as a child.'

'Why didn't you experience it?'

The question was a mere whisper between them.

'Because my mother died when I was five.' It took a moment to gather her composure, to blink away the threat of tears and force the painful truth past a constricted throat. 'I was put into foster care and never had a real Christmas—one with my own family, in my own home, with the people I loved most in the whole world.'

CHAPTER FOUR

Zuppa e Insalata…

or

Too Hot To Handle!

JOE didn't say a word. He simply rose from his seat and crossed to her side, tugging her out of the chair. He kept her hand snug within his own, never once releasing it. Maddie had never felt more secure than she did in that moment. They walked through the gated archway to the dance floor where the string quartet was playing the waltz from Tchaikovsky's *Sleeping Beauty* ballet. Joe released her hand, wrapping her within the protective circle of his arms. Then he drifted with her in a leisurely circle around the empty floor.

He lowered his head and his breath stirred the gardenia petals at her temple. 'Can you talk about your father, *cara?* What happened to him?'

'He wasn't able to take care of me,' Maddie replied in a neutral voice. 'It was all he could do to take care of himself. He'd remove me from foster care for brief periods of time, but it never worked out. He died about a year ago.'

'I see.' To her relief he didn't respond with pity, but kept his tone matter-of-fact. 'That explains all those injuries you nursed growing up. It wasn't brothers and sisters you bandaged, but other foster children.'

'It's amazing the kind of skills you pick up in foster care.'

'Such as?'

She shrugged. 'I learned to cut hair better than a barber, tutor math and science to the younger ones and bathe a baby.'

'So you were the dependable one.'

'Someone had to be. And I really didn't mind.'

'And, because of your father, you want to marry someone who can offer you a stable home environment.'

It was a hard truth to accept, let alone voice. 'That may be, but there's more to my relationship with Tupper than that.'

'Is there? Are you certain?'

Why, oh, why, did Joe have such a kissable mouth? And why did the expression in his eyes stir such a deep, passionate longing? Tupper never made her feel this way. 'I'm here to taste-test Christmas Eve dinner. Remember?' she asked unsteadily. 'You're reading too much into a simple holiday meal.'

'This isn't a simple meal and you know it,' Joe insisted. 'It represents everything you missed growing up.'

'I don't want to discuss it anymore. Tupper and his

family will be coming over to my home and we're going to have a wonderful evening. The sort of evening I've always dreamed of having.'

He pulled back slightly to glance down at her. 'Are you marrying Tupper or his family?'

'Tupper, of course.'

'And are you sure this dream of yours is what you really want, and not just an attempt to redress what happened in the past?'

'This isn't about my past. This is about my future.'

'Fine. Let's talk about that future.'

'It has nothing to do with you,' she argued.

'Now, that's where you're wrong. Don't you see? You want Tupper because he's everything your father wasn't.'

'And you're everything my father was!' she flashed back, instantly regretting the impetuous words. Joe had never done anything to warrant such an accusation. In fact, he'd been incredibly gentle with her. She fixed her gaze on a point over his shoulder. 'I'm sorry. That was uncalled for.'

To her relief, he didn't take offense. Instead, he cradled her closer and danced in silence for several more minutes. 'What was your father's name?' he asked at last.

'Profit. Profit Wallace.'

'And why do you think I'm like him?' Joe pulled back slightly, offering a teasing smile. 'Was he a handsome Italian chef?'

'He was a lot of things, including handsome. But he wasn't a chef. Nor was he Italian.'

'Perhaps if he had been he'd have understood the value of family.' And wouldn't have left his only child in a foster home; Maddie read the unspoken criticism. 'Tell me more about him.'

'I'd rather not.'

'I understand, *cara*. And I wouldn't push except for one small detail. You've claimed we're alike, and I need to know why. You've already said he was a flirt. I assume you think that applies to me as well?'

'A friend at work mentioned that you regularly grace the gossip columns,' Maddie confessed.

'I've dated women over the years. How else will I find the right one?' he asked reasonably. 'Does that qualify me for "flirt" status?'

'No, of course not.' She thought again of her father and those brief windows of time she'd spent with him. 'I guess it's when a man comes on to any and every woman who crosses his path, when he's insincere—'

'Whoa! Slow down.' He frowned in concern. 'Maddie, I don't know what sort of man your father was, but I've never made a promise I haven't kept. All my relationships with women have ended without tears or recriminations. I'd never do anything to hurt a woman.'

She searched his face with a troubled expression. 'Even unintentionally?'

'You mean, have I hurt a woman without meaning to? It's possible. But I have a mother who trained me well. Who trained all her sons well. I also had a grandmother who reinforced every lesson I'd ever been taught. Each of my three brothers is happily married to a wonderful, intelligent, delightful woman. The fact that I'm still unmarried is a source of great concern to all of them.'

'Then why are you still unmarried?'

He smiled tenderly. 'Because, *cara,* until last week I hadn't met you.'

'Don't,' she whispered. 'Don't complicate everything.'

His steps slowed until they were barely swaying in place. 'It's not complicated at all. In fact, it's quite simple. Let me show you how simple.'

He cupped her face, his fingers sliding deep into her hair. For a long moment he stared down at her, the dusting of gold in his dark eyes blazing with passionate promise. He made no attempt to disguise how he felt, allowing her to witness the full scope of his desire.

No one had ever looked at her with such blatant hunger, she realized in wonder. No one had ever shown her that she was so completely needed, or revealed such utter conviction in that need. He wanted her; she read it clearly. She didn't understand why, but her response came hot and hard, and hit with crippling impact.

His head dipped closer, and finally his mouth took possession of hers. It felt and tasted every bit as delicious as she'd anticipated. Firm. Decisive. Experienced. She was right about something else. In the two years she'd known Tupper, he'd *never* made her feel this good.

Her eyes drifted closed and she wound her arms around Joe's neck. She could sense his fight for restraint, feel the ripple that shuddered through him as he struggled to hold back. The instant her lips parted, though, the struggle ended. With a harsh groan, he possessed her mouth, his tongue surging inward, deep and hard and thorough. It wasn't enough.

She strained against him, wanting to feel all of him, wanting the hot brand of his touch on every inch of her. In that timeless moment, all her dreams, all her desires—all she'd ever wanted in life—existed within the seductive strength of Joe's arms. She wanted to stay there and never leave.

At long last he released her, and with the chill of their separation came the chill return of sanity.

'See how simple it is?' he asked gently.

She shook her head, frustrated, confused and oddly weepy. The gardenia flower became dislodged and she caught it before it hit the floor. 'What I see is how impossible this situation is.' She glanced upward and, acting on impulse, pushed the hair back from his forehead. 'How's your burn?'

He took the gardenia from her and tucked it behind her ear once again. 'Better thanks to you.'

His forehead did look better. 'It's almost gone,' she noted. 'Just a small bruise left.'

'Don't frown. It doesn't hurt anymore.'

'I'm glad.'

'Pardon me, Mr. Milano,' Giorgio interrupted from the edge of the dance floor. 'Your dinner is ready to be served.'

Joe kept his gaze fixed on Maddie as he replied. 'Thank you. We'll be right there.' He lifted an eyebrow. 'Well? Shall we finish our meal?'

'I'm not sure that's such a good idea. Perhaps we should just call it an evening.'

'You'd upset Giorgio if you left now. Not to mention Renzo.'

'Joe, please.'

Compassion filled his gaze. 'If I promise not to touch you again, will you come back to the table with me?'

She wished she could refuse. More than anything she wanted to return to the safety of her home, to go back to believing that she had her life perfectly mapped out. But what would running away solve? If she left now, she'd never be able to put this dinner together. Not on her own. And yet...

How could she work with Joe over the next few weeks? How could she watch that beautiful mouth curve into a smile and those hot chocolate eyes glitter with Christmas gold and still remain unaffected? And how could she possibly watch those marvelous, supple hands work their magic in the kitchen when secretly she'd be wishing they could work their magic on her?

That thought alone was enough to send her into a flat-out panic.

Joe held out his hand. *'Cara?'*

Run. Every impulse she possessed urged flight, to escape while she still had the chance.

She didn't hesitate for an instant. She linked her fingers with his.

Joe captured her hand, his relief so great he could taste it. He'd made a mistake, kissing her so precipitously. And, yet, nothing in the world could have stopped him. She was his, damn it, and neither Tupper Reed nor the ghost of Profit Wallace nor any other person would prevent him from making her his wife.

Giorgio arrived at the table the same moment they did. Although the main course—stuffed chicken breasts—looked delicious, Joe doubted Maddie had much of an appetite left. Neither did he, for that matter. For the first time in recent memory, he wanted nothing to do with food. What he wanted was to be alone with his woman, to hold her and kiss away her fears. Undoubtedly she wanted to be alone, too, he realized wryly. Completely alone, where she didn't have to worry about a stubborn Italian chef attempting to hold her and kiss away her fears.

'So what did you think about the main course?' he asked after five full minutes of silence.

'Okay.'

He frowned. 'The dinner. How is it?'

'Yes, fine.'

'The stuffing agrees with you?'

'No problem.'

'Hmm.' As far as he could tell she hadn't tried a bite of it. 'And the vegetables? Are you certain you want such a large selection? You might consider omitting one of them.'

'Whatever you say.'

His eyes narrowed at that telling remark. 'After we're married, you won't have to cook at all. Would that be agreeable?'

'Fine.'

'I'd like to train the children, though. You wouldn't have any objections?'

'Whatever—' She blinked. 'Excuse me?'

'The children. I want to teach them how to cook.' She stared at him blankly. 'What children?'

'The ones you agreed to have after we're married.'

'I agreed—?' She set her fork down with a sigh. 'I'm sorry. I haven't been paying attention to the conversation, have I?'

His mouth twitched. 'I don't mind in the least. I've had more success in the past five minutes than the past five days.'

For the first time in ages she smiled. 'Is that the secret of your success with women? You wait until they're preoccupied and then proposition them?'

'Will it work with you?'

Her smile widened. 'No.'

'Welcome back to the land of the living, *cara*,' he

said softly. 'I missed you. Try the vegetables and tell me what you think.'

She did as he requested. 'The glazed carrots are wonderful. Are they hard to fix?'

'They can be a little tricky. And the garlic potatoes? What do you think of those? They're fairly simple.'

Sampling them, she nodded in satisfaction, the creamy gardenia petals brushing the curve of her cheek. 'They're delicious.' She glanced toward the huge platter loaded with a selection of vegetables. 'Do you think the vegetables with hollandaise sauce are too much?'

'If you decided to omit anything, that would be my choice. The sauce has to be prepared last minute and it can curdle if you're not careful.'

'Okay. We'll cross that one off our list and go with the potatoes and carrots.'

'And we'll rework the stuffing.'

'It tastes fine to me.'

'We'll rework it.'

'We'll see.'

The arrival of the dessert prevented an argument. Maddie's face literally lit up when she saw the Christmas Mousse. No question, Renzo had worked magic. Set in almond tulip shells and made from white chocolate, the mousse was accented with a raspberry sauce and garnished with grated orange peel.

'It's beautiful,' she breathed. 'Too beautiful to eat.'

'I was afraid you'd say that.' With ruthless disregard, he scooped up a large helping of mousse and

held it out. 'Try some just to be certain you like it.'
He slipped the spoon between her lips, chuckling at
her expression as she savored the taste.

She sighed in delight. 'If you try and change a single thing with this dessert, I'll fire you as my official
wish fulfiller.'

'This one's a winner,' he concurred. 'All we have
to do now is discuss when we can get together to
practice the recipes.'

'Oh, right.' She looked at him uncertainly. 'When
are you available?'

'Every day until about three. What about you?'

'I'm not off work until five.'

Amusement lit his gaze. 'That'll make getting together a bit difficult, *cara*.'

'Only for the next five days. I'm taking a week off
starting next Monday and Tupper always closes the
office the week of Christmas. So as of Friday I can
accommodate any schedule you'd care to set.'

'Okay, how about this?... Until you start your vacation, we'll get together each night after I'm through
here. Can you handle the late hours?'

'I'll do whatever it takes.'

Whatever it took... He'd make damned sure it took
a lot. 'Then give me your address and I'll stop by
tomorrow evening before eleven.'

She hesitated, and he could see the concern forming
in her blue-gray eyes. 'But you'll have spent the
whole day cooking. Are you sure you want to—?'

'Spend a few more hours in the kitchen with you?

Positive. Besides, the majority of my time goes toward ordering supplies, putting together menus and creating new dishes. Oh, and—'

'Doing paperwork?'

He loved it when she relaxed enough to laugh. 'Exactly. Although I prepare the occasional meal when a VIP visits, or work the line when there's a backlog, I mainly supervise the kitchen staff. Doing some actual cooking will be a pleasure.'

She rested her chin in her palm. 'So, you really don't mind working with me on this dinner?'

'Not at all.'

'I'm glad.'

'You have a lot riding on this meal.' He didn't wait for her to confirm what he already knew. 'I hope you won't be disappointed if your plan doesn't work out the way you'd hoped.'

'It'll work out,' she replied steadily.

Joe caught the underlying message: it *had* to work out.

She sat back in her chair with a sigh. 'I should go now. Thank you for suggesting this. It was a brilliant idea. Would you introduce me to Renzo so I can tell him how much I appreciate his hard work?'

He was pleased she'd thought of it. 'But of course. And then, if you'd like, you can thank me again.'

She had trouble meeting his eyes. 'You promised to keep it business, Joe.'

'Did I?' He couldn't recall making any such promise. Not that it mattered. Before very much longer, she wouldn't remember either. 'Then, business it is.'

At least, for now.

Joe arrived at Maddie's door shortly before eleven on Monday evening. He'd offered to bring the supplies they would need for their first practice session and she was extremely grateful. To her surprise, he didn't head straight for the kitchen. Instead he paused in the doorway of her tiny living room. A line formed between his dark brows.

'You're frowning. What's wrong?' she demanded.

'Nothing's wrong.'

She eyed the living room, searching for the flaw he'd obviously uncovered. Everything appeared the same as always—couch, matching chairs, throw pillows and carefully selected bric-a-brac appropriate to the current holiday season. True, the drapes were on the flowery side and a bit overpowering for such a small room. But there was a reason for that. The living room in the magazine article had been much larger. She hadn't considered how the furnishings would look when squeezed into a tighter setting.

'You don't like it.'

'It's beautiful,' he replied. 'Picture perfect.'

She stilled, unsettled by his perception. 'You know, don't you?' she whispered.

For the first time, she saw the room as he did—saw how hard she'd tried to achieve the 'perfect' home and how badly she'd failed. Tears pricked her eyes.

Would she never get it right? Was she doomed to go without the one thing she wanted most in all the world?

Joe set his bag of groceries on the floor and tugged her into his arms. 'It's all right, *cara*. I understand. It's the home you never had. The home of your dreams.'

She buried her face in the crook of his shoulder. 'It looked so beautiful in the magazine. There was a mother in the photo, nursing her baby.' She waved her hand in the general direction of the couch. 'Over there.'

'You wanted to be that mother, didn't you? To have that child,' he murmured. 'And it would be a child you'd never leave. A child who'd grow up with a mother and a father who loved her.'

Hot tears pressed against Maddie's eyelids. 'My mother didn't mean to leave me.'

'No, sweetheart. She didn't. But you still ended up alone, being raised by foster parents. And you've been searching for a home and a family of your own ever since.'

It was as though he'd looked inside her heart and seen everything she'd ever felt or longed for. 'You aren't supposed to know these things about me.' A tear escaped and then another. 'No one's supposed to know.'

'Not even Tupper? Hasn't he realized the significance of this room?'

The tears flowed faster. 'No! He wouldn't understand.'

'But I do,' he stated simply.

It was true. He understood all too well. In fact, he'd learned more about her hopes and dreams in one short week than Tupper had during the six months they'd been dating. Maybe that explained why she'd kept the gardenia he'd given her; she had pressed the petals between the pages of her diary.

Gently Joe wiped the tears from her cheeks. 'Please, don't cry. I didn't mean to upset you.' And then he kissed her. Lightly. A kiss of comfort and tenderness.

Her lips parted in helpless response. She hadn't meant it as an invitation. Or perhaps she did, a response from the heart instead of the head. He wrapped himself around her, just as he had on the dance floor. She groaned, her need coming faster and far harder than before. Last time he'd kissed her, she'd wanted to feel every inch of him. This time he fulfilled that desire. He backed her against the nearest wall, his thighs and hips and chest surging aggressively against her.

He claimed her mouth with brief, urgent bites. 'I want to know you. All of you.'

'Yes.'

'I want to touch you.'

'Please.'

He spread his hands across her shoulders—those wonderfully strong, chef's hands—and ran them downward. Her breasts filled his palms, the tips pebbling with the strength of her desire. But it wasn't enough. She sensed his impatience, the overriding drive to brand her with his touch. She understood how he felt, because she felt the same way. She wanted to examine the width of his shoulders, follow the sculpted planes of his chest, put her mark on every bit of unfamiliar territory before exploring it at her leisure.

His fingers crept lower, across her abdomen, over the curve of her hips. He cupped her backside and lifted her against him. 'Do you feel me?' he whispered. 'Do you feel what you do to me?'

She slid along the length of him and closed her eyes, shivering. 'It isn't supposed to be like this.'

'It's supposed to be exactly like this. I want to make love to you, Maddie. I want to make you mine.'

Hearing the words spoken aloud terrified her. How had this happened? How could she have let the situation get so far out of hand? 'Joe, we have to stop.'

'No, sweetheart, we don't.'

'Yes, we do. Tupper...' The name cooled the air between them. 'I'm committed to Tupper.' And, unlike her father, she kept her commitments.

'Not yet you aren't,' Joe retorted forcefully. 'And if I have anything to say about it you never will be.'

'Well, you don't have anything to say about it.' She took a deep breath and performed a feat of Herculean proportions—she slipped free of his arms. 'I think we'd better get to work. That's why you're here. Remember?'

He studied her for a long moment, a furious protest sparking in his eyes. She waited in dread for him to lose his temper or to walk out and desert her. Instead, he snagged the groceries from off the floor.

'Lead the way,' was all he said.

Once in the kitchen, he took charge, putting the perishables away in the fridge before exploring the small room. All Maddie could do was stand by and wait for the inevitable. It didn't take long.

'Er...*cara?* May I ask you a question?' He poked his head in her pantry. 'Where are your supplies?'

She cleared her throat. 'Supplies?'

'Seasonings. Spices.' He began rummaging through her cupboards. 'Flour. Sugar. Salt and pepper. You know? Basic staples. Where do you keep them?'

'I'm not sure I have any basics. Except salt and pepper. That's on the dining-room table.'

He glanced over his shoulder at her. 'You have no staples?' he asked in disbelief. 'How do you cook without them?'

'Well...' She caught her lip between her teeth. 'That's an interesting question.'

Suspicion flared in his gaze. He opened more cupboards—very bare cupboards. Finally, he turned to confront her. The man who'd consoled her only moments ago had vanished, leaving behind a temperamental—not to mention ticked off—chef. 'Why don't you have anything to cook with?' came the rapid-fire demand. 'You don't even have any pots or pans. Why is that, please?'

She swallowed. Hard. 'Maybe it's because I can't cook.'

CHAPTER FIVE

Piatto Principale...

or

Dish of the Day!

'WHAT the hell do you mean, you can't cook?' Joe demanded.

'Just what I said.'

His brows jerked together. 'You mean you can't cook elaborate meals, right? You can fix easy items. Like... You can grill a steak, yes?'

'No.'

'Scramble some eggs?'

'Not a chance.'

He glared in exasperation. 'Boil water? Do you think you could do that?'

'You don't have to be so sarcastic. I could boil water if forced to. But the only thing I need it for is coffee and I have a machine that does that.'

'Then how do you feed yourself?'

'It's simple.' She marched past him and snatched up the telephone index on the kitchen counter. 'I pick a card and dial a number. Thirty minutes later there's a knock at the door. I answer, pay the delivery man, then sit down at the table and eat what he's brought. *Voilà!* I get fed.'

'Please tell me you're joking.' He took the index from her and flipped through it. 'You're not joking. *Dio!* You know all the delivery men by name. And what are these dates? Do you keep track of when they come?'

'No. Those are their birthdays,' she muttered.

'Their—' He seemed to have trouble breathing. 'And the names in parentheses?'

'Their kids.'

'"Gumdrop"? Larry from The Parthenon named his son Gumdrop?'

'Oh. That's his dog. He doesn't have kids.'

'And this?' He pointed to a notation on one of the cards. 'What is this beside Chet's name?'

She blushed. 'Blue scarf. That's…' She cleared her throat. 'That's what I knit for him last Christmas. A blue scarf. He doesn't like red.'

Joe closed his eyes. 'Of course he doesn't. I should have realized.'

'Kevin's the one who prefers red.' She flipped to the next card. 'See?'

'What the hell do you do, adopt every delivery man who comes to your door?' When she remained stubbornly quiet, he ground his teeth in frustration. 'And what about Tupper? Does he realize you can't cook?'

'Not yet.'

'You have to be joking! How have you managed to pull that off?'

'Most of the time we go out,' she reluctantly confessed. 'But the few times I've had him here I've had the food delivered before he arrives and then I warm it up.'

'And throw away the containers so the fiancé-to-be doesn't see them?' Her silence was all the answer he needed. His expression grew forbidding. Clearly he didn't approve of concealing such important information from the man she planned to marry. 'What an interesting relationship you two have,' he observed drily.

'Our relationship is none of your business!'

'You've made it my business,' he flashed back. 'Explain something to me, Maddie. How do you expect to prepare this dinner if you don't know how to cook?'

'That's why I have you, remember?'

'I thought you needed my help to practice the menu!' he roared.

'I do!'

'You don't need help. You need to have your head examined!' His accent increased on a par with his exasperation. 'These are difficult dishes. When you said you were having trouble with the menu, I assumed you expected me to offer some pointers or to show you how to handle some of the trickier recipes. You didn't say anything about teaching you how to cook.'

She folded her arms across her chest. 'Well, now you know I need a little more than just pointers.'

'Can you even operate the stove?'

'Yes,' she snapped. 'I just turn one of those round knobby things.'

'One of—' He closed his eyes. 'Oh, very good, Ms. Wallace. Excellent. You know to turn one of those round knobby things. And then what? *Dio,* you don't even have a pot to… To *cook* in!'

'I can buy a pot.'

'Tell me something, if you'd be so kind. How do you expect to learn all that's necessary in roughly three weeks?'

'I didn't think it would be that hard.'

'Really? Not so hard? If I came to you, never having so much as balanced my checkbook, could you teach me to be an accountant in that short a time?'

She winced, his question hitting the mark with uncomfortable accuracy. 'Are you saying you won't help?' He bit off a rather rude exclamation, then followed it up with a steady stream of rapid-fire Italian. She waited until he ran out of breath before asking, 'Is that a yes or a no?'

'What the hell do you think?' He glanced her way, then groaned, his anger fading as swiftly as it had flared. 'Don't look at me like that.'

'I'd appreciate an answer,' she said as dispassionately as she could.

'You know nothing about cooking and expect me to teach you how to prepare a five-course meal in about three weeks. And you're doing all this for a man you hope will ask for your hand in marriage. A man, I might add, you clearly don't love—'

'I do so!'

'And who knows nothing about you.'

'That's not fair—'

'Oh, really? What happens after you're married and he discovers how you've been deceiving him? Don't you think he's going to be a little upset when Larry and Gumdrop pull up with that evening's dinner?'

'I'm not deceiving him. I fully intend to tell him I can't cook.' Her chin jutted out. 'Eventually.'

'I think we'd better call it a night.'

She shot him a nervous glance. 'Are…are you coming back?'

Joe released his breath in a gusty sigh. 'Yes, sweetheart. I'm coming back. I'm your Christmas wish, remember?'

'Then why are you leaving?'

'Because there's no point in attempting this recipe when you don't have the basics we'll need to get started.' He glared at her empty cupboards. 'A pot, for instance. Which reminds me… Before I go, I'd like a spare key to your house.'

'Why?'

'So I can let myself in while you're at work. Tomorrow I'll hit the stores and drop off the necessary supplies before going to the restaurant.'

'You don't have to do that,' she protested, overwhelmed.

'Yes, *cara*. I do. I know what I want and where to

get it. I also tend to be rather particular about the ingredients I use.' Humor returned the gold highlights to his eyes. 'Besides, ordering supplies is part of my job. We'll get started tomorrow night. Agreed?'

'You're still willing to help me?' She couldn't quite believe it.

His expression turned serious. 'I won't desert you, Maddie. I gave you my word and I'll honor it.'

She could feel the threat of tears again, and turned abruptly away before he saw them. It would seem he had the same attitude toward commitment that she did. 'I'll get you a spare key.'

At the front door, he hesitated. 'I have a request to make.'

'Sure. Anything.'

His hands settled on her shoulders and he squeezed gently. 'There is nothing you can't tell me. Nothing you can say that will drive me away. So from now on I ask that you be honest with me. No matter how difficult you find it, tell me the truth.'

He didn't wait for her response, which was fortunate. Because the instant he left, she burst into tears.

'I'm really afraid, Joe,' Maddie confessed, picking up one of the aprons he'd brought.

'You watched Giorgio prepare the dressing. You saw how simple it was.' Joe approached and tugged the apron from her hands, wrapping it around her waist. 'I have every confidence in you,' he whispered in her ear.

She shivered at the touch of his warm breath. 'You're confident that I can fix something called Flaming Spinach, but not confident I can tie my own apron?'

'Ah, but that requires special talent.'

Her brow wrinkled in confusion. 'The salad?'

'No, tying the apron.'

She glanced over her shoulder at him. 'What sort of talent does that take?'

'The talent lies in using just enough knots so that you'll need my help when it comes time to remove it.'

He finished with the apron and she took a hasty step away. Just the thought of him touching her again put her in a flat-out panic. She felt for the bow at the upper curve of her backside. 'Is it really knotted?'

His lips twitched. 'Relax, sweetheart. I was just teasing. Shall we get to work? The salad recipe calls for brandy. Did you find the bottle I brought over earlier?'

'It was delicious, thank you.'

'You *drank* it?'

She slanted him a quick glance and grinned at his expression. 'Don't worry. I saved enough for the recipe.'

He chuckled. 'Ah… You're joking. I like that.'

'It seemed only fair, considering how much ribbing I've been taking.' She gestured toward the counter. 'I have the ingredients ready.'

'Excellent. Go ahead and start.'

'I can't.'

'Why? What's wrong now?'

'I couldn't find the measuring cups.'

'I don't use them.'

'But the recipe—'

'I don't follow magazine recipes, either.'

She planted her hands on her hips. 'Well, how am I supposed to know how much of each ingredient to use? Guess?'

'Works for me.' He put a saucepan on the stove. 'If you're not happy with that method, I'll approximate the measurements for you, okay?'

'Do you mind if I buy some measuring cups and spoons?'

'Whatever will make you most comfortable. What's in the recipe?'

'Bacon, drippings, onions, seasoned rice vinegar, lemon juice, sugar, mustard and Worcestershire sauce.'

'Sounds good. Tell me how much of each.'

To her amazement, he rapidly combined the ingredients without measuring a single one and then heated them. As the dressing approached the boiling point, he added the warmed brandy.

'Put your salad in the living room on a separate table. Then carry out the saucepan and ignite it, like this.' He took a long fireplace match and lit it before touching the tip to the brandy mixture. A hot blue flame leapt from the pan, licking above the rim. 'Normally I'd just tip the pan and light it off the burner, but I suspect you'd be more comfortable using a match.'

'You suspect right.' She stared uneasily at the pan. 'I pour it while it's still burning?'

'Just be careful. I wouldn't want you injured.' He smothered the flames with the lid of the saucepan and emptied the contents into a glass bowl. 'Now it's your turn.'

Although it offended her strict accountant soul not to measure the ingredients, she actually had fun approximating the amounts as Joe had done. 'That's the last of the sugar,' she warned.

'No problem. There's more in the pantry.'

While he went to get it, she tipped brandy into the saucepan to warm. She was just combining all the ingredients when he returned with the sugar.

'Now I light it, right?' she asked.

'Fire away.'

'Here goes.' Taking a deep breath, she touched the matchstick to the contents.

A blue fireball exploded toward the ceiling. Before she could do more than shriek, Joe had ripped a small extinguisher off the wall. Tearing out the safety pin, he squeezed the trigger. She heard a loud whoosh, and then the flames vanished beneath a cloud of white powder—powder that also covered her, the stove and half the kitchen.

Joe snatched the saucepan from her grasp and dropped it in the sink. 'Are you hurt? Did you burn yourself?' he questioned urgently. 'Do you need the vitamin E?'

'I'm fine. I'm fine.' A blizzard of white settled at her feet and she looked around, wide-eyed. 'What happened?'

'What the hell do you mean, what happened?' He grabbed the bottle of brandy. 'How much of this did you use?'

'I don't know! I just poured it, like you showed me.'

He didn't say anything for a long minute—she suspected he wasn't capable of uttering a single word. A thin white line formed around his beautiful mouth and his eyes turned so dark a brown they appeared black. He uncapped the bottle and lifted it to his lips, taking a long, slow swallow.

'I'll buy you those measuring cups first thing tomorrow,' he said at last.

'*Cara,* I wish you wouldn't wave the knife around like that. You don't want to cut off anything you might need later.'

'Sorry,' Maddie muttered.

'And, er, sweetheart…' The faintest hint of stress had entered his voice. 'You might want to check on those potatoes.' A loud hiss overrode his comment and he grabbed the boiling pot from the stove. 'Never mind. I have it. Would you mind turning the round knobby thing?'

She did as he requested, cutting the gas to the

burner. 'I never realized that potatoes could be so difficult to fix.'

He shot her an uneasy look. 'Perhaps you should consider serving them mashed.'

'But I like the garlic recipe.'

He dumped the potatoes into a colander. 'I'm afraid these are good only for mashing.'

'Again? That's the second bag we've gone through.' Maybe she shouldn't have spent quite so much time studying the shape of Joe's mouth and focused more on the potatoes. She grabbed a damp, stained notebook and pen. *Set timer and ignore Joe's mouth,* she jotted down.

'What are you writing now?'

'A reminder to keep an eye on the potatoes.'

'That's your third page of reminders and this is the simplest recipe of them all. At this rate, you're going to spend the entire evening reviewing that damn notebook instead of feeding your guests.'

'I'm trying to get organized.'

'If you'd stop taking notes and just pay attention—'

'I have been paying attention,' she objected. Could she help it if she'd been paying more attention to Joe than to his lessons? This was all his fault. If he hadn't kissed her, she wouldn't spend so much time remembering how his mouth had felt on hers—and wishing he would kiss her again. 'I have to write it all down or I might forget something.'

'You're forgetting anyway.' He ran a hand through his hair. 'This isn't getting us anywhere. You're exhausted. I'm exhausted. Why don't we continue this tomorrow night?'

She flipped her notebook closed with a sigh. 'Okay.'

'And sweetheart?'

'Yes?'

He snatched a quick, hard kiss. 'If you don't stop looking at me like that while I'm cooking, we're going to move our lessons from the kitchen to the bedroom.'

Before she could think of a single reason to protest such a delicious fate, he'd left.

'Cara...' Joe's voice rose. 'There's smoke coming from the pot.'

Maddie dragged her nose out of the notebook and stared at him blankly. 'I don't remember you saying the glazed carrots were supposed to smoke.' She poked her nose back into the notebook. 'Did I forget to write that down?'

'No, you didn't forget to write it down!' He ripped off his apron and slammed it onto the counter. 'You didn't write it down for a very good reason—they're not supposed to smoke!'

'Are you yelling?' she demanded.

'No, I'm not yelling!'

'Well, it sounds like yelling to me.'

He snatched the pot off the stove and glared at the contents. 'Trust me. When I start yelling, you'll be the first to know.'

'Gee, thanks.' She peeked over his shoulder and wrinkled her nose at the odor. 'It's not supposed to be all black like that, is it?'

He ground his teeth until they ached. 'Why, no. I vaguely recall learning that black glaze was a bad thing.'

'Sarcasm, Milano?'

'I— You—' He swore in Italian. It felt good. So damned good.

'Joe?' she whispered uncertainly.

He closed his eyes. 'I'm sorry. I shouldn't have lost my temper. Do you want to try the carrots again?'

'If we have enough ingredients.' She opened the door of the refrigerator and peeked inside. 'We're almost out of orange juice.'

'And we're low on sugar, but I think there's enough for one more attempt.'

'Joe?'

'Yes?'

'Thanks.'

The worry was back in her eyes, and he released his breath in a rough sigh. Tugging her into his arms, he gave her a reassuring hug. 'No problem. That's what I'm here for.'

'I don't want to change any of the recipes. You know that.'

'*Cara*, be reasonable.'

Maddie folded her arms across her chest. 'I am being reasonable.'

'Do I have to bring up the lemon salmon?'

The reminder had her reaching for a glass of water.

'Just do me one favor,' Joe urged. 'Sit down at the table and close your eyes.'

'But—'

'I just want to try a quick experiment. Please, Maddie. Have a seat.'

She did as he requested and closed her eyes. The instant she'd done so, he cupped the back of her head and snatched a quick kiss. 'Joe!'

'Sorry. Couldn't resist. Close your eyes again. Ah-ah. No peeking. Now open your mouth and taste this.'

She took a bite of cracker and pâté. 'It's fine. Satisfied?'

'Not yet. Keep your eyes closed and try this one.' He slipped another cracker between her lips. 'Well?'

'Oh.'

'Oh? That's it?'

'Oh, my.' The second pâté was almost as delicious as his kiss. In fact, the difference between the two appetizers was uncomfortably similar to the difference between Tupper's kiss and Joe's.

'My point exactly,' he said, satisfaction clear in his voice.

She opened her eyes. 'That last one… It's yours?'

'I just added a little to the recipe you clipped from the magazine,' he soothed. 'Well, what do you think? Are you willing to go with it?'

It was only a small change. And a delicious one, too. Did it matter if the recipe wasn't exactly as it had appeared in the magazine? To her amazement, she realized that she couldn't care less. 'I'd love to use your recipe.'

Joe ran a hand along the back of his neck. 'Try it again, Maddie. The eighteenth time is bound to be the charm.'

She heard the exhaustion in his voice and glanced at him in concern. 'How long have you been on your feet today? You look terrible.'

'I'm fine. Try the glaze once more. You're almost there.'

'You're not fine. And I'm through with the glaze. At least for tonight.' Turning off the burner, she grabbed his arm and towed him into the living room. 'Lie down on the couch. No, don't argue. Just do it.'

He gave her a sleepy grin and complied. 'Are you going to play nurse again? Which vitamins do we get to use this time?'

'No vitamins. Instead I'm going to give you a back massage. Turn over.'

He rolled onto his belly and folded his arms under his head. 'Is this another skill you learned while in foster care?'

'One of my moms was a physical therapist,' she admitted.

'What about my shirt? Don't you want me to take it off?'

Not a chance. 'Not a chance. This isn't a professional massage. I'd have to do that on a table. This is just a gentle back rub to help you relax.'

'It's a nice thought,' he murmured drily. 'But I'm afraid I won't be able to relax—not if you plan on touching me, that is.'

'Try.'

'Okay; I'll do my best,' he said, then asked, 'How many moms did you have, anyway?' His question ended in a groan. 'Ah, *cara*. That feels wonderful.'

'Eight.'

He heaved himself up on an elbow and looked over his shoulder. 'Eight! Why so many? Wait. Never mind. I know the answer to that.' He collapsed into the cushions once more. 'Your father, yes? Every time he gave you up, you'd go to a new home.'

'I made a lot of friends.'

'I'm not offering you pity, you understand. But I am sorry. Very sorry.'

'Thanks.'

He fell silent, slowly relaxing beneath her rhythmic strokes. It took every ounce of willpower to keep the massage from turning into something more intimate. He was so beautifully built. She would have found him impossible to resist if he had removed his shirt as he'd suggested. Even so, just kneading the hard expanse of sculpted muscles lit a painful fire deep in her loins. Fortunately, by the time she gave in to temptation and allowed her touch to turn into a caress, he'd fallen fast asleep.

At long last, she forced herself away from the

couch. Removing a spare blanket from the closet, she tucked it around his slumbering form and went to bed.

By the time she awoke, he'd left.

'My tulips are wilting,' Maddie announced with a groan.

'They're too warm.'

'Last time they were too cool. Now they're too warm. How am I supposed to get the timing right?'

'Unfortunately, there's only one way. Experience.'

'Oh, great. We only have a week until Christmas Eve. That doesn't give me a lot of time to gain experience, now, does it?'

He wrapped an arm around her shoulders. 'Almond tulips are hard to make, even for a professional. Do them the day before and make double the number you need. That way, if one breaks or another wilts, you have spares. And be sure you store them in an airtight container. If they don't turn out, serve the mousse in a parfait glass instead of the almond tulips.'

She rested her head in the crook of his shoulder. 'But if they wilt I can reheat them, right?'

'Yes. But don't try and do it the night of your dinner party. Leave too much until last minute and you'll spend all your time in the kitchen instead of with your guests.'

Guests. She pulled free of Joe's arms with a guilty start. Her guests were Tupper and his family—which meant that she had no business allowing her relationship with Joe to get so personal. Especially when she hoped to be announcing her engagement in the near future.

'Maybe we should save the tulips for another day and try the Christmas Mousse,' she suggested self-consciously. Joe didn't comment, but she could see the awareness in his eyes. She saw something else, too—a passionate determination that almost had her tumbling back into his arms.

He inclined his head. 'Okay. Mousse it is. Now, the tough part about this recipe is getting the temperature of the sugar right.' He set measuring cups on the counter. 'Mix the sugar and water together and start heating it. Make sure you shake the saucepan as it warms.'

'Why do I shake it?'

'If you stir it with a spoon, the sugar adheres to the side of the pan and crystallizes. You'll end up with little balls of sugar.' He stood behind her, peering over her shoulder. She fought to stay focused. She'd been burned by sugar once before and had no interest in it happening again. 'Easy, *cara*. Tilt the pan slowly. Watch the color. Once it gets hot, the process goes very fast. One minute you have brown sugar and the next—'

'Black, right?'

'Right.' He reached around her and turned off the heat. 'Now we whip the egg whites and add the sugar to it. Go ahead and separate the eggs.'

She grinned. 'I like this part.' In fact, it was one of the easiest jobs Joe had taught her. Setting the electric beater to its highest setting, she whipped the whites into soft, fluffy peaks. She glanced at the plate of cubed white chocolate positioned at her elbow. 'When do we put in the good stuff?'

'After the sugar. Actually, we can start adding that now.' He leaned a hip against the counter and popped a cube of chocolate in his mouth. 'Turn the speed down and add the syrup a little at a time. Then add the chocolate.'

To her delight, it was a snap. The next step was whipping the cream. Like the egg whites, she enjoyed watching the liquid transform into stiff white peaks. 'What's next?' she asked over the whir of the beater.

'We fold the whipped cream into the mousse.'

'Got it.' She picked up the white chocolate mixture. 'No, wait!'

The warning came an instant too late. Maddie tipped the mousse into the mixing bowl full of whipped cream. It hit the high-speed beaters, and instantly globs of white splattered everywhere, covering Joe, Maddie and a good portion of the kitchen.

CHAPTER SIX

Dolce…

or

Meltdown!

'OH, NO,' Maddie said with a groan. 'No, no, no.'

She peeked cautiously at Joe and winced. Whipped cream and white mousse covered his face, neck and chest. He hadn't moved a muscle since she'd switched off the beaters, but had simply stood there, staring at her with blistering black eyes. At long last, he moved. Moved fast.

She held up her hands, backing away. 'I'm sorry! I'm really, really sorry.'

'I'm not.' He backed her up against the counter, locking her into place with his hips. 'I'm not sorry in the least.'

She risked a quick, upward glance. 'You're… you're not?'

'No. Because if you hadn't done that, I wouldn't have been forced to do this…' He cupped her face with mousse-splattered hands and kissed her—hard. 'And I've been waiting to do that again for a very long time.'

'You're not angry?'

'I'm furious.' He punctuated each word with deep, lingering kisses. Hungry kisses. Kisses that grew more passionate with every one she accepted. 'Furious that I've kept my hands off you for all this time.'

'You haven't kept your hands off me,' she whispered, lifting her face for another kiss.

'Not entirely. But I've shown amazing restraint.' He swept her mouth clean of mousse. 'I'm also furious that you continue to practice a meal meant to entice another man.'

'He's my fiancé-to-be.'

'That infuriates me, too. But the worst part of all is that you haven't given up on this insanity and let me make love to you.'

'I can't.' She shivered. 'We can't. You know that.'

'All I know is how I feel when you're in my arms,' he said roughly. 'You feel it, too. Admit it.'

'I don't feel anything,' she lied with undisguised desperation.

'Do you think I'm blind? That I can't tell how you long to touch me? That I can't see the desire burn in your eyes? That I don't sense you watching me when you think I'm unaware?'

She paled. 'I never meant to—'

'I'm quite certain you didn't.' He cut her off with infinite gentleness. 'But that doesn't change the fact that you want me.'

Tears washed into her eyes. 'It's wrong.'

'No, *cara*. It's very right.'

'Tupper—'

'Isn't your husband. He isn't even your fiancé. He's a man you work with, a man you've dated. A man you thought you loved.'

'I do love him!'

'It's been three weeks since we first met. Hasn't the time we've spent together proven that what you feel for him isn't love? Friendship, yes. Comfort, perhaps. But he doesn't touch your heart.' Compassion crept into Joe's gaze. 'And that's why you consider him so safe. Since you don't love him, he can't hurt you.'

'Stop it! I don't want to hear any more.' She blinked back tears, focusing on the forceful sweep of his jaw as she fought to control her emotions. 'You... You have whipped cream on your chin.'

'Do I?' Laughter glittered in his eyes. Laughter and something else—something deeper and more profound. An emotion that started her trembling again. Slowly, he lowered his head. 'Do me one small favor.'

She drew a shaky breath. 'What?'

'Kiss it off.'

For a long moment, she simply stood and stared. She felt the air tremble in and out of her lungs, felt herself sway closer. And then her mouth closed over the dab of whipped cream. Ever so softly she sucked, feeling the rasp of stubble against her tongue.

He inhaled sharply and her name escaped him in a harsh, guttural exclamation. 'You're killing me.'

'Should I stop?'

'Not a chance.'

'You have some mousse right...here.' She nudged his collar to one side and found the smear of white at the juncture between his neck and shoulder.

'I can't see it.'

'Then maybe I should take care of it for you.'

She stood on tiptoe and delicately cleaned the spot, the mousse melting in her mouth. She could feel his pulse pounding against her cheek, a heavy thunder that echoed the rapid beat of her own heart. Unable to resist, she finished by sinking her teeth into his taut, warm skin.

He exploded into motion. Fastening his hands around her waist, he tossed her onto the counter. 'Sit still,' he bit out. Reaching behind her, he found the tie of her apron and yanked it. 'You won't need this anymore.' He swept it from her waist, dropping it to the floor.

'It's not just my apron,' she protested. 'Everything's a mess.'

'I'm well aware of that. So, we'll take it one step at a time. Starting here...' Cupping her face, he trailed a scorching path along the curve of her jaw to just beneath her ear. 'Relax. This is going to take a while.'

He reached into a drawer beneath her legs and removed a striped dish towel. Wetting it at the sink, he carefully rubbed dabs of mousse and whipped cream from her face. He paused on occasions to give the chore more personal attention, kissing away a spot on her temple and then above the arch of her eyebrow, and finally in the hollow at the base of her throat.

'Your turn,' he said, handing her the towel.

She offered up a prayer for strength, but even as she said it she knew the prayer would go unanswered. Unable to resist, she copied his actions. She pushed his hair back from his brow, combing through the heavy waves. The strands were delightfully thick and vibrant, twining about her fingers with a life all of their own. Once she'd cleaned his brow, she used the opportunity to explore the arch of his cheekbones and run a fingertip along the slight crook in his nose. A hint of shadow darkened the lower portion of his face, abrading her palm as she removed the last of the whipped cream.

'You've never touched a man like this before, have you?'

She shrugged self-consciously. 'Just when I put the vitamin E on your burn.'

'Then take your time. I don't mind in the least.'

She gave in to sweet temptation, tracing the crinkles at the corners of his eyes and the indentations bracketing his mouth. They were signs of laughter, and she caught her lip between her teeth. Her father used to laugh all the time—a deep, contagious laugh that invited others to join in. The first time she'd seen Joe, he'd offered a broad, hungry grin. She struggled to remember the last time she'd heard Tupper laugh and couldn't. But then, his was a more serious disposition.

'Your sweater's a mess,' Joe murmured.

'So's your shirt.'

'No problem.'

Never taking his eyes from her, Joe unbuttoned first the cuffs, then the front, every movement swift and fluid. Yanking his shirt free of his slacks, he tossed it to the floor beside her apron. Her throat constricted. He was every bit as beautiful as she'd anticipated— broad and sculpted, his bronzed skin stretched taut across firm muscle and sinew. Corded biceps gave evidence of his strength, and she remembered how easily he'd lifted her onto the counter. Her attention drifted lower. Dark hair filled the gap between his flat nipples, ending just above his abdomen.

'Did you get all the mousse?' he asked.

Her gaze jerked upward, held by the undisguised desire raging in his dark eyes. She'd been studying him, she admitted with painful honesty. And he knew it. In fact, he'd encouraged it. He wanted to spark her awareness of him, kindle the fire she had worked so hard to bank.

'The mousse?' he prompted.

She gave his torso a final, swift glance. 'You're clean.'

'Good. You're next.'

She didn't protest as he slid his hands beneath her sweater. Heaven help her, she should have. But, aside from a bitten-off exclamation, she didn't utter a single word. Inch by agonizing inch, he bunched the sweater upward. Pulling the wool away from her face, he swept it over her head and sent it along the same path as his shirt and her apron. It took every ounce of restraint not to fold her arms across her chest as he examined her.

'Hang on,' he murmured. Moving to the sink, he rinsed the dish towel in warm water again. Then he stepped between her knees and cupped her chin, tilting her head to one side. 'You did a good job with that mousse,' he commented as he brushed the towel along her collarbone.

She shuddered beneath the damp caress. 'Are you done?'

'Not even close.' He lowered his head to her shoulder, feathering a string of kisses toward her neck. She felt the brief flick of his tongue and then he dipped lower.

She stifled a moan. 'There can't be any mousse there,' she protested breathlessly. 'My sweater—'

'Must have had some great big holes.' He cupped her silk-covered breasts, nuzzling the soft skin rising above her bra. 'There's whipped cream everywhere. I can taste it.'

'You can't possibly.'

'No?' He reached around her, and she heard the clatter of the glass mixing bowl banging against the beaters. An instant later he pulled his hand back, a huge white dollop clinging to the end of his fingers. Mischief glinted in his eyes. 'I think you're mistaken.'

'Don't!' Her voice escalated in a muffled shriek as he smeared the cream across the upper curve of her breast. She fought for breath, hardly daring to move as he lowered his head once again.

'Told you I could taste it,' he said, his mouth following the trail of whipped cream.

'You shouldn't. We shouldn't. Joe—'

She had to stop him. But even as the distracted thought crept into her consciousness her thighs tightened around his hips. She felt a groan rumble deep in his chest, and he slid his hands along the top of her thighs and then around to cup her bottom. He tugged sharply, positioning her firmly against him. She dropped her head to his shoulder, burying her face against his neck.

'You feel good,' he muttered roughly. 'So damned good.'

'So do you.' She dragged air into her lungs, fighting to say something to distract them before they strayed too far along such a dangerous path. 'I'll bet you never realized mousse could be this much fun.'

'I'll never fix it again without remembering tonight.'

'That good, hmm?'

'And then some.'

'Really? You sure we can't improve on it?' Maddie groped behind her for the mixing bowl. Her hand connected with the slippery contents and she scooped out a handful. Before he realized what she intended, she rubbed it in his face. 'Better than shaving cream,' she decided, dropping a quick kiss on the tip of his nose. 'Tastier, too.'

He grinned—that wicked, heartbreaking grin that had become so endearingly familiar. 'So, you want to play, do you?'

'Only if I can win.'

'Ah, *cara*... In this game, we both win.'

He wrapped his arms around her and kissed her, his mouth warm and passionate and certain. She parted her lips, her tongue sparring with his. And it was then that she realized how right he was. They did both win in this sort of duel.

'Now you're covered in whipped cream, too,' he murmured against her mouth.

'Which means you'll have to clean it off again.'

'Later.'

His arms locked around her back and then he felt for the clasp of her bra, separating the hooks and eyes. She caught the silk to her chest before it could fall off. For an endless moment, they remained motionless, staring at each other.

'Joe,' she whispered.

'Don't be afraid, *cara*. Don't you realize yet how much I love you?'

Her throat tightened and she started to reach for him, hesitating at the very last instant. If she touched him now, she would be committed. There would be no turning back. It came down to a clear-cut choice: by giving herself to Joe she would be deceiving Tupper. And even though they hadn't formalized their relationship, guilt ate at her—as did the fear of following in her father's footsteps.

'When you come to me, it's with a whole heart and no doubts,' Joe said, as though reading her mind. He dropped his hands to his side, taking a step back, and she realized he wasn't going to kiss his way into her bed. Instead, he would give her the time and space to reach a decision.

Every instinct urged her to choose Joe. To forget the past, to ignore her fears, and give herself to him.

Tupper took the choice out of her hands.

The phone rang and Joe closed his eyes, a muscle jerking in his jaw. 'Should I even bother asking you to ignore that?'

'No. I have to answer it.' She wiped the mousse from her face with the dish towel and slipped off the counter, clutching her bra to her chest. Joe came up behind her and rehooked the back just as she picked up the receiver. 'Hello?'

'Hi, it's me.'

She cast Joe an uneasy glance. 'Hello, Tupper.'

'Working late again.'

For an instant she thought he was referring to her, and felt her cheeks burn with shame. Then she realized he meant himself. 'You're *still* in Spokane? Is something wrong?'

'Not really. Just trying to get some business settled before the holidays. But I'm afraid I'll have to stay on an extra week. Fortunately, Joy's been a tremendous help.'

'Oh, good—'

'I'd be in serious trouble if it weren't for her. You

never told me what a wonderful sense of humor she has.'

'Yes, she—'

'Or what a whiz she is with spreadsheets.'

'I guess that's because I didn't know.'

'Oh. Well…' He cleared his throat. 'Listen. About Christmas Eve. Would it be too much trouble if a few more family members came?'

Maddie took a deep breath, fighting a wave of panic. Joe frowned at her expression and slipped an arm around her shoulders. 'Okay?' he mouthed.

She nodded. 'How many more?'

'More?' Joe exclaimed softly. 'He wants you to feed more people?'

She waved at him to be silent. 'I'm sorry, Tupper. What did you say?'

'I'm not sure how many,' he repeated. 'Two or three. You don't mind, do you?'

'Tell him no!'

'No, of course not.'

'Dammit, Maddie!'

Tupper released a sigh of relief. 'Great. And, ah… Would it be a problem if Joy came along? I wouldn't ask, except—' He lowered his voice. 'She doesn't have anywhere to go, and she's been such a help these past couple of weeks.'

Maddie tried to ignore Joe's tight expression. 'The more the merrier.' To her surprise, he disappeared in the direction of her bedroom. When he returned, he was carrying a clean blouse.

'That's kind of you, Maddie. Thanks.'

'It's a special night,' she said brightly. 'Right?'

Tupper hesitated for a split second. 'Sure. After all, it's Christmas Eve. Look, I've got to run. I'll call later this week. And I'm sorry I won't be back as soon as I expected.'

'I understand.'

He was quiet for a moment. 'Yeah. You always have. Goodnight, sweetheart.'

'Goodnight, Tupper.'

She returned the receiver to the cradle, staring at the phone for several long seconds. He'd called her sweetheart. He didn't often do that. Joe called her sweetheart occasionally—the few times he didn't use *cara*. For some reason when Tupper spoke the endearment it didn't have the same resonance, the same passionate conviction.

It didn't make her want to crawl deep into his arms and never leave.

'I gather there'll be more guests,' Joe said, tossing her the blouse. 'How many?'

'Tupper wasn't sure. Two or three. Maybe four.'

'Ten? You're supposed to serve ten now?' Joe shook his head. 'This is getting out of hand.'

'What's the difference if it's six or ten?' she questioned apprehensively, slipping her arms into the teal blue silk and buttoning it. 'I just prepare more, right?'

He glanced at her hesitantly. 'What if I come over Christmas Eve to help?'

'I want to do this myself. You know that.'

'Just a little help.' He pinched his fingers together. 'See? Just this much. What do you say?'

'It wouldn't be the same. Don't you get it? If I'd wanted someone else to do the work, I'd have hired a caterer.'

'Why?' A hint of concern entered his voice. 'Why are you so obsessed with doing it yourself?'

'Because...' She closed her eyes in defeat. 'Because I'm afraid.'

'Afraid?' He tilted her chin, forcing her to meet his gaze. 'Afraid of what?'

'Afraid that I'll fail. That if I don't succeed this time, I never will.'

'I don't understand. Why weren't you taught when you were younger?'

'They tried. The first foster home I was sent to...' She swallowed hard. 'I...I burned it down.'

'You *what?*'

'It was an accident. I was trying to help.' She glared at him. 'Stop laughing. It wasn't funny. In fact, it was really traumatic. They sent me to another home and my new foster parents wouldn't let me near the kitchen.'

'I don't blame them,' he retorted drily. 'If I'd been smart, I wouldn't have let you near it, either.'

'Yeah, well... Now I've decided to confront my fears. If I let someone do the cooking for me, I'll never learn.' She shrugged. 'And I want to learn.'

'Why? Just tell me why.'

'Because I don't want fear to control the choices I make in life.'

He thought about it for a moment, then said, 'If you're conquering your fear of cooking, why can't you conquer your fear of marrying someone like your father?'

'Since I'm not marrying someone like my father, there's nothing to conquer,' she snapped. 'Tupper is nothing like Profit.'

'Neither am I. That doesn't change the fact that if you marry Tupper instead of me your marriage will fail. I guarantee.'

'You don't know what you're talking about.'

'Yes, I do. Maybe it won't end the first month or the first year or the first five years. But, one day, you'll wake up and realize that you can't live without love. And all your fears will come to pass. Only it won't be Tupper walking out that door. It'll be you.'

'No! I won't be like my father. Once I give my word, I'll keep it. I've known Tupper for two solid years. I know what sort of man he is—what sort of husband he'll make.'

Joe's mouth twisted. 'Yeah, right. Stable, dependable and secure.'

'What's wrong with that?'

'It won't be enough. Not without love.' He pulled her into his arms, fierce determination marking his expression. 'Maddie… Haven't you figured it out yet? I love you. I have from the first minute I saw you.'

'We've only known each other a matter of weeks,'

she protested. 'You can't make those sort of decisions in such a short time. It's not real. It can't be.'

'No? And what if I'd known you for months instead of weeks? What then?'

'You'd have lost interest and moved on to someone else.'

'Like Profit did with his women?'

She closed her eyes, shying from the comparison. 'Do you have any idea how frightening it is to give up everything you've worked so hard to attain?' she questioned. 'To start all over again?'

'Yes, *cara*. I do.' He cupped her face, his thumb caressing her cheek. 'I gave up everything when I moved here, as my parents did before me. I left all that was familiar to risk something new.'

'But at least you had family waiting for you.'

'So do you,' he stated with quiet conviction. 'I'm here for you. And my family is your family. All you have to do is take that final step.'

'And if I don't? What happens then? Do you walk out and leave me?'

'How many times do you need to hear it? I won't leave you.' His smile almost broke her heart. 'I'm your Christmas wish. Remember? You're stuck with me. Just tell me what you want and it's yours.'

'I want…' Her mouth trembled, but she forced herself to say the words. 'I want you to teach me to cook dinner for ten.'

The gold in his eyes dimmed, but he didn't argue. 'Fine. Then that's what I'll do.' He released her.

'Come on. Let's try the mousse again. We'll need to double the recipe in order to have enough.'

He headed for the kitchen. And he didn't look back.

CHAPTER SEVEN

Caffè e Conversazione...

or

Hot and Steamy!

THE final week before Christmas flew by. Although matters didn't get quite as far out of hand as on the night they had practiced the mousse, the tension between them grew more palpable with each passing day.

Maddie found that concentrating on the menu became a near impossible task and, as a result, her mistakes became legion. With each additional one, Joe's temper frayed a little more, finally erupting two days before Christmas Eve.

'You weren't listening!' he snapped.

'I was so listening. Two pinches of salt and a quarter cup of sugar. That's what you said.'

'You're right. That's exactly what I said. Unfortunately, that's not what you did.'

She rounded on him. 'How do you know?'

'Taste it.'

'Why?'

'You'll see. Go ahead and taste it.'

She scooped up a helping of raspberry sauce and tried it. 'Oh!' She made a face. 'What happened?'

'You used a quarter cup of salt and two pinches of sugar.'

'I reversed it?'

'Brilliant deduction, Ms. Wallace.'

'How did that happen?'

'How did—?'

'And don't start swearing at me in Italian again.' She planted her hands on her hips. 'Just because I don't understand the language, doesn't mean I don't know what you're saying.'

'Then I'll swear in English. Dammit, Maddie! You have to pay attention to what you're doing.'

'I was paying attention,' she argued. 'But in case you didn't notice both the containers have an 's' on them. They're easy to confuse.'

'Salt is always in the smaller container, sugar in the larger.' He grabbed her by the apron strings and towed her to the counter, pointing at the two. 'See?'

She glared in exasperation. 'Well, how was I supposed to know? Haven't you ever gotten them mixed up?'

'No.'

'Oh, that's right. You're a cordon bleu-trained chef. You don't make mistakes.'

He ignored her sarcasm. 'Even cordon bleu-trained chefs make mistakes.'

His restraint only increased her anger. 'Then why are you giving me such a hard time?'

'Because if you make too many mistakes your precious dinner will be ruined.'

She stripped off her apron and tossed it onto the counter. 'Then it'll be ruined,' she retorted evenly. 'Look, I'm doing the best I can. If that isn't good enough, than you won't have to worry about my telling Tupper I can't cook. He'll find out the hard way.'

Joe's mouth tightened. 'For your sake, I hope not. Get out the ingredients, Maddie. We'll try again.'

'No. We're done.'

He hesitated for an instant. 'Fine. Then I'll see you tomorrow.'

'No,' she repeated. 'I mean we're completely done.'

He turned to face her. 'You don't want me to come back?'

Looking into his infuriated brown eyes was the most difficult task she had attempted since she'd met him. 'You've spent nearly three weeks teaching me how to prepare these dishes. If I can't do them by now, I'm not likely to figure it out in the next forty-eight hours.'

'That's not the reason you want me to leave,' he said roughly. 'Tell me the truth.'

She wrapped her arms around her waist. 'You know the reason,' she replied in a pained voice. 'I need time to think things through. And I can't do that with you here. You're too…distracting.'

'I don't want to distract you. I want to make love to you. Hell, I want to marry you. You know that.'

'You do right now. But what about next month? Or next year?'

'My feelings won't change,' he stated adamantly.

A laugh escaped before she could prevent it. 'Oh, Joe. What am I going to do?'

He removed his apron and dropped it onto the counter beside hers. 'I'll tell you what you're going to do. You're going to kiss me goodbye. Then you're going to get to bed at a reasonable hour. In the morning I want you to try the recipes on your own.'

'Is that it?'

'No. Promise you'll call if you need me.'

'And if I don't call?'

'I'm not walking away from you.'

That said, he thoroughly distracted her with one last kiss.

Joe paused outside Maddie's door, wondering for the umpteenth time if he was doing the right thing. She had told him repeatedly that she didn't want his help. So why was he standing on her porch on Christmas Eve, just hours before her guests were due to arrive?

He closed his eyes. He knew damned well why.

Because he loved her.

Because he didn't want her to face this dinner alone—without someone there who understood how tough this would be for her.

Be honest, he silently ordered. There was one other very vital reason. He lifted his fist and banged on the door.

The truth was...he'd come in the vain hope that she would turn down Tupper's offer of marriage.

The door flew open and Maddie stood there, her breath coming in frantic little gasps. She wore a white terry robe and very little else. Her dark brown hair was piled in a lopsided tangle of curls on top of her head. Flour dusted a bright red cheek. And her misty blue eyes reflected sheer, unadulterated panic. Joe thrust a hand through his hair, torn between laughter and the urge to sweep her up and carry her off to bed.

She took one look at him and burst into tears. 'I—' She pointed toward the kitchen. 'Dinner—' She drew a weepy breath and grabbed the lapels of her robe. 'Dress—'

He stepped over the threshold. Slamming the door shut, he pulled her into his arms. 'Let me guess. You're running around like a crazy woman. Dinner is only half-done. And you haven't even showered, let alone dressed.' He tilted his head to one side and gave her a slow smile. 'Is that about the extent of it?'

'Yes!' she sobbed.

'Okay. Here's what we do. I'll take a look in the kitchen to make sure nothing burns or boils over.' When she started to protest, he planted a kiss amid the tumble of curls crowning her head. 'I'm not going to fix dinner for you. I'll just keep an eye on things while you shower and dress.'

She wiped her eyes with the sleeve of her robe. 'You don't mind?'

'Would I be here if I did?'

She caught her lip between her teeth, something remarkably like hope creeping into her expression. 'Why are you here, Joe?'

'Because you need me,' he said simply. 'I'm your Christmas wish, remember?'

Tears gathered in her eyes again. 'Maybe I should write that down,' she suggested unevenly. 'I keep forgetting.'

'Maybe you should.' He ushered her in the general direction of the bedroom. 'Go get ready. Is the table set?'

She spun in her tracks, horror dawning in her gaze. 'The table! I completely forgot.'

'I'll take care of it,' he soothed. Anticipating another argument, he quickly added, 'I won't be doing the actual dinner. I'll just be lending a little bit of help.'

'Oh, Joe.'

She flew back into his arms and gave him a brief, tantalizing kiss. A kiss that reminded him of how much he stood to lose if she married Tupper. The next instant she was gone, leaving him with nothing to hold onto but an armful of memories.

Fighting the urge to follow her into the bedroom, Joe headed for the kitchen. He switched off the burner under the bacon she'd been frying and transferred the strips to paper towels. Then he looked around, checking the status of the various dishes. It wasn't nearly as bad as he had feared.

The pâté hadn't been unmolded, yet. But that could

wait until the last minute. She'd already prepared the soup, he saw with relief, as well as the garlic potatoes and glazed carrots. They wouldn't take long to reheat—which left the salad, the chicken breasts and stuffing. He nodded in satisfaction. She should have just enough time.

After tying an apron around his hips, he rummaged through the refrigerator, removing fresh spinach and the ingredients for the stuffing. He'd promised not to help, but washing spinach and chopping vegetables was prep work. And prep work didn't count as actual cooking. Maddie would still be doing that.

As soon as he had julienned his way through the celery and carrots, chopped the chives and sautéed the mushrooms and leeks, he tackled the table. To his surprise, the decorations were totally different from the photos in the magazine article. He couldn't help but wonder why.

Checking his watch, he realized they didn't have much time left until Tupper and his family arrived. He crossed to Maddie's bedroom door and tapped. '*Cara?* Are you almost ready?'

'Coming.'

She opened the door and he stood and stared. '*Sei bella,*' he whispered.

'Is that good?' she asked uncertainly.

'Yes, sweetheart. It's very good.'

She'd donned a form-hugging red dress that showed off an incredible amount of leg. And all he could think about was how she had wrapped those long legs around his hips, how he'd cupped her whipped cream covered breasts in his hands. Dammit! She wore the dress for the benefit of another man, Joe reminded himself. For Tupper. He wished the knowledge would stir his anger—anything to divert the burning need that filled him. But it didn't. He couldn't be angry with her. Not on their last day together.

He reached out and touched her hair. It framed her face, curving in a soft bell at her shoulders. 'You left it down.'

She shrugged. 'It seemed like a good idea.'

'But it's not Saturday or Sunday. It's not even Friday night.'

'I…I made an exception.'

'You told me you never make exceptions.'

'I did this time.' She turned her back to him, peeking over her shoulder. 'Would you mind zipping me?'

'My pleasure.'

He took his time, caressing the supple length of her back as he slowly pulled the tab upward. She shivered ever so slightly, and he knew he couldn't let her go without another kiss. He slipped a hand around her neck, his fingers splayed across her collarbone. 'Maddie.'

'Dinner…' But even as she murmured the reminder she leaned back, her spine pressed against his chest.

'Dinner will wait one minute more.'

'You shouldn't be here.' Slowly she turned in his arms. Her eyes had darkened, the blue almost swallowed by gray. 'Why did you come?'

He offered a crooked smile. 'There's nowhere else for me to go.'

'Do...do you want to stay for dinner?'

The words seemed torn from her, and he shook his head. 'I didn't come for that.'

'Then, why—?'

'You know why.' He lowered his head, tracing a silken path from her shoulder to her lips. 'I came for you.'

He covered her mouth with his, muffling her half-hearted protest as he drank in the sweetness. Heaven help him, she tasted so good, the flavor of her lips unmatched by anything he'd ever concocted in the kitchen. He started to release her, but she clung to him. Her hands cupped his face and she held fast, giving herself without hesitation or restraint, responding to the play of tongue and teeth with unstinting generosity.

A painful urgency filled him, a desperate need to fight for the woman he loved. But he kept it under firm control. He would fight tomorrow—and he would win. Tonight belonged to her.

The doorbell rang twice before the sound succeeded in driving them apart.

Maddie pulled free of his arms, staring in abject horror. 'They're here! I'm not dressed. Dinner's not ready. What am I going to do?'

'Finish dressing. I'll get the door.'

'No, wait!' She stopped him before he could leave

the room, lifting a trembling hand to his face. 'You have lipstick on your mouth.'

He couldn't help smiling. 'Really? You don't.' The doorbell rang yet again. 'Hurry, *cara*. If I don't answer soon, they'll leave.'

'Go ahead and get it. I'll just be a minute. Will you put them in the living room and serve them some pâté?' She disappeared into the closet. 'Tell them I'll be right there.'

'No problem.'

He left her bedroom and crossed to the front door. A multitude of Reeds stood in the brisk Seattle wind. 'Merry Christmas,' he greeted them. 'Sorry to keep you waiting. Come in, please.'

The first one across the threshold was a tall, pleasant-looking man in his early thirties, followed close behind by a young blonde in her mid-twenties. The man stuck out his hand. 'I don't believe we've met. I'm Tupper Reed. And this is a co-worker, Joy Jessup.'

'Joe Milano. It's a pleasure to meet you.' He shook hands, then gestured toward the living room. 'Make yourself comfortable. Maddie is running a little behind. There's champagne punch on the side table, or coffee, if you'd prefer.'

After greeting each guest in turn, Joe excused himself and headed for the kitchen. Inverting the pâté onto a platter in a single smooth movement, he added an assortment of fresh vegetables and crackers before rejoining the Reeds. The questions started the minute he walked into the living room.

'You're that chef on TV, aren't you?' Joy asked as he set the platter on the coffee table beside a stack of plates, napkins and butter knives.

'Are you cooking tonight's dinner?' Tupper's mother questioned.

'Where *is* Maddie?'

'Are you joining us this evening?'

Tupper asked the final question. 'Just how did you two meet?'

Joe smiled cheerfully. 'Yes, I'm that chef on TV. No, Maddie prepared this meal all on her own; we just reviewed menus together. She's in the bedroom dressing. I'm sorry to say I have other plans for this evening, so once she joins you I'll be leaving. And I know her because she bought me at an auction. I'm her Christmas wish.'

'Bought you?' Tupper asked, an odd expression dawning on his face.

'Perhaps I should have said she bought my expertise. The rest of me just came along for the ride.' Joe gave Maddie's fiancé-to-be a direct look. 'I gather tonight is a special occasion. She purchased my help to make it as perfect as possible.' A curious silence followed his response. A silence he didn't like one little bit. He glanced around the room. 'This is a special evening, isn't it?'

'Yes, of course,' Tupper replied uneasily. 'We just didn't realize she'd gone to quite so much trouble.'

'She's worked very hard.' Joe offered his most professional smile. 'Now, if you'll excuse me, I'll see if she's ready.'

She emerged from her bedroom just as he approached. 'Go ahead and visit with your guests for a bit,' he suggested. 'I'll wait for you in the kitchen. It shouldn't take long to finish the dinner preparations. Once you sit down to eat, I'll make myself scarce.'

Maddie joined him ten minutes later. 'What did you say to the Reeds?' she questioned curiously. 'Tupper and his family were giving me the oddest looks.'

'They asked how we'd met and I explained about the auction.' He frowned at the chicken breasts waiting to be stuffed. 'Maybe I shouldn't have said anything.'

'No. It's all right. I'd already told Joy about it.' She glanced nervously around the kitchen. 'My mind's gone blank. I don't know where to begin.'

'Put the potatoes in the oven, get the soup warming on the stove and finish the stuffing.' He wrapped her in an apron, making sure it covered every inch of dress. 'You can put the chicken on to broil right before you serve the salad.'

'What about the white sauce for the chicken? When do I do that?'

'You timed it, remember? It's written down somewhere in that notebook of yours.'

'Oh, right.' She flipped rapidly through the pages. 'It only takes five minutes.'

'Which means...?'

'I can make it after I'm done eating the salad.'

'Excellent. You're doing just fine. Go ahead and get the bowls ready for the soup course. The serving tray's right here. I can carry it out for you, if you'd like.'

She followed his instructions, all hesitation gone. He smiled at her intent expression, remembering how awkward she had been when he'd first started working with her. She had come a long way. He leaned against the counter, thrusting his hands in his pockets so he wouldn't be tempted to snatch a kiss as she passed.

Joy appeared in the doorway of the kitchen just then, and he was relieved that he'd shown such restraint. 'Is there anything I can do to help?' she asked.

Maddie smiled warmly. 'Thanks, but I have it under control. I'm glad you could come tonight, though.'

'Thanks for inviting me.' She lingered for a moment longer, looking as though she wanted to say more. Then she shrugged. 'Call if you need any help.'

'I will.' After Joy left, Maddie stood in the middle of the kitchen, frowning in concentration. 'There's one more thing I'm supposed to do before serving the soup.'

'Think, sweetheart,' Joe murmured encouragingly. 'You can do it.'

She glanced up, triumph bright in her eyes. 'The salad dressing. I'm supposed to combine all the ingredients so all I'll have to do is heat it up and add the brandy. Right?'

'You got it.'

'I've already fried the bacon,' she muttered to herself. 'All I need to do is dump everything into the saucepan.' She rummaged through the cupboard and found the pan she needed, placing it on the stove. Then she measured out each ingredient.

He watched in satisfaction. 'You're looking good. Very professional.'

She paused long enough to shoot him a smile. 'I was taught by the best.'

The soup came next. Once she determined that it was hot enough, she ladled portions into the individual bowls while Joe transferred them to the table. Just before she went to sit down with her guests, he untied her apron and tossed it to one side.

'I should go now,' he said.

She gave him a nervous look. 'Can you wait until after the salad course? Just in case something goes wrong.'

'Nothing will go wrong.'

'Please.'

He couldn't refuse, not once he heard that tiny catch in her voice. 'I'll stay,' he finally agreed. 'But only until you serve the salad.'

The next twenty minutes were excruciating. Joe could hear them as they sat down, hear Tupper tease Maddie about having 'bought' herself a chef, hear her laugh in response. And all the while he wanted to march into the dining room and yank her out of her chair and into his arms. He wanted to proclaim in front of Tupper and Joy and all the Reeds that Maddie belonged to him.

Instead, he silently endured his own private hell.

Finally it came time for her to prepare the salad. She took the bowl of fresh spinach to the side table she had set up, then returned to the kitchen to heat the dressing.

'Good luck,' he whispered just before she entered the dining room. This time he didn't fight the urge to snatch a kiss—a kiss she returned in equal measure. 'Hurry, before it cools,' he prompted at last.

Once she'd positioned herself at the side table, he stood where he could watch her ignite the brandy mixture. He planned to give Giorgio a blow-by-blow description of how well she did. She glanced his way at the crucial moment and winked. And then she set the dressing aflame. He grinned at the exclamations of pleasure from her guests. Giorgio couldn't have done it any better, and Joe intended to tell House Milano's *maître d'* just that.

She popped into the kitchen immediately afterward, flushed with pride. 'Did you see?' she whispered excitedly, slipping the chicken breasts under the broiler. 'I did it. No fires, no extinguisher, and best of all— the house is still standing.'

'It was perfect. You did very well,' he complimented in all sincerity.

Shutting the oven door, she hurried to his side and threw her arms around his neck. 'It's all due to you. Thank you, Joe. Thank you so much.'

'I was happy to help.' Joe closed his eyes. It was time. Gently he disengaged himself from her hold. *'Cara...'*

'Don't say it,' she whispered. 'Please, don't.'

He gritted his teeth, fighting to ignore that soft, urgent plea. 'I have to leave you now.'

CHAPTER EIGHT

Arrivederci!

or

The way to a man's heart…

MADDIE took a step backward, fighting the over-whelming urge to fling herself into his arms again. Two days ago she'd asked Joe to leave—had needed the solitude to consider their situation. But now… Now she realized that this was really, truly the end. When he walked out of the door this time, he wasn't coming back.

She made a helpless gesture. 'Do you have to go?' she asked, knowing his answer before he uttered it.

'You have everything under control. You don't need my help anymore.' He inclined his head toward the dining room. 'Join your company. They're waiting for you.'

Her throat felt strangely constricted and her eyes burned worse than when she'd scorched the carrots. 'I could set another place for you.'

He was beside her in two swift strides. 'What do you want from me?' he demanded in a furious un-dertone. 'Shall I sit at your table and lift a glass to celebrate your engagement? I can't do that. Shall I eat your food and smile while you and Tupper and all his relatives set a date for your wedding? Forget it. I'm not that altruistic.'

She flinched from the picture he described. 'I'm sorry,' she whispered. 'I didn't think.'

He smiled with heart-stopping tenderness. 'You don't need to think. All you have to do is kiss me goodbye.'

It was the most difficult task he'd ever set her, and, yet, how could she refuse? He'd asked so little of her and given so much in return. She stood on tiptoes and pressed a trembling mouth to his. To her dismay, only their lips met. He didn't slide his arms around her as she'd hoped. Didn't cup her face in his hands or feather his thumb across her cheekbone. Nor did he lift her to the counter and cover her in whipped cream and mousse and candy-coated kisses.

Instead their lips brushed, clung and then parted.

He stepped back and she could only gaze at him, stricken. 'I—' Her voice broke. Still, she managed to say, 'Thank you for giving me my Christmas wish.'

'But I haven't given it to you. Not yet.'

'You taught me to cook dinner. You came over to make sure it went well. That was my Christmas wish.' She stared at him uncertainly. 'Wasn't it?'

'No, *cara*.'

Her brows drew together. 'Then what was my wish?'

He grinned, that wonderful, predatory grin. 'Don't you remember?'

'Apparently not.'

'Ah. In that case, I'll keep your wish a while longer. If you remember what it is and still want it...' He trailed off with a shrug.

'What?' she demanded. 'What should I do?'

'Come and get it. You know where to find me.'

'That's it?' She glared indignantly. 'You're leaving? You're going to walk out without even giving me my Christmas wish?'

He chuckled. 'I'm afraid you're on your own. Have a wonderful dinner. Oh, and give my regards to your guests.'

He removed his apron and set it on the counter with a finality that brought tears to her eyes. 'Joe—'

He didn't look at her. 'Merry Christmas, sweetheart.' He headed out of the kitchen, pausing at the very last second. 'Oh, and Maddie?'

She waited, a desperate hope clawing for release. 'Yes?'

'Better flip those chicken breasts or you'll need that fire extinguisher after all.' And then he was gone.

Torn between chasing after him and burning down the house, she reluctantly chose the less hazardous of the two. Crossing to the oven, she pulled out the broiler pan, swearing beneath her breath. The chicken was a perfect golden brown. She scowled at it. So what if it was perfect? What did she care? Joe had just walked out the door and...

She wrinkled her brow. And what in the world had she wished for? She struggled to recall, coming up with the same answer every time. As far as she knew, she'd asked Joe to teach her to cook tonight's dinner and that was it. *Think, darn it! What else could it be?* Working automatically, she flipped the breasts and returned them to the oven.

'Maddie?' Joy appeared in the doorway again. 'Are you sure there isn't something I can do?'

This time Maddie didn't hesitate. 'Actually, there is,' she admitted. 'Would you help me serve dinner?'

Ten minutes later they had the main course on the table. Maddie smiled automatically at her guests, all the while searching her memory. Her wish... Her wish... What in the world had she wished for? But no matter how hard she tried she kept coming up with the same answer. Dinner. She'd wished for the dinner she was currently enduring.

Some wish, she thought glumly.

Where the next thirty minutes went, she never could recall. When she awoke to her surrounds, she found herself sitting at the dining room table, a plate full of food still in front of her, silent guests all around—and, worst of all, no Joe.

She blinked in confusion.

'Maddie?' Tupper asked tentatively. 'Is everything all right?'

'Everything's fine. Why?'

'You haven't said a single word all night. I was

worried—' He glanced at Joy and his relatives. 'We were worried that something might be wrong.'

She placed her knife and fork on the edge of her plate. 'To be honest, there is something wrong.'

Joy smothered an exclamation. 'I knew it. I just knew it.'

'You see...' Maddie frowned. 'I made a wish and can't remember what it was.'

No one said a word.

'And I've been sitting here for the longest time, trying to figure it out.'

'A wish,' Tupper repeated in utter bewilderment.

Everyone exchanged puzzled—not to mention concerned—glances.

'What sort of wish was it?' Tupper's mother asked hesitantly.

'It was a Christmas wish.'

Again there was an odd moment of silence. And then Tupper's mother offered diffidently, 'Joe told us *he* was your Christmas wish. Does that help you any?'

Maddie's lips parted and she fought to draw air into her lungs. *Of course!* How many times had he said it? 'I'm your Christmas wish, remember?' 'He's my Christmas wish.' Tears filled her eyes. 'How could I have forgotten?'

'Maddie, what is it?' Tupper asked in alarm. 'What's wrong?'

She stared, seeing him clearly for the first time. He was everything she'd ever wanted in a man—stable, dependable, guaranteed to give her the security she craved. Only one thing was missing. She didn't love him. She liked him, respected him, enjoyed being with him. But she didn't love him.

She'd given every scrap she possessed to Joe.

Which left one major problem. Joe was gone and Tupper was here.

'Tupper, there's something I have to tell you,' Maddie announced.

He gazed at her warily. 'What is it?'

'I can't marry you. I'm so sorry.'

'It's Joe, isn't it?'

She simply nodded. 'I love him.'

'I understand—perhaps better than you might think. You see, there's something I have to tell you, too.' Taking a deep breath, he pushed back his chair and stood. Crossing to Joy's side, he dropped a hand on her shoulder. 'I asked Joy to marry me last night. I didn't mean to deceive you.' He gave an awkward shrug. 'It just happened.'

Fear and hope were reflected in Joy's apprehensive gaze and Maddie couldn't conceal her relief. Thank heavens it would all work out. 'It's all right. Honest,' she hastened to reassure them. 'I'm so glad you two got together. Really, I am.'

'You're sure you don't mind?' Joy asked nervously.

'I'm positive. I hope you'll be very happy.' Maddie stood as well, realizing in that moment that Joy would be the perfect wife for Tupper. He needed someone a little irreverent, a bit bold and possessing a keen sense of humor. Besides, she could cook, which would delight Mrs. Reed. 'Will you all excuse me? I have to go now.'

'You're leaving? But why?' Tupper asked in bewilderment.

'I'm sorry. I have to find Joe. There's mousse in the refrigerator. Help yourself. And if you wouldn't mind locking up when you're through, I'd appreciate it.' She offered up a radiant smile as she edged toward the door. 'I really have to run.'

'Would someone please explain to me what's going on?' she heard Tupper's father complain as she ducked from the room. 'First he's going to marry the one girl. Now he's going to marry the other. And what the hell's a moose doing in the refrigerator?'

Tupper caught up with her in the hallway. 'Wait. Please. I—' He hesitated, clearly at a loss for words.

She tilted her head to one side. 'We haven't ended our relationship very well. Is that what you wanted to say?'

'Something like that.' He took a deep breath. 'I did plan on asking you to marry me tonight. And then...'

'Then you took Joy to Spokane.'

'I fell in love with her,' he said simply. His mouth curved into a lopsided smile. 'I didn't plan to. It just happened. But I am sorry I didn't talk to you about it before tonight. At the very least, I should have cancelled the dinner.'

'I understand. It all happened so fast. And, to be perfectly honest, I'm glad you didn't cancel. If you had, I'd never have met Joe and you'd never have discovered how special Joy is.'

'Crazy, isn't it?' His smile faded. 'What about you? Is everything going to be all right?'

She reached for a parcel that was sitting on the hall table and then for the doorknob. 'That's what I'm going to find out.'

Maddie knew precisely where Joe had gone after he'd left her—House Milano. With luck, he'd be waiting for her to show up. At least, she hoped so.

By the time the elevator stopped at the top floor of King Tower, she was shaking with nerves. As always, walking into the lobby of the restaurant was like stepping into paradise. This time, it was a Christmas paradise, with holly and red satin bows and the crisp scent of fresh-cut evergreen. Giorgio had assumed his customary station by the reservation desk.

'Merry Christmas, Ms. Wallace,' he said, giving her a courtly bow. 'We've been expecting you.'

'Don't you think it's time you called me Maddie?' she asked with a smile.

'Thank you, I'd like that.' He relieved her of the Christmas gift she'd brought for Joe before helping with her coat. 'I understand your dinner was a smashing success.'

'I wish you'd been there. You'd have been quite pleased. I didn't burn anything down.'

'Most impressive.'

'I...I assume Joe's here?'

'He's been pacing the length of the restaurant for the past two hours.' Giorgio indicated the brightly wrapped Christmas present. 'Shall I put this under the tree or would you prefer to give it to him now?'

'I think now might be best.'

'Excellent. Then I trust you intend to put him out of his misery some time in the near future?'

'I'll do my best.'

'We'd be most grateful.'

Once again a band played to a nearly empty restaurant—Christmas songs this time. She bypassed the dance floor and walked through the gate into the private section, pausing at the bottom of the stairs leading to Joe's table. *This was it.* Taking a deep breath, she climbed to the top, her gaze sweeping the darkened area. And then she spotted him.

He stood in shadow, his back to the windows. The instant he saw her, his eyes flashed with gold sparks. 'You had me worried, *cara.* I'd begun to think you wouldn't come.'

'I just dropped by to pick up my wish,' she told him with a shaky grin.

He lifted an eyebrow. 'I gather you remembered what it was.'

'Actually, Mrs. Reed clued me in.'

'Really? That must have been an interesting conversation.'

'It certainly brought matters to a head.' She paused by the couch, running a finger along the silk brocade.

'I'm afraid I was a terrible hostess. I left before serving the dessert.'

'What a shame.' A sensual gleam crept into his gaze. 'As I recall you make a particularly delicious mousse.'

'Not very filling, though.' She peeked at him from beneath her lashes. 'It left me hungry for more.'

'You've forgotten, *cara*. I'm a chef. You'll never have to worry about going hungry again.'

She dropped the present she'd brought for him onto the couch. 'You'll keep me well fed?'

'Count on it. You're going to be so well fed, you won't be able to move for a week.'

'We're not talking about food, are we?' she asked in a husky voice.

'I certainly hope not.' He left his stance by the window, approaching with slow, deliberate strides. 'So you came to collect your Christmas wish. What is it you want?'

She didn't hesitate. 'You. You're my Christmas wish, remember?'

'I remember. You're the one who forgot.'

'I won't forget again,' she promised. 'I recorded it in my notebook.'

A smile cut across his face and he reached out, combing his fingers through her loosened hair. 'You left it down for him.'

'You're wrong. I left it down for you. I was going to wear it up. But when you arrived...' She shrugged. 'I wanted to surprise you.'

'You succeeded.' His hand settled at the curve of her neck, his thumb stroking her jawline in small, teasing circles. 'And the table decorations? They weren't the same as the magazine layout. Why, Maddie? Why did you change them?'

'Because those decorations were part of a different memory. A special one.'

'What memory?'

Her throat tightened, but she persevered. The very least Joe deserved was her honesty. 'The night we ate here. You tried so hard to give me my dream. You prepared the menu I asked, decorated the table to match the pictures. You even had gardenias. If I'd tried to duplicate it for Tupper it would have tarnished all that you'd done for me.'

'What about Tupper?'

'I thought I loved him. I really did. I guess I was afraid that if I broke my commitment to him I'd be just like my father. Then I realized something.' She gave him a direct look. 'You can't make a true commitment without love. And I didn't love Tupper. He was a man I'd cut out of a magazine, just like the recipes. He represented what I thought I wanted out of life.'

'And what do you really want?' Joe asked tenderly.

'You.'

'Why?'

'For the most important reason of all.'

'And what's that? Security…? Dependability…? Or is it stability?'

'It's because I love you.'

The words hung between them, soft as a whisper and sweet as an angel's kiss. It was all he needed to hear. He opened his arms, catching her as she flung herself against him.

He kissed her then, a deep kiss, filled with both passion and demand. She wound her arms around his neck, holding on with all her strength. She never wanted to let go, never wanted to be parted from him. Their tongues tangled, mated and withdrew, only to begin the dance once again. She was starving for the taste of him—a desperate, naked hunger. She wanted to touch him, hold him, make love to him. Her breath shuddered in her lungs, and he drew back.

'It's all right,' he murmured, tracing the path of tears she hadn't realized she'd shed. 'Everything's all right now. Just as soon as my relatives arrive, we're going to have an old-fashioned family celebration. You'll like them. They're good people.'

'They're coming here?'

'We always close the restaurant for Christmas. It's our time to spend with each other.'

'Do they know about us?'

'They know.'

'What have you told them?' she whispered.

There was no hesitation, only unmistakable certainty. 'I told them the truth—that I love you and plan to make you my wife.' He cupped her face, the gold in his eyes like liquid sunshine. 'Will you marry me, Maddie Wallace?'

'You know I will.' She caught his hand in hers and pulled him over to the couch, gesturing toward the Christmas present she'd left there. 'It's for you.'

He tugged her down beside him as he unwrapped it, lifting out the scrapbook he found inside. Only one page had been filled—with pressed gardenia petals. 'From our dinner together,' he said quietly. It wasn't a question. 'I remember tucking a gardenia behind your ear the night you dined at House Milano.'

'I pressed the petals in my diary later that night. I never understood why until today, when I realized how much I loved you. I bought the book—so we could start commemorating our life together.' She gave him an impish smile. 'I thought about tucking some of that mousse inside. Fortunately for you, I decided it would be a bit too messy.'

'I can't tell you how pleased I am to hear that.' Then he grew serious. 'No more magazine photos?'

She shook her head. 'I don't need them anymore. Those were daydreams. This is reality. And I'd rather have reality if it means having you.'

He pulled her into his arms and held her until the sound of excited voices finally drew them apart. 'Your family's arrived,' she murmured.

'No, *cara*. They're our family now.' Clasping her hand in his, he led her toward them.

Dona Milano was the first to step forward. 'Introduce us, Joe,' she requested with a warm smile.

'This is my fiancée, Maddie Wallace,' he replied quite simply. 'She's my own Christmas wish.'

ALL THE TRIMMINGS

Lindsay Armstrong

Dear Reader,

Christmas comes but once a year—or so I tend to think gratefully when the shops are crowded, the roads are clogged and here in Australia the temperature soars. Every year we promise ourselves a cold Christmas dinner but never can bring ourselves to abandon the traditional roast turkey and ham even as we swelter.

I have a very old, fold-up plastic tree that I get out and wrestle into shape, to the delight of those who remember it from their childhood. And every Christmas morning there's a mound of presents under it—to the round-eyed amazement of the newer, little members of the clan.

That's why I love Christmas, when I finally get to the day! It's such a family time.

Lindsay Armstrong

LINDSAY ARMSTRONG'S
AUSTRALIAN CHRISTMAS CREAM

(Serves four)

3 eggs, separated
2 tsp sugar
2 tsp gelatin
150mL/¹/₂ cup hot water
Juice of one lemon
150mL/¹/₂ cup milk
450g/16-oz can of passion fruit, drained
Glacé cherries, nuts to decorate
Whipped cream mixed with chopped fresh mint

Lightly beat the egg yolks and sugar in a bowl. Put the hot water in a separate bowl and dissolve the gelatin in it; keep stirring to blend properly. Add this to the egg yolks, along with the lemon juice and milk, stirring them in gently. Finally, blend in the passion fruit pulp. Leave the mixture to stand in a cool place until almost set, and then whisk it well. In a separate bowl, whisk the egg whites until they are stiff and then fold them into the cream mixture. Pour the mixture into a decorative bowl and chill really well. When ready to eat, decorate with red and green glacé cherries and nuts of your choice, and serve with whipped cream.

CHAPTER ONE

'Merryn—it's only three weeks to Christmas!' Sonia Grey said.

Merryn Millar looked wry. 'You must be a mind-reader; I was just thinking the same.'

They were seated on the broad back verandah of the Grey home, which overlooked the Brisbane river from the heights of Hamilton Hill—a home Merryn had grown up in although she was no relation. She'd been orphaned at the age of four and Tom Grey, Sonia's husband, who had died a year ago, had been her father's best friend. Tom and Sonia had taken her in and brought her up as one of their own. Which was why she was here now, repaying some of her dues.

'Merryn,' Sonia said earnestly—she was an elegant sixty-year-old, although the pain and complications of her recent hip replacement had added new lines and stooped her a bit—'I can't tell you how grateful I am for all this, but—'

'Darling,' Merryn said patiently, 'we've been through it all before and, contrary to your beliefs, I'm enjoying being here with you.'

'But you could be flying around the world. You could even be having a cold, snowy Christmas.'

'Flying—stewardessing anyway—is not quite the

glamorous occupation many take it for, Sonia. By comparison this is some well earned rest and recreation.'

'Well, you certainly look very glamorous these days—are you sure taking six weeks off to look after me is not going to harm your career? I'm sure I could have managed with Rox and Michelle's help, you know.'

Merryn wrinkled her brow as she thought of Sonia's two daughters, Roxanne and Michelle, both married, both with young families, and shook her head. 'I don't think it would have worked somehow,' she said, with a humorous little glint in her grey eyes. 'Will you stop worrying? I'm not bored, and I'm not pining to be jetting off anywhere; I am content. And I've been thinking about Christmas—I suppose you want the whole family to have it here?'

'Of course,' Sonia said. 'We always do. We have so much room here. Oh, yes.'

Merryn looked around. It was a beautiful old two-storeyed house with a large garden and lots of trees. There was a swimming pool and a tennis court and its position on the hill above the river gave not only spectacular views towards Moreton Bay but caught what breezes there were in this hot and humid part of the world. It was also far too big for Sonia now, since Tom's death, but Merryn knew what a wrench it would be for her to leave it, and it had been a year of trauma anyway. Besides which, Tom and Sonia's only son, Brendan, had inherited it, but he appeared to have no intentions of claiming it yet...

'I was thinking that this year we should have a cold Christmas lunch,' Merryn said a little abruptly.

Sonia laughed. 'My dear, you don't know—well, you probably do—how many times I've threatened to do that!' She stopped and sighed suddenly. 'But—'

'I know, you've made it a wonderful tradition, with roast turkey and ham and all the trimmings. But we can still do the same with cold meat and salad, seafood, ice cream and fruit salad and all feel a lot better for it,' Merryn said. 'It's an exhausting enough day as it is.'

'You're right, although I am coping much better with my walking frame now. But, no, it is a bit ridiculous to have a traditional meal when it's so hot—not even a Christmas cake, though? Surely we couldn't have Christmas without a cake? I do have a fruit cake put aside, and...'

Merryn laughed and reached for a pad and pen. 'Of course we'll have a Christmas cake. I'll start making lists. Let's see...there'll be two, four, six adults, and seven kids at last count.'

Sonia counted on her fingers and murmured, 'Rox and David, you and me, Michelle and Ray, Damien and Dougal—' She broke off with a wry smile at the thought of Michelle's ten-year old twins, who were gaining a reputation for being twin terrors. 'Mandy and Alison, Sophie and Dix, and Miranda—her very first Christmas!' Sonia continued fondly, only to add with a sudden tinge of sadness, 'If only Brendan could be here.'

Merryn heard herself say calmly, 'Didn't he say there was no chance?'

'Yes, he did—if I'd known that being a civil engineer was going to take him away from us so much, I'd never have agreed to it!'

Merryn looked at her affectionately. 'It was all he ever wanted to be.'

'I know.' Sonia looked gloomy. 'But I've only seen him four times in the last three years—and the last time was at his father's funeral. How many times have you seen him, Merryn? You couldn't even be at Tom's funeral.'

Merryn sighed. She'd been on the other side of the world and unable to get home in time. 'Uh—I guess it's…three years since I've seen Brendan.'

'Such a pity,' Sonia sighed. 'I keep praying that one day these ancestral halls will echo with the sound of his children, but…' She stopped and shrugged.

'I'm sure they will, one day,' Merryn consoled her, and changed the subject. 'So, we haven't left anyone out? We'll need at least four kilos of prawns,' she murmured, and made notes.

'Well, there is someone I thought of inviting— Steve, Ray's brother. I think he's a really nice young man. I know Michelle thinks the world of her brother-in-law and you like him too, don't you, Merryn?' Sonia remarked innocently.

Merryn grimaced inwardly—not because she disliked Rox's brother-in-law but because she was well aware that Sonia was indulging in some matchmaking, possibly spurred on by Steve's exhibiting some discreet interest in her. But she agreed without a tremor. 'OK, that's seven adults and—'

'Why don't you make it eight, a nice round number?' a voice said from behind them.

Unbeknownst to them, the owner of that voice had been there for a few minutes, taking in the peaceful scene on the verandah above the green, lush garden, with its mango trees and the family of rosellas swooping and chattering around a tall umbrella tree as they vied for its delicious fruit, and the sun started to set. Taking in, with a narrowing of his eyes, the girl who sat beside his mother making notes, wearing a loose, filmy, pale yellow dress with her dark hair falling to her shoulders like a river of rough silk.

He could only see her profile but it was a face he knew well enough. Only now it seemed to him to have matured, and the lovely line of her throat, the smooth, rounded curves of her shoulders and arms beneath the halter neck of her dress were a change from the gangly girl he remembered. He found himself wondering how else she had changed. She always had had long dark lashes framing those light grey and often grave eyes, and a square jaw—surely that couldn't have changed too?

Then he'd spoken, and they'd both turned convulsively to see the tall figure standing in the doorway— the tall, well-built man with thick tawny hair and quizzical hazel eyes who was Brendan Grey. The man who had been like an older brother to Merryn for as long as she could remember...

'*Bren!*' Sonia attempted to stumble up, sheer, delirious joy on her face. 'Oh, Bren—are you home for Christmas?'

Brendan Grey strode to his mother's side and took her in his arms. 'I'm afraid so,' he said gently. 'Think you can put up with me?'

'Oh, Bren,' Sonia said with tears on her cheeks, 'you must *know* how much this means to me!' She buried her face in his shirt.

Brendan Grey looked over his mother's head and said, 'Why, Merryn, you've grown up!'

Grown-up, Merryn thought later, when she was cooking dinner. I'm twenty-*four*—how does he contrive to make me feel as if I'll *never* be really grown-up in his eyes? Surely twenty-four to thirty-three is a totally different matter from, say, fifteen to twenty-four? Surely a nine-year age difference narrows with time, in other words?

She took three lean juicy steaks from the fridge and spent the next minutes forcing herself to concentrate on the meal she was preparing, on the Idaho potatoes she would fill with sour cream and top with chopped chives, the ratatouille she'd prepared in advance to go with the grilled steaks, and the banana cream she'd made for dessert.

Brendan and his mother were in the lounge having

a pre-dinner drink and catching up—he'd laughingly
declined a family reunion that evening, pleading jet
lag and the fact that his army of nieces and nephews
deserved a clear head. 'Let it just be us, tonight,' he'd
pleaded, and his mother had been secretly only too
happy to comply.

It was left to Merryn to think, *Just us,* with a certain
amount of bitterness as she set a table on the verandah, lit a fat candle in a glass dome for light, and a
citronella candle to ward off the mosquitoes. She put
out wine glasses and stood a bottle of champagne in
a silver ice bucket, knowing that Sonia would expect
nothing less for the return of this beloved son. Then
she stopped and sighed, took a deep breath and rang
the little crystal bell.

Much to her dismay, Sonia discovered that excitement
had taken away her appetite, and she was forced to
retire early. She did so with many protestations that
she was fine, really, but as Merryn helped her to bed
it was plain to see she was exhausted and in some
pain.

'How is she? I mean really,' Brendan asked
abruptly when Merryn came back and brought coffee
out to the back verandah.

'She's going to be fine. It will just take time,'
Merryn reassured him as she poured the fragrant Blue
Mountain coffee. It was completely dark now, and the
flying foxes that lived upside down in the mango trees
had replaced the rosellas with their familiar chitters

as they settled for the night. It was also hot and still, so the candle burnt steadily and its pale smoke lingered on the air.

'This is very good of you, Merryn.'

She glanced at him as she sat down, but couldn't read his eyes. 'It's not, you know. It's the least I could do for her after all she did for me.'

'All the same,' he said slowly, then shrugged. 'I feel guilty.'

'Why? If it's because I'm not one of the family that makes *me* feel—rejected.'

His lips twisted. 'Merryn, the last thing I want to do is make you feel rejected. Have I ever treated you as an outsider?'

'No,' she said honestly, and looked at him again. 'You've always treated me as a kid sister. Haven't you?' There was a curious undercurrent to her words and she wondered if he understood—if *she* understood what she was trying to establish.

'I certainly fixed your punctures for you, taught you to play tennis and to swim, and protected you when Rox and Michelle teased the life out of you,' he said wryly. 'Talking of my sisters—how are they? You can tell me truthfully.'

Merryn couldn't resist the answering glint of humour that the question evoked. 'Well, Michelle is very matronly and proper these days, but I suppose that's hard to avoid with four kids. On the other hand, Rox is the same madcap despite three kids. Uh—and they still fight.'

Brendan Grey grinned. 'I suspect they'll fight to the grave, Rox and Michelle. But tell me about yourself, Merryn—and how come you look so grown-up all of a sudden?'

Merryn gritted her teeth briefly. 'Well, I've been flying for three years now—the last eighteen months on overseas services.'

'So that accounts for the new you,' he murmured as he scanned her candidly and at leisure.

'Did no one mention it?'

'Yes, now I come to think of it, the last time I was home they did. I just couldn't visualise it, I guess. So, I imagine other things have changed as well?'

'Such as?'

'I'm reminded of your high school ball.'

Merryn felt the colour steal into her cheeks and was grateful for the dim light of the candle. Because at seventeen and a half, although looking her best in a beautiful new dress, she'd been claimed by an awful bout of nerves and a terrible shyness on the night of her high school ball. It had been Brendan who had found her in her bedroom—Brendan, at twenty-six and so many light years ahead of her in experience and everything else, who had taken the time to coax her out of it, who had told her she looked as pretty as a picture and that there would surely be boys fighting over her. Brendan who had persuaded her to go.

She made herself smile. 'Yes, I've got over all that. Thank goodness.'

'Does that mean there are now many men in your life?'

'Some,' she said.

'Anyone serious?'

It was said lightly and in just the way an uncle might enquire after a favourite niece. 'Well, perhaps,' Merryn heard herself say with a touch of tartness and a complete disregard for the truth. 'But how about you? Your mother was saying only today—'

'I heard,' he broke in ruefully. 'Something about the patter of little feet down these ancestral halls. But no, I've no plans along those lines.'

'Why?'

He regarded her quizzically. 'Why?'

'I mean—why not?' Merryn said self-consciously. It was a stupid question, she realised, but it was also something she wanted to know.

'Because there's no one I have any intention of marrying at the moment,' he replied wryly.

Merryn thought of the women Brendan had been involved with before he'd gone overseas, all beautiful or exciting, mostly both, and shook her head perplexedly.

'It doesn't make sense?' he said with a lift of an eyebrow.

'Well, no,' she conceded. 'I mean, I'm sure it doesn't make sense to your mother.'

He stretched and clasped his hands behind his head. 'Which is why I feel a little guilty, actually. Especially when I see her like this. But, amongst other things, it's not easy to persuade a wife to endure the kind of lifestyle I have. It means either living in some God-forsaken parts of the world, or living here alone a lot of the time.'

'Is that how you plan to spend *all* your life?' she asked with a frown.

He stared past her for a few moments, then smiled. 'Probably not. Look—' he stood up '—let me help you with the dishes. Then, if you wouldn't mind, I'm going to follow my mother's example and have an early night. I've been travelling for days.' He stretched again, this time skywards. 'I feel permanently crouched into a sitting position!'

Merryn stood up as well, and gathered their cups. 'Don't worry about the dishes,' she said prosaically. 'I can do them.'

He came round the table and took her chin in his hand. 'You always were a sweet kid, Miss Merryn,' he said, using the name he'd called her when she was a bewildered four-year-old. And he kissed her lightly on the lips. 'But from tomorrow,' he added, 'I shall— well, at least take the warring weight of my sisters and their offspring from your shoulders during this festive season.' He turned and went inside.

Merryn, on the other hand, put a hand to her lips, and, after the slightest hesitation, abandoned the dishes for the time being in favour of a walk in the garden.

There was an old swing under one of the mango trees and she sat on the smooth wooden plank that formed its seat and held the ropes. But she didn't swing. Instead she laid a cheek on one hand and closed her eyes. Why had he come home? Why had he written to say there was no hope of getting away, so she'd felt quite safe about these six weeks, then turned up out of the blue? Why, most of all, hadn't he changed?

No, she thought, why haven't I changed? How can you fall in love with a man when you're *only* fifteen and *never* change? She sighed and amended that. Of course she'd changed, quite radically, from the shy teenager she'd been. It was only the quiet, secret longing that flowed like a river in her for the one man who was unattainable that hadn't changed.

It had been, and still was, an understanding of all the facets of his personality—the light, carelessly brilliant side of Brendan Grey as well as the deeper, quieter moods few saw, and the sometimes savage impatience that didn't allow him to tolerate fools lightly, the determination that had driven him into conflict with his father, who'd come from a long line of lawyers and had desperately wanted his only son to step into his shoes and take over the family firm.

But law had held little fascination for Brendan. It had always been roads and bridges and dams, and then a growing preoccupation with physics and maths that had led him to civil engineering. And he'd fought not only family disapproval and disappointment, he'd fought his way up to having his own consultancy firm, based overseas and with a world-wide reputation—

which was why he spent most of his life overseas and in places unsuitable for a wife.

The thing is, Merryn mused on that hot, still night as she sat on the swing under the old mango tree, I didn't *really* expect it to go on for so long. I thought I must be cured of Brendan one day... Is that why it came as such a shock tonight—today—to be told I'd grown up but told in such a way that it made me feel as if I could never grow up enough for him?

And was it a shock to find that he has no more intention of discussing his real, inner life with me than he ever had? And what about the rest of it, the desire to be held and kissed and loved? Yes, you're right, Brendan, she thought with an inward shiver, I have grown up, only you don't know how much... Oh, why did you have to come home? And how will I cope?

For a few moments after he opened his eyes, Brendan Grey couldn't place himself the next morning. Then the familiar pattern of the old pressed-iron ceiling made sense, the sunlight and the humid air streaming in through the curtains he'd left open were deeply familiar. They spelt a Brisbane high summer, and he knew he was home.

He grimaced and rolled over to bury his head in the pillow, because he shouldn't really be at home from a business point of view. He should, at the most, have made it a flying visit for his mother's sake, yet he'd taken a whole month off in the midst of a tricky contract—why?

Because the delight, the challenge, the wonder, the sheer satisfaction of constructing dams that would be the lifeblood of communities, roads and bridges that would be the same seemed to have palled a bit? Yes, he acknowledged. Only I don't know why the hell it should have crept up on me like this.

Then the sound of someone diving neatly and cleanly into the pool below his window wafted in with the sunshine, and he groaned because he knew it would be impossible to sleep in now. He rolled back and shoved his hands behind his head—Merryn. It would have to be Merryn having an early morning swim.

Merryn, he thought with a frown in his eyes. Who would have believed it? That all the years of at first no front teeth and then braces, the years of pigtails, impossibly stick-like arms and legs and at times that sheer, paralysing shyness could have metamorphosed into this Merryn?

Well, that's not quite true, he answered himself. There was always intelligence behind those huge grey eyes. And the ability to be quiet, plus a hint of inner strength in her. And there *must* have been more than a hint of this Merryn by the time she left school— why didn't I notice?

He shrugged and got up to look out of the window. She was swimming steadily and exactly as he'd taught her, but it was no longer a skinny girl cleaving through the pool in lap after lap.

It was an intoxicatingly clear, fine day, he saw,

and he turned to pull a pair of togs from his unpacked bag.

The first intimation that she was not alone in the pool
came to Merryn when the water spouted, upsetting her
even stroke, and then a tawny, plastered head rose
beside her.

'Oh, it's you!' she gasped, then sank and came up
spluttering. 'I thought you'd sleep in.'

'Sorry—yes, it's me. And you always were an early
bird, weren't you?'

She trod water. 'Are you blaming me for not being
able to sleep in?'

'I heard you,' he said reproachfully, then grinned
at the indignation in her eyes, with their long lashes
spiked wetly together. 'To be honest, I was already
awake—just—then I heard you dive in, and it was no
use trying to go back to sleep because the idea of
missing an early-morning swim on this kind of day
was not to be borne.'

'Oh. You had me worried for a moment.'

'And annoyed,' he said softly, and paused. They
were in the shallows now and he looked down at her
curiously.

'What?' she said involuntarily.

'I don't know, but I have the oddest feeling I *do*
annoy you these days, Miss Merryn, and I can't help
wondering why.'

'That's ridiculous,' she parried swiftly, and pulled
herself out of the pool in one lithe movement.

'You've only just got home and I hadn't seen you for three years before that,' she added, reaching for her fluffy pink towel.

He stayed where he was, watching her, taking in every line of her slim, golden figure in the plain black superbly cut bikini she wore before she wound the towel deftly around herself. Deftly and almost defensively? he wondered. 'So you aren't?' he said at last, and the muscles of his broad shoulders rippled as he pulled himself out of the water.

'No,' Merryn said as she thought, Don't, for heaven's sake, give yourself away! She wrung out her hair and ran her fingers through it. 'Why on earth should I be?'

He shrugged. 'Perhaps you think I've neglected my mother—is that it?'

She heaved an inward sigh of relief. 'I could hardly think that now—she's ecstatic—but, no, I never did anyway,' she responded quietly, and only then saw the trap yawning at her feet. She sat down sideways on a cane lounger.

He said right on cue, 'Then it's something else.'

'Bren—' she swallowed '—it's nothing. Just your imagination. Or perhaps it's surprise—you did arrive like a bolt from the blue,' she added with an attempt at humour.

'Move up,' he murmured, and when she did after a moment he sat down beside her. 'Are you sure? I really wouldn't like to think there are mysterious undercurrents between us, Miss Merryn.' He picked up her hand and studied it; the nails were beautifully manicured but there were no rings.

'Quite sure.' She cleared her throat as it came out a touch huskily. 'Um…'

But he said, 'Tell me about this special man in your life?'

She tensed, and he felt it through her hand. 'Well—well, not so special yet but I think he could be,' she heard herself say. 'He—well, he's Michelle's brother-in-law, Ray's brother, Steve, actually. Did—did you meet him when you came home for your father's funeral?'

Brendan frowned but didn't release her hand. 'The medical student?'

'He's a registrar now.'

'Is he?' It was said without any inflection, and Merryn suddenly remembered that Ray and Brendan had never particularly liked each other. In fact, she herself didn't particularly like Michelle's husband, Ray. He was a lawyer and had gone into the Grey family firm in Brendan's place; he had suffered serious delusions of grandeur as a consequence, as had Michelle.

'He's not like Ray,' she said hurriedly.

'I should hope not,' Brendan replied evenly. 'A more pompous ass I've yet to meet.'

'I don't think he's an *ass* precisely, but you're right.' She chuckled. 'Very pompous.'

'These things can run in families.'

'Oh, now—'

'They can be latent,' he said.

'But there's no sign of it in Steve at all,' she protested.

'What does Michelle think of it?'

Merryn opened and closed her mouth, then stopped to wonder just what Michelle *would* think were she to have the slightest inkling—which she hadn't. At least not that Merryn in any way returned what she probably only took for a very mild interest in Merryn on the part of her brother-in-law anyway. 'I—why should she object?' she said slowly.

'I don't know—you tell me?'

Merryn pulled her hand free and clasped it to her other hand, then her mouth dimpled at the corners and she said wryly, 'She does like to organise—*everything* these days.'

Brendan cast his eyes heavenwards. 'She would have made a good major-general. How do you put up with her?'

'I—well, I ignore her,' Merryn confessed. 'And I'm determined to have my own way over Christmas Day, by the way!'

'I heard you.'

'But don't you think it's a good idea?' She turned to him impulsively. 'It's so much less trouble to have a cold lunch, and you know what your mother's like. She's quite sure nobody can cook a turkey as well as she can, or do a walnut stuffing the way she can, or glaze a ham to utter perfection the way she can. She'd be panting to get into the kitchen and pining away if we barred her. Whereas salads and so on are so much easier not only to make but to digest in this heat, and I can do it all. Before she's even out of bed if necessary,' she added with a grin.

'I think it's an excellent idea,' he murmured, taking in her shining eyes and the imperious tilt of her chin. He smiled as if at some inner thought, then said, 'Are you sleeping with him? Steve?'

Merryn blinked, and before his gaze the candour disappeared from her eyes and the old reserve came back. She stood up and he didn't attempt to stop her. Her towel fell open with the movement, showing him once again that lovely golden body in its brief bikini. But she gathered it back with composure and said quietly, 'That's none of your business, Bren.'

'No? I admit it's been three years, Miss Merryn, but you always used to tell me about the important things in your life.'

'I'm not your kid sister any more—I never was.' But for some reason she bit her lip before turning to walk coolly away from him.

He watched her go with a narrow, considering expression. Then he stood up and dived into the pool.

CHAPTER TWO

BY LATE that day Sonia had retired to bed and Merryn was feeling distinctly limp—it had been an exhausting day. The family had descended on them *en masse*—all delighted to have their brother or uncle Bren in their midst again. That was to say Rox and Michelle had arrived with their children, but not their husbands, it being a week day.

Merryn had been moved to think that they were a close family, despite their tendency to fight, as she'd watched first Michelle, who was tawny-haired like her brother, and tall and beautifully turned out, and then Rox, who was petite, fair and gamine, embrace him with obvious delight.

Mind you, she'd cautioned herself, this glow of delight probably won't last for ever, and we could be back to normal fairly soon.

The children, those that attended school just into their school holidays, had been in fine form too.

At one stage the subject of Christmas Day had come up, with, as it turned out, both Rox and Michelle having definite ideas of their own. But Merryn had stuck to her guns and Brendan had backed her up. For a moment Michelle had looked mutinous. Her plans had included having Christmas Day at her house, which had immediately spurred Rox on to suggest that they have it at hers. All of this had caused Sonia to start to look anxious and weary, but Michelle, on the receiving end of a warning hazel glance from her brother, had given in with no more than a narrow, not entirely friendly glance in return.

The moment had been broken by the discovery that Damien and Dougal, armed with a pair of sewing scissors, were giving free but compulsory haircuts to the younger children, some of whom thought it was great fun, others of whom were moved to noisy tears as their silky locks bit the dust.

The fiasco this had produced had been tremendous, with Rox and Michelle exchanging hard words not only on the subject of whose children were naughtier but on who was the better mother. Merryn, nursing Miranda, Rox's beautiful, placid three-month-old, had placed her cheek against the baby's, soft as down, and laughed soundlessly.

'Bloody hell!' Brendan said now, coming into the kitchen after seeing them all off as the sun started to set. 'I need a drink. If that's an advertisement for marriage and parenthood, I can't help thinking I'm well out of it.'

'They're not so bad when their fathers are around,' Merryn offered with a grin.

'I should hope not! Don't tell me you're not exhausted?'

'I recover quickly. Why don't you take Sonia up a drink? I'll tidy up and start dinner.'

'I've got a better idea. Why don't I get us some take-away?'

'That's sweet of you, but don't worry,' Merryn said quickly. 'I've got a casserole that only needs heating up. I made it this morning before they arrived.'

'Good thinking,' he replied with a grin. 'OK, I'll take her a drink and sit with her. I might—would you mind if I had my dinner up there with her?'

'Of course not,' Merryn said warmly. 'She'd love that. I'll bring it up.'

'Why don't you bring yours as well? No point in you eating alone down here.'

'Bren,' Merryn said slowly, 'I was wondering, seeing as you're here, whether you'd mind if I went out?'

He raised an interrogative eyebrow at her. 'With Steve?'

'No.' She paused, wondering whether she'd bypassed a golden opportunity. 'No, it's late-night shopping tonight and I haven't even started buying my Christmas presents yet, that's all.'

He looked wry. 'Neither have I—and of course I don't mind, but you can still eat with us.'

'I thought I might have something out to save time.'

He glanced at her. 'Tell you what, why don't you grab your coat and hat and go now? Metaphorically speaking. You've been cooped up in this house for a fortnight now, from what I can gather, and I can deal with a casserole.'

'Well…'

But he surprised her by possessing himself of her hand and planting a light kiss on her brow. 'Do as you're told, Miss Merryn—off you go.'

About three hours later, she parked her smart little car in the garage and struggled into the house beneath a load of shopping bags.

A glance up at the second floor had told her that Sonia's room was in darkness, but the television was on in the family room and, as she staggered down the passage, Brendan came out of it.

'My dear Merryn,' he drawled, and relieved her of most of the bags, 'you didn't have to do it all in one night.' He put the parcels down on the settee, flicked the television off with the remote control and switched on a lamp.

'All? This is only the children,' she replied indignantly. 'There are seven of them, in case you've forgotten.'

'How could I?' he murmured wryly. 'Anything you'd like?'

'I'd like nothing so much as a cup of tea,' she said ruefully. 'How's Sonia?'

'Fine. Asleep. Two cuppas coming up.'

When he came back with a tea tray, Merryn was sitting in the middle of the floor surrounded by her purchases. 'I've gone educational for Dougal and Damien,' she explained as she looked up from a children's encyclopaedia. 'I *know* they like to read when they can be persuaded to sit still, and these give instructions for making simple telescopes and things like that. What do you think?'

'I think something needs to be done about them.' He put the tray down and poured her tea. 'A reform school, perhaps?'

Merryn grinned and showed him her presents for the rest of the children.

'What about these?' He indicated the other packages after he'd duly admired everything on display.

'That one is odds and ends to put in their stockings that we hang from the mantelpiece. And that one is wrapping paper, cards and so on.' She sipped her tea, sitting cross-legged on the carpet, and raised an eyebrow at him as he sat opposite her on a footstool and looked at her quizzically. 'What?' she murmured.

'You look—exceedingly pleased with yourself.'

'I always enjoy Christmas shopping, especially for the kids.'

'I should have thought to ask you to do mine.'

'I will! If you like.'

He laughed. 'On the other hand, I'm going to have to find myself *something* to do!'

Merryn gazed at him consideringly and pictured him sitting alone in this room, watching television—a scenario most unlike Brendan. She frowned suddenly. 'How long do you plan to stay?'

'A month.'

Her eyes widened.

'That long?'

'Yes, that long. At least, that's when I've made my return booking.'

'Business must be slow,' she observed after a moment.

'No, business is not slow. I shouldn't, by rights, be here for more than a week.' He dropped his gaze to the cup in his hands.

'So why?' she said simply.

He paused, then said dryly, 'I'm not quite sure. I seem to be subject to a certain restlessness of the soul—but I haven't had a decent holiday for years, so maybe that's all it is.' He shrugged, as if he felt constricted, then settled.

'How will they manage without you if that's the case?' Merryn asked when she'd digested this with a frown.

'I've ordered a fax machine.' He grimaced. 'So I won't be entirely unavailable.'

'You don't have to stay here for the whole month,' she said after some thought. 'I mean, you could go somewhere where you could have a real holiday. Laze on a beach, that kind of thing.'

'Trying to get rid of me, Merryn?'

'No,' she replied coolly, 'of course not. But I can't help thinking you might go mad stuck here for a month,' she added candidly.

He looked her over thoughtfully. She'd changed into slim white trousers and a khaki silk blouse for her shopping spree, and tied her dark hair back with a pewter scrunchie. And she contrived, even after three hours of intensive shopping, to look cool and casual but elegant. Her make-up was minimal but the whole was perfectly groomed—from the sheen and order of her hair, the way her clothes fitted and sat, her slim hands and manicured nails to her pewter flat shoes. Was it a way of life with her now? he wondered. To be able to be cool and composed under all circumstances?

He said abruptly, 'Your young man was here.'

'My…?' Her grey eyes widened.

'Steve.'

'Oh. What for?' She winced inwardly as soon as the words left her lips.

'Merryn—certainly not to see me, I imagine,' he said ironically. 'Although, having heard I was in residence, he had decided he might be able to take you to the movies.'

'He should have called first.'

'So I told him. He asked me to ask you to ring him.' The irony was still there in his eyes, plus something else that was sardonic and slightly scathing.

Merryn moistened her lips and thought irrelevantly that the old house was very quiet and peaceful. But for some reason Brendan, sitting opposite her in navy shorts and a white T-shirt, with the lamplight turning the hairs on his arms and legs to gold and turning his thick hair to a lighter bronze than normal, was not at peace with himself or anyone.

It crossed her mind to wonder suddenly whether there was a woman at the root of his confessed restlessness. A woman that, for once, he couldn't have? But why should I think that? she mused. Except that it might explain a certain cynicism towards anyone else's romance? Surely he can't object to Steve simply because he's Ray's brother, and, anyway, what does it matter to him?

As all this passed through her mind she discovered that it generated a spirit of defiance in her, or, if not that precisely, a spirit of contrariness...

'You still don't like him, I gather,' she said flatly. 'But—'

'But it's none of my business,' he mimicked, and smiled. 'So you told me. It's not that I don't like him, it's just that I find him very ordinary.' He shrugged and put his cup down on the table beside him.

Merryn tightened her lips and forgot that she too found Steve very unexceptional and ordinary. 'He's also very *decent,*' she said tautly. 'He's hard-working, he really cares about his patients—'

'If you think taking all that to bed with you for the rest of your life is the answer, Miss Merryn,' he said with a gentleness that was lethal, 'you're in for a sad awakening.'

'Are those the words of an expert on the subject?' she shot back.

He grimaced. 'The words of someone fairly experienced,' he murmured.

'And that's why you're here now, dishing out advice, not to say preaching to me on the subject, when you don't have a wife, when you appear to have *no one?*'

His brows rose, but only with amusement. 'You're very cross, Merryn. Why?'

She smiled thinly. 'And you're not going to answer the charge, are you?' she retorted. 'Only sit there being all male and superior. Look, if the restlessness you mentioned is another word for plain boredom—if that's why you're taking it upon yourself to act like a father—'

'Biologically speaking, that's impossible. I'm not old enough to be your father,' he interjected mildly.

'Or like an older brother, which, as I've told you, you're *not,*' she flung at him furiously, 'then the sooner you find yourself something to do, or, to be more specific, some woman to entertain you, the better off we all might be!'

'Now why,' he said lazily, 'do you think I need a woman?'

Merryn breathed deeply and counted beneath her breath. 'Most men do.'

'That sounds exceedingly trite, Miss Millar,' he said, with a wicked little glint in his eye.

Merryn made a sound of pure frustration and started to shove her presents into bags.

'But, then again, you could have become quite an authority on men for all I know.'

Her hands stilled as the words hung on the air between them. And although she searched his eyes stringently for signs that she was being infuriatingly teased, her certainty faded slowly—because there seemed to be only a genuine enquiry in those hazel depths.

'I...' But suddenly she didn't know what to say.

'You resent me asking you that? You seem to be pretty free with your assumptions about *me*,' he said with quiet mockery.

'Look...' Merryn hesitated. 'Perhaps I shouldn't have said it, but I can't think why else you'd be...at a loose end like this. I—'

'Footloose and fancy-free, you mean?'

'Well, I actually wondered whether you'd fallen for someone you couldn't have.' She opened her hands in a flower-like gesture, then looked at him a little warily. 'Sorry, but I *also* thought it might be why you were—somewhat cynical on the subject of romance in general.'

'Did you, now?' he responded, with his lips twisting. 'Then I'll set your mind at rest. I'm not pining for someone I can't have, and I'm not looking for anyone. I'm simply...' A wry smile lit his eyes for a moment. 'Yes, at a bit of a loose end. But—' the smile died '—I'm also concerned that this butterfly, this new *you*, who must have so many opportunities now, should want to ally herself with Ray's dull and stodgy bloody brother.'

Merryn stared at him blankly but perceived with inner clarity that her strategy for coping with Brendan Grey had been ill-conceived to say the least. Because he was right about Steve? No, he wasn't! Well, not entirely—but how to go on now? She blinked and said, 'Your mother likes him. She never resists an opportunity to matchmake. Are you sure it's not your vendetta with Ray that's making you think like this?'

'Merryn—'

'No—look, you barely know him!' She stood up, gathering bags at random. 'Nor am I about to *marry* the man. This is not fair, Brendan. I'm going to bed.'

He stood up and quite politely helped her pack things away. But then he took the bags she was carrying out of her hands and piled them on the settee.

'What are you doing?' she protested.

'This.'

Which was to take her into his arms.

'I… You…' She trailed off incredulously.

'You've accused me of preaching at you, you've accused me of being a womaniser and you've told me you're serious about a man who obviously doesn't fire you up in the slightest—'

'You—how can you *know* that?' she protested, but with a tinge of pink entering her cheeks.

'I might have thought otherwise if there'd been just a faintly visible tinge of pleasure in you to think that he'd called and wanted to take you out—there wasn't,' he drawled, and waited a moment, but she was speechless.

'So I thought I'd give you a demonstration of what to go for when you fall in love, Miss Merryn. You see, a man can have all the most admirable traits of decency and so on, but unless he sets you alight like

this—don't have a bar of him,' he said softly, and
lowered his head to kiss her.

How did I get myself into this? The thought shot
through Merryn's head and was almost immediately
followed by the question in reverse—how do I get
myself out of it? And *why* is he doing it? But nothing
altered the fact that he was doing it, and she was quite
simply and quite suddenly engulfed by a trembling
sense of need, by the knowledge that this was all her
dreams come true, this was the only man she had ever
wanted to be kissed by.

She hadn't got to twenty-four without experiment-
ing with others, of course, only to find herself left
with an oddly hollow little feeling, a let-down feeling
even though they'd been nice... How could it be so
different? How could she fit against his body so well
and feel so slender and smooth and *alive* when it had
never happened to her before? How could she feel so
warm and wonderful and so receptive? To his hands
on her hips, his mouth on hers, to all the strong lines
of his body and the fresh minty taste of his breath.

How could she be dying, as he kissed her gently,
then more and more deeply, to press closer, to wind
her arms around his neck and run her fingers through
his hair, to have him open her blouse and touch her
breasts...

And not only that, she realised. There was the urge
to get onto the same plane as Brendan Grey, to soar
with him in mental unity—two people who needed

each other, not only physically, but needed also to explore each other's minds and moods, their love.

Then panic struck her abruptly and she tore herself free. He put out a hand to steady her and almost absently smoothed her collar. He said, barely audibly, 'If you're going to tell me I shouldn't have done that, you're right. But if it opens your eyes to what you should be looking for—'

Merryn stayed to hear no more. She left her presents on the settee and ran up to her room. She locked her door in a furious, futile gesture then slumped onto her bed and rocked herself backwards and forwards, more angry with Brendan Grey than she'd thought possible. And finally, after she'd changed, she got into bed with a piercing sense of sorrow in her heart.

'I'm just a bit worried about Bren,' Sonia said the next morning at breakfast.

They were alone on the back verandah. Brendan had gone out early.

Merryn contemplated saying a few bitter things but instead murmured only, 'Why?'

'I've never seen him like this.' Sonia frowned. 'Have you?'

'I haven't seen him for three years.'

'But before that—you two used to have quite a rapport, I thought.'

Merryn smiled mechanically. 'Only an older brother—kid sister one. I think he used to feel sorry for me.'

'He was unexpectedly sweet with you—well, not unexpectedly,' Sonia amended. 'We all grew to love you as one of our own—who wouldn't? But I thought it was more than that.'

'Thought—?'

'That you understood Bren better than his own sisters at times.'

'I...' Merryn paused and decided to bypass this. 'He did say he hasn't had a proper holiday for years. Could that be the problem, do you think?'

'I don't know.' Sonia frowned. 'I seem to detect a prowling, almost tiger-like discontent in him.'

Merryn shivered inwardly at this analogy because it seemed to fit what had happened the night before so aptly. It might have only been that, after all, she mused painfully. It's almost as if a tiger has come padding into our paddock, with all the latent explosive qualities tigers are renowned for.

'I know!' Sonia sat up suddenly. 'I'll enlist Rox and Michelle. Get them to give a welcome home dinner for him or something like that. They still move in all the old crowd mostly, and they looked quite disappointed about Christmas Day, didn't they? This will give them something else to think about and it might just help to get Bren back into the swing of things!'

Merryn opened her mouth to say that Brendan was perfectly capable of getting *himself* back into the swing of things if that was what he wanted, but there was more enthusiasm and zeal in Sonia's eyes than she'd seen for a while so she held her peace.

'But we won't tell him what we're doing—not yet at least—' Sonia stopped abruptly at the sound of a car.

Two minutes later Brendan strolled onto the verandah, glanced at his mother and Merryn, narrowed his eyes and said, 'All right, spill the beans!'

'What on earth do you mean, Bren?' Sonia enquired.

'I mean that you two look as guilty as two little girls who have just been caught raiding the cookie jar.'

Sonia laughed. 'That's ridiculous!'

'Is it? I wonder,' he murmured. 'Morning, Merryn.'

'Morning, Bren,' she answered briskly.

A faint smile played on his lips as he studied her, and for an awful moment Merryn thought he was going to mention the happenings of the night before— calmly bring it out into the open, as if it was something that would benefit from a public airing. There was certainly no hint of guilt or unease in his manner. Who are you kidding? she wondered. When was Bren ever not at ease, except, perhaps, with himself?

But she held her breath until he spoke again, and refused to look at him now. All he said, though, was, 'What do you think of this?' And put a brochure down on the table.

Sonia picked it up with a frown. 'Is it—it's a tree house.'

'It's a play house, more accurately, a free-standing one. But we could put it under one of the mango trees so the kids can not only climb up the steps from the ground but climb in and out from the tree.'

'You mean—you've bought it?' Sonia said rather dazedly.

'I've bought the kit, beloved. And I intend to build it with the help of those monsters—young Damien and Dougal. Merryn put me in mind of it, as a matter of fact. It can be my Christmas present for all of them.'

'I think that's simply wonderful, Bren!' Sonia enthused. 'It'll give you something to do at the same time—when does the kit arrive?'

'This afternoon—'

'And I've had another brilliant idea! I can furnish it for them as *my* Christmas present.'

Both Brendan and Merryn surveyed Sonia affectionately as she positively glowed with enthusiasm and went on excitedly, 'Merryn—could we go shopping today, do you think?'

'Of course, darling,' Merryn said softly, for this was the first time Sonia had voluntarily suggested leaving the house since her operation.

They came back from their shopping trip laden and laughing although the bigger items were to be delivered.

'I can see we'll have a busy time ahead of us,' Merryn remarked as they unpacked their purchases, which included material for curtains for the tree house.

'I know,' Sonia replied ruefully. 'But I do feel as if I've got the Christmas spirit at last. By the way,' she added conspiratorially, 'I've set everything up with Michelle and Rox—next Saturday night, and you're invited.'

'I…what about you?'

'No, no—this is to be a young gathering!'

'But I don't like to leave you—'

'That's all taken care of as well,' Sonia said firmly. 'I'll ask my friend Mary Eaves to stay the night. She's a widow as well—we'll be fine! I gather,' she added, 'Rox and Michelle are taking the opportunity to get out their glad rags—formal, in other words. Why don't you shout yourself something simply stunning to wear, Merryn? I'd very much like to make that my Christmas present to *you.*'

'You don't have to,' Merryn protested. 'And—'

'But I insist, my dear!'

Merryn sighed, for on occasions Sonia could be just as stubborn as any of her offspring. 'You're very sweet, but—have you told Brendan?'

'I'm leaving that to Rox and Michelle—I can't see any real problem, though, can you?'

'I…no,' Merryn said slowly, but sounded unconvinced.

As it happened, her doubts were justified.

CHAPTER THREE

'Whose flaming idea was this?' Brendan said six days later—the day before the party.

I knew it, Merryn thought. They'd decided to keep the party a secret from Brendan, a surprise, but Damien and Dougal had apparently spilled the beans. Damien and Dougal had spent the previous days hammering, banging and building under their uncle's tutelage and were loving every minute of it—for which the whole family had given silent thanks and Merryn and Sonia had given thanks of another kind. Brendan appeared to have relaxed and be enjoying himself.

Until now, that was, as he faced his mother and Merryn as they were about to start lunch.

'I…uh…what's wrong with it?' Sonia asked meekly.

He pulled out a chair—they were eating on the verandah—and sat down with some savagery. He was obviously hot, there were some wood shavings in his hair and he was quite obviously annoyed. 'Michelle's, I'll bet. It sounds just like her. Why did you let her go ahead with it—the last thing I want or need is a welcome home party complete with black tie.'

Merryn put a plate in front of him. There was cold

301

meat and salad on the table, as well as a pitcher of fruit juice and some warm rolls.

'Why not?' Sonia said bewilderedly.

He ignored her and turned to Merryn suddenly. 'Unless it was *your* idea?' he said abruptly.

Merryn sat down and helped herself to potato salad.

'Merryn?' he ground out.

'No, it wasn't,' she answered calmly, although inwardly she was fuming at his tone and at the fuss he was obviously going to make. 'What makes you think that?'

'You were the one who advised me to get myself a woman,' he said through his teeth. 'I thought this might be a ploy of your devising to implement just that idea.'

'Bren!' Sonia registered both shock and confusion. 'What on earth are you talking about? Anyway, it was my idea.'

He swung back to his mother incredulously. 'Your—whatever for?'

'I thought you were bored. I thought—I was a bit worried about you, that's all.'

Brendan said something beneath his breath but his mother went on regardless. 'Bren, you wouldn't upset all their plans, would you? They're so excited about it and it's been quite a feat, organising it at such short notice. It's also taken their minds off Christmas Day—'

'All right!' A tinge of amusement crept into his

eyes as he scanned his anxious mother. 'Enough said—so long as you promise me no more surprises.'

Sonia heaved a sigh of relief. 'And of course you can take Merryn. We've chosen her an exquisite and stunning new dress—my Christmas present.' She turned her attention to the cold meat.

Merryn raised her eyes from her plate then wished she hadn't. Because it was to encounter a look of irony and cynicism in Brendan's.

'Stunning is the word,' he said dryly the next evening as he drove them to Michelle's house.

'Don't you like it?' Merryn asked mildly. 'Sonia picked it and insisted on paying for it—not that I needed or wanted to be thanked like this, but it seemed to make her happy.'

The dress was of an ivory very fine silky knit. It was sleeveless with a slit up the back and it clung to her figure and set both it and her golden skin off perfectly. She wore pearls in her ears and round one wrist, and beautiful taupe high-heeled suede sandals. Her hair was swept back at one side with a tortoiseshell and pearl barrette. Her only other accessory was a tiny suede purse. Her make-up was discreet, as always, but she'd used eye shadow and mascara so her eyes were luminous and huge, and her lips glowed like petals and exactly matched her nails. There was the faintest tinge of her favourite perfume lingering on the air.

Brendan was wearing a black dinner suit and, to be

honest, although he appeared to be annoyed by *her* appearance, she'd taken a sudden breath at the sight of him because he looked so tall and distinguished.

'I've no doubt Steve will be happy as well. I'm sure he'll be there,' he said sardonically.

'Only until midnight,' Merryn replied tranquilly. 'He goes on duty then.'

'I see. So you'll be just like Cinderella. You'll have to resort to me and this pumpkin coach to get home.'

Merryn gritted her teeth. 'Some pumpkin coach,' she retorted of his mother's shining black BMW. 'Why are you trying to pick a fight with me?'

'Am I?'

'Yes! This *wasn't* my idea.'

'Well, it's very definitely not my idea of fun, perhaps that's why.' He drove off from a traffic light with supreme impatience.

'One evening!' Merryn marvelled.

'One evening,' he said through his teeth, 'of being gushed over by every available single woman they've been able to lay their hands upon—how the hell can you imagine I'm going to enjoy that? And don't tell me,' he warned ominously, 'that that isn't a basic part of my mother's concern or one of the prime purposes of this so-called welcome home party.' He eyed her scathingly.

Merryn grimaced. 'In this mood they probably won't gush for long,' she said.

She saw his knuckles tighten on the wheel, then all

of a sudden he relaxed and started to laugh. 'Tell you what,' he said, 'why don't we do a flit?'

She stared at him.

'Go somewhere on our own,' he explained patiently, as if to a child. 'We could have dinner, dance—and still be home by midnight.'

'You're not serious?'

They were stopped again, at another light, and he turned to look at her fully. He let his eyes drift over her, in fact, and the lovely dress, and then he said, as if it still came as a surprise to him, 'So poised. I gather you've forgiven me, Merryn?'

She swallowed, but didn't pretend to misunderstand. 'What did you expect me to do?'

'I don't know.' His eyes lingered a moment longer, then he drove off. 'But, whilst you may have forgiven me, you've also taken pains to avoid me since I kissed you—in case you thought I hadn't noticed,' he added with a glint of humour.

'I thought that might be wise—seeing we seemed to be at such cross-purposes,' she said calmly.

'Strangely enough, that wasn't how it felt when we kissed each other,' he observed.

'Yes, well, you told me yourself how experienced you were.'

'So you think that's all it was?' He pulled into a parking space outside Michelle's house, which was aglow with lights.

'I've told you what I thought it was,' Merryn said after a little pause—and with an effort, because he was too close for her peace of mind. Close enough to be a living reminder of that kiss, to torment her with memories of the feel of his arms and body, of his mouth on hers.

'You didn't say a word,' he murmured, his eyes on the fall of her hair.

'I said it all before you... I haven't changed my mind. Your mother...agrees with me.'

One eyebrow shot up. 'You told her?'

'No, of course not. But she also thinks you're dangerously bored.'

She said it all barely audibly, and with her heart beating unevenly, and she saw the lines beside his mouth, which she would have loved to have smoothed with the tips of her fingers, crinkle as he smiled with wicked amusement.

Then he sat back. 'You could be right. You know, you haven't changed all that much, Miss Merryn. You were often a grave, thoughtful little person. And I could often detect from just one look out of those big grey eyes when you disapproved of me. Shall we go in? I promise to behave myself.'

It was a kaleidoscope of colour, Michelle and Rox's party.

The house was an old Queenslander, with verandahs all around, and they were hung with Christmas decorations and lights, shimmering baubles and greenery. In the main lounge, which had been cleared for dancing, there was a tall tree spangled with tinsel and stars and lit with fairy candles.

Michelle herself was magnificent in apple-green silk, with her already portly Ray by her side. Rox glowed in bouffant yellow taffeta, with David at her side, and for once the sisters seemed to be in accord. There was not a child in sight.

Brendan accepted a drink from his brother-in-law Ray, and no one would have guessed that they disliked each other. Merryn, still reeling inwardly from the events in the car, saw Steve and walked over to him.

It was some curious compensation to see the way his brown eyes lit up as she approached. He might not be tall and dynamically attractive, she thought briefly, but he was not dangerous either.

Thus it was that she spent the first part of the party, comfortably in Steve's company. Well, not entirely comfortably, she amended to herself. Because of a curl of guilt that Steve might read more into it than she wanted him to? She also couldn't help herself being aware of Brendan all the time, of how he was handling this despised party. There was only one word for it, she decided, brilliantly.

How could he do it? she wondered. *Why* was he doing it after all he'd said? *Why* was he circulating amongst the single women, dancing with them, greeting old friends—always the centre of attention and within a circle of interest? *Why* hadn't he contacted anyone before now?

And it stunned her to find that, annoyed with him she might be, hurt that she couldn't be his soul mate she might always be—but she still worried about him. As she always had. She couldn't help feeling now that there was something wrong in his world, and she couldn't help the concern it brought her...

Then eleven o'clock struck, they were called to the buffet and Steve told her regretfully that he would have to leave. 'But we should do this more often, Merryn. Can I take you out next week? I have a free night on Wednesday.'

'Steve...' She paused, then thought a little helplessly, Why not? 'I wouldn't mind going to the movies, but—'

'Take it slow, Steve?' he suggested. 'Don't worry, Merryn. I know you haven't fallen in love with me, but that doesn't mean to say it mightn't happen one day, does it? Goodnight.' And he kissed her lightly on the brow.

Oh, dear—oh, no! Merryn was saying to herself silently as she watched him go, then turned abruptly to find Brendan at her side, looking down at her curiously.

Her cheeks flamed and she closed her eyes exasperatedly, but he took her hand and said, 'May I take you into supper, Miss Merryn?'

'I...why?'

'Well, in the old days I believe it was a mark of singular interest to take someone into supper. And as there's no one I'm singularly interested in I'd rather not compromise myself, you see,' he said gravely, but with his hazel eyes alight with mocking amusement.

'That's…'

'Twaddle?' he suggested. 'Don't you believe it, Merryn. All sorts of…castles in the air can be built on a simple thing like that. Or going to the movies,' he added softly as he found them a place around the crowded buffet table. 'Here—if you hold the plates, I shall endeavour to get you your heart's desire. In the way of food.'

Merryn sighed inwardly, recognising only too well his mood and the fact that there was nothing to be done once he was in a mood like this, and held the plates obediently.

There was a feast laid out. Cold chicken, hot delicious little meatballs, savoury rice, butterfly prawns, curry, two types of pasta, salads and vegetable dishes, ham and pineapple… 'I don't know where to start,' she murmured.

'Then leave it to me,' he suggested. 'I must say, my sisters have excelled themselves.'

'So you should say, Bren,' Rox put in, happening to overhear, 'I'm worn to the bone!'

'Dearest Rox, I'm eternally grateful! As I'll demonstrate shortly—this way, Merryn,' he murmured, and steered her away.

'Where?'

'I refuse to balance my food on my knees,' he said dryly, and led them into the dining room which was not in use and therefore dark, quiet and peaceful. He switched on one lamp and said, 'Stay here, I'll be right back.' He closed the door behind him.

Merryn hesitated, then put her plate down on the long table. It was a big room so most of it was in shadow, and it contained Michelle and Ray's valuable collection of porcelain urns and vases which was probably why it was not in use, she reflected. It was also always off-limits to the children.

'There.' The door opened and Bren reappeared with a bottle of wine and two crystal glasses.

'Why are you doing this?' Merryn enquired curiously.

'I need a break,' he said laconically and held out a chair for her. 'You must admit—' he sat down and unfurled a napkin, '—that I've been the perfect party animal up until now.'

Merryn chuckled unexpectedly and took a sip of the ice-cold wine he'd poured. They ate in a companionable silence for a while, then she put her elbows on the table and looked at him with her fork about to spear a peeled prawn. 'What's wrong, Bren?'

His lips twisted and he sat back. 'I thought I told you.'

She speared the prawn and ate it, then put her fork down. 'It seems to me to be more than a "certain restlessness of the soul". It seems a bit darker than that.'

His eyes narrowed. 'Why do you say that?'

'Well, I do know that while you're not a party animal you're not a complete recluse either. And I do know that while you're *not* a womaniser there have been women in your life—'

'If you're referring to my late teens, do you really think you should hold that against me?' he said dryly.

'No. And I wasn't. But this—the way you've come home but almost as if it's against your will, and the way you carried on about this party—is strange.'

He was silent, turning the stem of his wine glass around in his long fingers.

'And,' she went on, taking another sip of wine— for fortification? 'you would be the last person I would have suspected of—doing what you did the other night.'

'Kissing you, you mean?'

'Yes. I…always thought I might have meant more to you than to be on the receiving end of that kind of thing.'

'You do,' he said abruptly. 'And if you can *prove* to me that Steve is the special man for you—'

'He's nice, you know,' she broke in, wishing fervently at the same time that she hadn't started all this in the first place.

'Nice? Is that all you can say about him?'

'Look—' she pushed her plate away, '—let's not get onto that tack again. It's you we're supposed to be talking about.'

'Merryn—' Brendan Grey stopped and stared into her eyes. Stopped as he wondered if she had any idea of how beautiful she was, sitting there so quietly and composedly in her lovely dress with that midnight hair, sitting there with her concern for him showing plainly in those grey eyes, as if he *were* an older, wayward brother. As if it could not be possible for her to imagine that the impulse that had led him to kiss her had been irresistible.

But why had it been so irresistible? And why should the thought of her and Ray's brother be so unacceptable? Had she any idea that she was like two separate people for him? Miss Merryn, who until a few days ago he had always remembered as a thin, serious little girl, and *this* Merryn?

He gritted his teeth suddenly and thought, No, she's right—if that part of you that's seriously beginning to wonder why there isn't more to life and love than you've encountered so far is also seeking some sort of temporary solace from a beautiful woman, it should *never* be her.

And he remembered suddenly how, one night, after he'd had an awful row with his father, she'd appeared in his room in her pyjamas, with her hair in plaits, and put her favourite thing in the world on his desk: a battered little grey wooden mouse with its whiskers painted white, its eyes red, its tail and feet pink. He'd known she always slept with it under her pillow and had had it since a baby. And she'd only said, 'Keep it for tonight.' Then she'd disappeared as silently as she'd come. He'd picked it up and turned it over in his hands and found himself feeling curiously warmed and consoled.

'It's a pity you haven't got a mouse to give me,'

he said, barely audibly, but her eyes widened. 'No,' he went on as her lips parted, 'you're right, Merryn. I…there is nothing seriously wrong with me. Other than having spent too much time living in too many out of the way places, where often the only thing *to* do is work. I think I've lost the art of relaxing. I think I *had* become a bit of a recluse. That's all—and prone to mischief,' he said ruefully. 'I apologise.'

Merryn sat back and wondered why she felt cold suddenly. Because she'd been hoping she'd given him the opening to tell her he'd fallen in love with her? You fool, she thought. Have you secretly been nurturing that little hope since…that night? Yes. Well, it's the only other explanation that might have fitted…

'Merryn?' He said her name quietly and looked at her interrogatively.

She looked back blankly.

'You shivered,' he said slowly. 'But you couldn't possibly be cold on a night like tonight.'

'Did I?' She stood up and picked up her plate. 'I can't imagine why. Don't you think we ought to get back?'

'One thing.' He stood up and his gaze rested on her almost quizzically. 'One request, at least. While I work my way back to being civilised, could you see *your* way to not—withdrawing from me?'

She opened her mouth, then closed it to stifle the cry that rose within. A cry of pure pain.

'You always used to—be there,' he said, although

now there was nothing quizzical in his eyes, just a sober request.

'I...yes, Bren, of course,' she said quietly.

The door opened and Michelle stood on the threshold—an irritated Michelle. 'What on earth are you two doing locked away in here by yourselves?' she demanded, with her hands on her hips.

'Planning to steal your Ming vases,' Brendan replied with a perfectly straight face. 'We've just worked out how to bypass the burglar alarm.'

'Bren—oh, you are mad!' Michelle laughed, however. 'Look, we're just about to drink a toast to you—'

'Michelle, if you have any sisterly affection for me at all, don't do that. Tell you what—' he took his sister's hand and led her out '—why don't I propose the toast?'

'But Ray's all set to—'

'I can imagine,' he said wryly, and tossed a comically incredulous look over his shoulder at Merryn, 'but I insist on thanking you all for this *wonderful* party publicly. Now, don't argue, it's been an amazingly argument-free period for us Greys—let's not spoil it!'

Merryn followed after a moment, and she watched him make a toast to his sisters and their husbands and give a light, brilliant, witty speech that had people laughing helplessly. Then the lights were dimmed, the music was turned up and the party got going again—

but she slipped away into the kitchen, found herself a plastic apron and got to work on the colourful mess.

Rox found her and tried to remonstrate with her. 'You don't have to do this, Merry!'

'Yes, I do, it's my contribution,' she replied placidly. 'You and Michelle have been magnificent, but you deserve to enjoy yourself now.'

'It's going really well, isn't it? I think Bren's thoroughly enjoying himself. All right, if you insist,' she said with a cheeky grin, and planted a kiss on Merryn's cheek. 'Steve's gone anyway,' she added airily, and departed.

Then, later, Ray found her and said, 'You don't need to do this, Merryn!'

'I'm doing it because I want to, Ray. By the way, where are the kids?'

'They're all at Rox's with a babysitter—oh, well, if you're sure you don't mind. I'm sure Michelle will appreciate it. What a pity Steve had to work,' he added—and departed.

What is this? Merryn wondered, with her hands suspended in soapy water and a frown in her eyes. A conspiracy? And why are they all coming out of the woodwork now? Because I'm home for six weeks? But how do they know I have any interest in Steve? Not that that ever stopped the Greys, particularly Michelle, when they got the bit between their teeth. She shook her head bewilderedly...

'Ah, there you are, Cinderella! How appropriate.

But I think we can decently leave this party now—
it's two-thirty in the morning.'

It was Brendan, with his shoulders propped against
the doorframe as if he'd been watching her for a
while.

Merryn rinsed and dried her hands and reached up
to take the apron off. 'I think I've made a significant
impact,' she said with a glint of humour. 'If you're
ready?'

He straightened. 'Ready, willing and able.' His lips
twisted. 'To get home to bed, that is.'

There was little traffic on the road as they drove
home, beside the river for a while, then up the hill
through the quiet, leafy streets.

'I didn't lay eyes on one of my nieces or nephews,'
he said suddenly, as if it had only just occurred to
him.

'They hired a babysitter and herded them all together at Rox's.'

He looked wry. 'I wonder if they had to pay the
babysitter danger money?'

Merryn laughed. 'Well, there were no urgent phone
calls so I guess they're all all right.'

'You know what it would be nice to do now?' he
said as he turned into the drive.

'No?'

'Go for a swim.'

'You go. I think I'll go straight to bed.'

He drove into the garage, switched off the car but

made no move to get out. 'The thing is, I feel a bit guilty about you tonight, Merryn,' he said after a pause.

'Why? I mean, you don't have to.'

'All the same I do.' He switched on the overhead light. 'I can't help feeling I made it a difficult night for you.'

A bubble of mirth, despite herself, escaped from Merryn's lips.

'You agree?' he queried, with an odd little look that she couldn't decipher in the depths of his hazel eyes.

'Well, it wasn't the most relaxed I've been going to a party,' she said wryly.

'That's why I feel guilty. Especially to think of you in your beautiful new dress ending up doing the dishes.'

Merryn rested her head back tiredly. 'I'll survive,' she murmured.

'That makes me feel worse,' he said very quietly. 'Come for a swim—you must be feeling hot and sticky. I am. And you must be feeling let down—I'd quite understand if you were feeling particularly annoyed with me after all the fuss I made.'

She turned her head to look at him and saw, with her heart constricting, lines of tiredness on his face— but more than that there was an affection in his eyes, and just the simple fact that this was Brendan, who could be impossible and then go out of his way to charm you to make it up.

'You don't have to do this,' she whispered.

'Yes, I do.'

'And I suppose you won't take no for an answer?'

'I'd rather not.'

Merryn sighed. 'Will you promise to let me go to bed after I've had a short swim?'

'Scout's honour.'

'All right. But we'll have to be quiet so we don't wake your mother.'

'I wasn't planning to yell and shout.'

This is not such a bad idea, Merryn thought as she floated on her back and watched the stars. The water, while not cold—it never did get really cold in mid-summer—was still refreshing. There were a million stars in the sky and she gradually felt the tensions of the night being soothed away.

'Merryn?' Bren said softly from the side of the pool, where he was sitting with his legs dangling in the water.

She turned over and swam towards him. 'Yes?'

'I've made us a nightcap.' He indicated a small tray beside him.

Merryn blinked and hazarded a guess. 'Irish coffee?'

'Uh-huh. Don't let it get cold.'

She rested her arms on the stone coping of the pool and accepted the glass in its silver holder. 'This is very grand. And very nice,' she added after a sip, licking the cream off her lip.

He grinned down at her. 'One of my few culinary

accomplishments, if you can call it that. What were you thinking? When you were floating on your back staring at the stars?'

A breath of breeze stirred the trees. 'I was picturing myself thirty thousand odd feet up there, hurtling through the night.'

'Do you enjoy it, Merryn?'

'Yes. I wouldn't be doing it otherwise.'

'Silly question,' he said wryly. 'Let me rephrase—what made you choose it as a career? I'm sure it's not all glamour, although you do fit into that mould—perfectly now.'

She shrugged and smiled. 'No, it's not all glamour, but it is an opportunity to travel, which I always wanted to do. And I guess—well, it's rather difficult to put into words, but to be successful at it takes a variety of skills that I...I didn't really know I possessed. PR skills first and foremost—'

'You mean you need to be skilled at handling people?'

'Yes. And children. You need patience, you need stamina and so on.'

'And how do you fight off the passengers? The male ones? Not to mention male crew?'

She glinted a wry look upwards. He'd swum before making the coffee, and he was sitting there just in a pair of board shorts, with his hair damp and tousled, and suddenly he reminded her of a much younger Brendan. 'You can always do it, you know. You just have to be firm.'

'Do you always do it?'

'So far I've managed to evade every single one of them that I didn't want to be propositioned by.' She put her glass down and pulled herself out of the pool to sit beside him.

'And those you did?'

'As a matter of fact there hasn't been anything serious,' she answered after a time. 'A couple I liked—but that's one of the disadvantages of it, I guess. You're always on the move.'

He glanced at her. Instead of her bikini she'd chosen a one-piece dark blue swimsuit. He hesitated before he said, 'Does it fill you with contentment, though? To be always on the move, always taking care of other people?'

'Do you—are you saying you see it as a shallow occupation?' she countered.

'I wasn't being critical at all,' he said after a pause. 'I was wondering, though, how you see the rest of your life?'

'I see,' she said slowly, 'that I won't be happy to do it for ever, actually being a flight attendant, but if you're good enough you can go into the training side, or the sales side—there are quite a few opportunities when you decide to hang up your wings.'

'What about the being a wife and mother side of things?'

She was silent for so long he turned to her again. 'Merryn? Is something wrong?'

'No. But sometimes I wonder if I haven't been conditioned to be a loner, you know. Not,' she said swiftly, 'that it's anybody's fault—your family couldn't have done more for me and I'll always be so grateful—but…having never had anyone who really belongs to me…perhaps I just can't visualise it.'

She thought she heard an indrawn breath, then he said, 'Not even Steve?'

Least of all Steve, she thought wearily, and once again cursed herself for ever having told that lie. And cursed herself doubly for allowing an Irish coffee and starlight and this version of Brendan Grey, who once would have understood what she was trying to say, to trap her into revealing her inner secrets.

'I—I don't know, Bren.' Her shoulders slumped suddenly, but she attempted to put a brave front on it. 'If there was a moon I could accuse it of making me maudlin, but there isn't so it must be the coffee. I'm going to bed, but you were right—this swim was a good idea. Goodnight.' She got up quietly and vanished inside.

CHAPTER FOUR

'ONLY one week to go,' Merryn said.

She was hanging curtains in the play house; Brendan was hanging a door. Children had been barred from it so that the furnished interior would come as a surprise on the big day.

'Uh-huh,' he said through a mouthful of nails.

'Do you need a hand?'

'If you could just hold it...straight like that, it would actually be a big help.'

They worked together in silence for some minutes as he attached the door to its hinges. Then he said, 'That's it. Good girl. Unlike my previous helpers, you're a model assistant.'

'I'm not sure how you coped with your previous helpers,' she said wryly.

'You know the worst thing about them? They never stopped talking,' he said with a grin. 'I'm sure they can talk under water—I used to hear them talking at me in my sleep. Yes, only a week to go until Christmas—have you got a minute or two?'

'Sure.' She sat down at the small table and looked at him enquiringly. It had been a curiously peaceful time since the night of Rox and Michelle's party. No mischief, no dangerous, tiger-like prowling had been detectable in Brendan Grey. He'd worked away on the play house and also started to build a small pond and waterfall beside it, suitable for sailing little boats in or just getting wet without anyone worrying that they would drown themselves, as he'd explained to his mother and Merryn.

For the rest of the time he'd been content to be quietly at home, reading, playing tennis during the day with Merryn, playing cards in the evening with Merryn and Sonia, or listening to music, even watching television or just talking. What he had *not* done was take up the strands of his previous social life so temptingly presented to him per the medium of Rox and Michelle's party, although he had spent a part of each day receiving and sending business faxes and had gone out a few times to meet people in the same business.

It had puzzled Merryn at first, and she'd fully expected it to pall after a couple of days. But there'd also been no more references to Steve, not even when he had taken her to the movies, and, to his mother's joy, he'd found a Christmas tree even bigger than Michelle's, he'd got out all the boxes of Christmas decorations and he and Merryn had decorated the house together.

'Do you remember offering to help me with my Christmas shopping?'

'I do.'

'Well, I'm at a loss concerning my sisters and my mother.'

'I'd be only too happy to help,' Merryn said with an imp of mischief dancing in her eyes. 'In fact you could leave it all to me if you really wanted to.'

'Well, Rox and Michelle I'd be happy to leave to your taste and judgement, but I want something…rather special for Sonia. Could I come with you, in other words?'

'Shopping? Of course. When you say special, have you got any ideas?'

He frowned. 'I thought of a painting—she loves art.'

Merryn clasped her hands together and her eyes shone with enthusiasm. 'You must be a mind-reader! There is an artist she's interested in whose work is on display at the Jabiru Gallery at Sanctuary Cove. She was talking about him only last week. She was disappointed to think that his exhibition will be over before she feels comfortable about a longish drive down to the Coast.'

'Do you think we could tootle down to Sanctuary Cove, Merryn?'

'We'll have to concoct some excuse if you want it to be a complete surprise,' Merryn said slowly. 'But, come to think of it, Sanctuary Cove would be a good place to shop for Michelle and Rox.'

'Leave it to me—would tomorrow suit you?'

'Why not? Yes.'

'Does she know where we're going?' Merryn asked the next morning as she sat beside Brendan in the black BMW.

'She only knows that you're helping me with my shopping.' He looked wry. 'She was delighted, and she's got Mary Eaves coming over to give her a hand with some baking so we don't need to worry.'

It was a fine, blinding day, and Merryn had on a cool, sleeveless button-through floral dress and sandals, and had a big raffia hat trimmed with flowers resting on the back seat. Brendan was similarly casual in white trousers, a navy sports shirt and espadrilles.

They talked desultorily but with that new-found comfort as he drove down the Pacific Highway towards Sanctuary Cove, a lovely resort on the water just north of the Gold Coast.

'I can't remember the last time I came here,' he said as they wandered through the colourful shopping village.

'It's fun, isn't it?'

He looked down at her, then took her hand. 'Yes.'

Merryn felt her heart constrict in a familiar way but made herself breathe evenly. Just one day with him on my own, especially now he's like this, like the old Bren, can't hurt, can it? she thought. Surely I can be natural too?

Two hours later they were sitting at the St Tropez restaurant on the waterfront, outside under the awning, a couple of satisfied shoppers. The painting they'd chosen for Sonia was boxed and in the car and the spare chair at their table was piled with exotic carrier bags. Merryn was sipping an iced fruit juice and Brendan a beer.

'That was lovely,' she said with deep satisfaction. She took her hat off and ran her fingers through her hair, a movement that tautened the thin fabric of her dress across her breasts. 'You've been very generous towards your mother and sisters, Bren,' she added a little wickedly.

He shrugged and turned to gaze out over the marina, with its forest of masts and sleek motor cruisers, and wondered again if she knew how delicious she was. How that to shop with her, something he didn't normally enjoy, had been a new experience as she'd handled fine leather, silk, porcelain and perfumes in those slim, elegant hands and made her wants known with quiet grace. If she knew how she'd paused thoughtfully, holding up an item with its recipient obviously in her mind's eye, and then chosen things he'd known his sisters would love but would not have thought of himself. She had been a delight to watch.

He shrugged. 'I'm glad you approve, but the style all came from you.'

'That's probably because I'm a woman buying for women,' she responded wryly. 'But the painting was your idea, and so was the play house—both pretty inspired gifts, if you ask me. Sonia will love it. She adores landscapes, and that particular one of the Dalby area is not far from where she grew up.'

'I know—how lucky was that? That leaves me with

only one person to buy for now—' He broke off as the waitress came to take their order for lunch, then added, 'You.'

Merryn smiled at him. 'As a matter of fact, I'm in the same boat—only you left. But...' She paused, then said quietly, 'Perhaps...being able to be like this again is all we need to do for each other, Bren? I mean, it is like a gift.'

'Does it mean so much to you, Merryn?' he said after an age.

'Yes. Are you...?' She took a breath but didn't evade his eyes. 'Are you really happy again? I know that sounds a trivial and trite way of putting it, but I guess you know what I mean.'

His lips twisted. 'Yes, I do. No, I'm not. But that's not your fault.'

Her eyes widened. 'You haven't...'

'Shown it?' There was irony in the depths of his hazel eyes but it was self-directed. 'Sorry about that, it was rather juvenile.'

'I—' She sat forward abruptly. 'It must be something you can put a name to now, though? A more definitive name?'

'You're right, it is.' He smiled unamusedly. 'I don't want to simply work for the rest of my life. I need— and this took me by surprise, Merryn, although it may not you—I need a woman. But one I want to spend the rest of my life with. At least, I'm pretty sure that's what it must be.'

She gasped.

'Strange, isn't it?' he agreed dryly.

'No, of course not,' she said dazedly. 'It's very natural, actually.'

'But not what I particularly thought would happen to me.'

'I—you asked *me* this but hadn't *you* ever thought of being a husband and father?'

'Yes, although I found it hard to actually visualise—could we be two of a kind?' he said, with a smile lurking at the back of his eyes.

Merryn blinked several times but could think of nothing to say.

'I suppose the logistics of it have always been a problem too. I'm attracted to faraway places, the more difficult the terrain the better I like it. Or did,' he added with a shrug.

'You could always change that—couldn't you?' she suggested. 'There must be roads and bridges and dams to be built here at home. Can I...?' She paused. 'Can I tell you what I really think?'

'Please do.'

But she waited as their lunch was served—grilled fish for him, a Caesar salad for her. 'I think,' she said slowly as she toyed with an anchovy, 'that when the right woman comes along, it will all resolve itself.'

Brendan raised a wry eyebrow. 'I'm sure you're right—at least, that's the accepted theory.'

She grimaced. 'But you don't subscribe to it? You think, talking of trite—'

'I'm probably a little cynical—I guess *that's* why it's come as a bit of a shock.'

'Cynical about women?' she asked, raising her eyes to his.

Their gazes caught and held. 'Sometimes,' he said at last.

'I should have thought many of them would be perfectly willing to be anything you wanted them to be.'

'That—doesn't altogether recommend itself in the end,' he said dryly.

Merryn's mouth dimpled at the corners. 'So you're looking for a challenge as well as someone to live the rest of your life with?'

'I gather the irony of that amuses you?'

'Sorry.' But her eyes danced. 'I mean, while I'd like to be a friend who could help, sometimes there are times when you're a woman first—or a man first, if you know what I mean.'

A reluctant smile tugged at his lips. 'Yes,' he replied, 'I know exactly what you mean.'

They ate in silence for a few minutes, but it suddenly seemed to Merryn as if the gloss had gone from the day. She couldn't put her finger on exactly why it should be different, or what she might have said, but when he spoke at last she knew that things had gone wrong.

He changed the subject completely. He spoke about boats, asking her if she was a boating person, and when she said she had little experience of them, confided that he'd often had the desire to sail around the world but suspected that it was one of those unreasonable desires everybody had, such as writing a book. Then he looked at his watch and suggested they think of driving home because he'd told Sonia they wouldn't be late.

Merryn agreed quietly.

It was as they were coming off the Gateway Bridge onto a busy road not far from home that the car behind them attempted to overtake, found itself with no room and forced Brendan to drive into the pavement. The impact caused Merryn to hit her head—and that was the last thing she remembered for a short while.

When she came to, Brendan was crouched on the pavement with her in his arms, an oasis in the chaos around them. Two more cars had crashed, as well as the one that had caused the accident, and there was traffic building up all around...

'Bren...' she whispered and licked her lips. 'What happened?'

She felt a strong muscular surge run through his body as he held her closer and closed his eyes. Relief? she wondered as she started to remember and attempted to sit up.

'Don't be a fool,' he murmured, and kissed her hair. 'Stay still.'

'But...'

'But nothing. I don't think anyone's seriously hurt, although there are a lot of seriously ruffled tempers about, but the police have arrived so they can sort it out. How do you feel?'

She explored the side of her head with her finger-tips and winced as she encountered a lump. But other than that she seemed to be fine, as she told him.

'Thank heavens.' But his hazel gaze was still concerned as it roamed over her. Then he said, 'Look, we might as well make ourselves comfortable. This could take some time.' And he picked her up and carried her to a bus stop bench that now had a black BMW bumper resting against it. He put his arm around her and drew her into his side as they sat and observed the mayhem.

Once, Merryn buried her face in his shoulder, because although it shouldn't have been funny it was at times. He rested his chin on her head and she could feel him laughing too.

Eventually a platoon of policemen got the traffic flowing again and came to take a statement from Brendan. Then an ambulance officer insisted on checking Merryn and recommended that she go home but to be on the look-out for concussion or delayed shock. The sun was sinking as Brendan reversed the only superficially damaged car off the pavement and drove them slowly home.

Sonia was waiting for them. 'I thought you two might have eloped!' she said, with her frown of concern fading.

Merryn took a breath and looked up into Brendan's eyes, only to see a look of such startling intensity she was almost blinded by it. But what it meant she couldn't for the life of her tell, and it was gone almost

instantaneously. Then Sonia's eyes fell on the car still
parked in the drive and swift understanding dawned.
'Oh, no—are you all right. *How…?*'

'We're fine,' Brendan hastened to assure her. 'At
least, Merryn might have a headache but that's all.
Come inside. There's nothing we can do about it today.'

'If you think I give two hoots about my car,' Sonia
said indignantly, 'you don't know me very well,
young man!'

Brendan laughed, and, as if it was becoming second
nature to him, picked Merryn up and carried her inside.

'You don't have to,' she protested

'And you'll just do as you're told, young woman,'
he replied, still grinning. He put her down on a settee
in the family room, looked down at her for a moment
as if he was in two minds, then said only, 'Stay
there—it's my turn to see to dinner tonight.'

'I thought you only made Irish coffee,' she said
ruefully.

'That's true, but I can use a phone.'

Merryn blinked.

'Pizza,' he said significantly. 'But I might just be
able to toss up a salad to go with it.'

'Bren, you don't have to order pizza,' Sonia said,
coming into the room. 'Anyone would think I was
completely disabled!'

'Dearest,' her son replied, 'I know you look upon
it as a mortal sin, the eating of take-away food, but

there are occasions when it can be warranted, when it can be quite pleasant and, provided you don't make a habit of it, it will not even destroy the moral fabric of our lives. Besides which, I happen to have a yen for pizza. If it would make you happier, you can make the salad.' He strolled from the room.

'What's put him in this mood?' Sonia whispered conspiratorially.

'I'm not even sure what kind of mood it is,' Merryn whispered back. 'But I think you'd better let him have his way.'

Sonia chuckled. 'I think you might be right. Are you sure *you're* all right? You do look pale.'

'No, I'm fine.' Merryn stood up. 'I'll just go and freshen up.'

But in the haven of her room she looked at herself in the mirror after she'd washed her hands and face and was perturbed by what she saw. There was a dazed sort of look in her eyes that she suspected had nothing to do with her fleeting bout of unconsciousness and everything to do with the sheer heaven of being held and comforted by Brendan Grey...

It was a happy though short evening as Brendan introduced his mother to the delights of pizza and they got out the Christmas wrapping paper and made a start on the growing mountain of presents.

'I don't think we should leave them under the tree,'

Merryn said at one stage—which was where they were starting to pile up.

'Why not?' Brendan enquired. 'That's where they always used to be.'

'Not before you were about twelve,' his mother replied. 'Merryn's right—it's an unbearable temptation and, anyway, Father Christmas arrives in the depth of the night, don't forget. Unless—Bren!' She looked at him excitedly.

'Oh, no.' Brendan shook his tawny head. 'If it's what I think you have in mind, the answer is no!'

'You don't know—'

'Yes, I do, and nothing on earth would induce me to dress up as Father Christmas. You'll have to rope in either Ray or David for that little pleasure.'

Sonia subsided.

'Or why not Steve?' he added dryly. 'If he wants to be part of this family, he should earn his keep.'

Sonia blinked. 'Well, I might do just that—but, no, I can't now! He rang yesterday to tell me that he has to work on Christmas Day, which is really sad, but he can't help it, I'm afraid.' She looked at Merryn.

That was when Merryn decided she'd had enough, although it wasn't anything she said that alerted Brendan. But perhaps the barely perceptible movement she made did. Because he looked at her suddenly, looked at his watch, then stood up and held down his hand to her. 'Bed for you, I think, Miss Merryn. I know it's not that late, but it's not every day you get a bump on the head and black out.'

'Yes, of course,' Sonia agreed.

Merryn took Brendan's hand and allowed herself to be helped up, but then she said composedly, 'Thanks, but I can get myself up the stairs. I really am all right.' She bent to kiss Sonia, then smiled at Brendan and walked out of the room.

But he followed her right to the door of her bedroom. She turned to face him uncertainly.

'You look so tired,' he said softly, and raised a hand to touch her face.

'It's been—' She stopped abruptly.

'A difficult day?' he suggested.

'Well, no.' She twisted her hands together because it had been, but what was the point of saying it? 'It was a lovely day to start with—thanks for lunch. And dinner.'

'Merryn—' he frowned '—are you trying to tell me something?'

'What?' she whispered.

His fingers roamed down her cheek. 'How can I know,' he murmured, 'unless you tell me?'

It ran through her mind that what she would love to say was, Stay with me, Bren. Hold me again. Soothe me to sleep and when I wake up feeling better make love to me. Take me away with you wherever you have to go; I'll cope...

'Merryn?'

But although she swallowed several times, she couldn't speak.

'Look,' he said, 'get into your pyjamas and I'll bring you something.'

'No—'

'Don't argue, Merryn.' He turned on his heel.

She was in bed in a pair of maroon silk pyjamas with white piping when he returned with a glass of milk and a tablet.

'Got it from Sonia,' he said, putting the glass on her bedside table and handing her the tablet. 'It'll help your headache.'

'You didn't worry her? This…is just reaction, I guess.'

'No, I didn't worry her. But I've got the feeling it's more than reaction. I'm sorry if what I said about Steve upset you.'

Her eyes widened.

He smiled slightly. 'That surprises you? That I should apologize?'

'Yes,' she said honestly.

He looked wry. 'I must be more arrogant than I thought I was. But watching you today, Merryn, made me realise that—'

'Don't tell me—I've grown up,' she said a little tartly.

'Well, you have.' He fingered the coverlet. 'And you've done it with the kind of inner grace that generally means you've got things under pretty good control. So, who am I to come barging in and trampling around on your—choices?'

He'd been looking down at the fine cotton between

his fingers, but suddenly he raised his gaze to hers.
'That's what occurred to me today,' he said, with a
glint of that self-directed mockery she'd seen once
before in his eyes.

'Bren…' But the words stuck in her throat—the
words she would have loved to utter—and she wondered why, then knew almost at once that if she ever
did say them, and he had to tell her that he could
never think of her as a wife, it would ruin everything
between them… 'Bren, I don't know what's wrong
with me tonight,' she said slowly, 'but I promise you
that tomorrow I'll be back to normal.'

He seemed about to say something important, but
said only, 'Drink your milk.'

She did so, swallowing the tablet and lying back
tiredly.

'Sweet dreams, Merryn,' he said after a moment,
standing up.

'Thanks,' she answered huskily. 'Could you turn
off the light?'

He did so and closed the door—in time, she hoped,
not to notice the sudden tears on her lashes.

She fell asleep quite soon, but just before midnight
she woke with her heart pounding and her mouth dry
from an old, old nightmare she hadn't had for many
years—to do with losing her parents in a car accident.
She thrashed aside the bedclothes and was at her door
before she was properly awake, then she was stum-
bling down the stairs, anything to escape the images
in her mind. There was a light on in the lounge and

she ran into the room—and Brendan, still fully clothed and already on his feet, fielded her.

'Merryn, Merryn.' He pulled her close, 'What on earth—don't tell me you still get those dreams?'

'Bren…' She trembled and shook like a leaf in his arms. 'You remembered—no, not for years.'

'You poor kid,' he murmured, and, picking her up, sat down on the settee with her. 'It must have been what happened today that stirred it all up. Why didn't I think of that?' he added with savage impatience.

'It's not your fault,' she said shakily, moving her cheek restlessly on his shoulder.

'Merryn.' He passed a hand over her hair. 'Hey, it's OK—relax, little one.'

And gradually the feel of his hand stroking her hair, the warmth and strength of his body and arms, cut through her trauma, and she fell still and started to breathe evenly. She even found the composure to ask, 'What are you doing up so late?'

'Nothing much.'

'Not just sitting here? That doesn't sound like you.'

'No?'

She twisted her head to direct a smile up at him. 'Not like the Brendan Grey I used to know.'

He raised a wry eyebrow then quite naturally kissed her lightly on the lips. 'Was I such a hell-raiser? I don't seem to remember that.'

'No. But you had an awful lot of energy. I'm surprised you haven't taken up one of your old sports if nothing else.'

He laughed, then sobered. 'As a matter of fact I was contemplating changing my booking.'

'To go back?' Merryn said after a startled pause. 'Oh, no!'

'You don't think that's a good idea?'

She bit her lip. 'Your mother— You wouldn't go before Christmas? You—' She broke off confusedly.

'Of course not, but—look, don't say anything to her. It was just a thought.'

'Oh, Bren.' She tilted her face to his again, 'I *wish* I could help.'

He stared down at her sombrely. 'Unfortunately you're the one girl who can't, Merryn. Look, I've had an idea—why don't I make us up a bed down here? We can watch the *Late Show* together,' he added with a grin, in a lightning change of mood.

'I...' She looked at him helplessly.

But that was exactly what he did. He found an old mattress and some pillows and sheets, as well as opening a bottle of wine and bringing a platter of cheese, crackers, olives and fruit.

'A midnight feast?' Merryn found herself unwittingly charmed and soothed.

'A bit more sophisticated than what we used to have,' he said wryly, and poured the wine. 'Make yourself comfortable. How's your head?'

'I'd forgotten all about it,' Merryn confessed.

'OK.' He sat down cross-legged beside her on the mattress—he was still fully clothed. 'Now, we have a choice between some really old movies, although...'

He paused and smiled. 'What about Laurel and Hardy?'

'Yes, please!'

Two glasses of wine and much laughter later, as they lay side by side holding hands, Merryn fell asleep.

When Brendan realised this, he eased his hand out of hers and turned the television off with the remote control. Then he stood up and tidied their feast, but stopped with his hand on the one lamp that was lit and stared down at her.

There was something absurdly young, he thought, about the way her dark lashes fanned her cheek, and something small and very vulnerable about her slim figure curled up in her maroon pyjamas. A different Merryn, he mused, from the poised girl she so often was. An orphan who didn't think she knew how to have someone of her own. And yet only today he'd told her, and believed it, that she was handling her life well.

That was before she got knocked out, he reminded himself. And before she came running down here shaking like a leaf and with horror-stricken eyes. And you might believe she's handling her life well but you still have difficulty with Ray's brother...

He stood lost in thought for several minutes, then she moved restlessly and he switched off the lamp and lay down beside her, taking her gently into his arms. But he thought, I shouldn't be doing this...

* * *

Sunlight was streaming over them when Brendan woke the next morning, but it wasn't that which had woken him. It was the sound of an indrawn breath, then footsteps advancing into the room.

He lifted his head and squinted at the pair of feet that had come into view. Feminine feet in open-toed shoes with painted toenails—feet that planted themselves inches from the pillow. And Merryn stirred in his arms.

Then the owner of those feet spoke, and his sister Michelle said in outraged tones, '*Brendan!* How could you? It's not decent in the first place, but if you *had* to seduce her surely you didn't have to do it in *public!*'

CHAPTER FIVE

'WHAT the hell do you mean?'

Merryn struggled to sit up as Brendan barked the question at his sister. She pushed her hair behind her ears and rubbed her eyes.

'Isn't it obvious?' Michelle responded, and turned to Merryn. 'I'm really surprised at *you*,' she said arctically, 'but I suppose that's why you and Bren locked yourselves away the night of the party. Tell me this, Merryn, don't you think it's a bit unkind to Steve to lead him on when you're carrying on with Brendan?'

'*Carrying on* with me,' Brendan repeated savagely, springing up and towering over his sister. 'You bloody fool, Michelle, just look at me. I'm fully dressed, in case you hadn't noticed!'

'That doesn't mean anything—'

'And do you seriously believe either of us would choose the lounge floor to disport ourselves? You must be mad!'

'Then tell me what you were doing!' Michelle shot back.

'Look—' Merryn scrambled up '—we had a midnight feast, as a matter of fact.'

Michelle laughed unkindly and scrutinized Merryn's pyjama-clad form scathingly. 'That's a new name for it—you were sleeping in his arms! But then you always did have a crush on Brendan, didn't you, Merryn?'

'I... I...' Merryn felt a burning tide of colour rise to her cheeks, and she turned on her heel suddenly and marched out.

But even from her bedroom the row that ensued was audible. Brendan told Michelle he'd always known she was a fool but not even he had suspected just how big a fool. This prompted Michelle to drag up every grudge she'd ever held against him and to conclude by saying that she, her husband and her children would not be participating at any Christmas event held in this house that he would be attending.

'One should be grateful for small mercies—your kids are uncontrollable, your husband bores me to tears and you, yourself, Michelle, are not only insensitive, domineering and lacking in humour, but you bore me to tears, too! It would give me great pleasure if you did stay away, and why don't you make sure your dull-as-ditch-water brother-in-law does as well?'

At this point Sonia limped into Merryn's room with wide eyes and a horror-struck expression. 'What...*why?*'

Merryn sat down on her bed and rubbed her face distractedly. And tried to explain. She finished by saying, 'But she—Michelle—thought we were...well—'

'Making love?' Sonia said, surprisingly grimly for her. 'Do you know, there are times when Michelle is unbelievable? And so I will tell her.' She limped out determinedly.

Merryn stared after her, then blinked and buried her face in her hands as she contemplated a bleak and disastrous Christmas, not to mention how on earth she was ever going to face Brendan again. Then she got up and began to dress hurriedly, conscious of one overwhelming urge—to get out of the place for a while.

Five minutes later, as she drove down the road, she thought they probably weren't even aware that she'd left; no one had rushed out to stop her.

But it was a tense, miserable day she spent, shopping for food and trying to distract herself, and when she drove back at about four o'clock that afternoon only Brendan was home...

'Where the devil have you been?' he snapped when she walked into the kitchen.

'Out,' she murmured, dumping fresh fruit and groceries on the table.

'And it didn't occur to you that my mother might be worried sick about you?'

She eyed him. He was lounging at the table with a pot of tea in front of him, wearing a checked shirt and khaki shorts. 'No. It didn't,' she replied evenly. 'She knows I'm over twenty-one—where is she?'

'At Rox's. Miranda's come down with some sort of ailment.'

Merryn stopped unpacking bags. 'Serious?'

'I doubt it. The doctor has said not but she wanted to see for herself.' He raised a wry eyebrow.

Merryn shrugged and turned away. Sonia took her grandchildren's health very seriously and always insisted on being on hand when she could.

'Merryn?'

She reached up to pack away some tinned foods then tucked her white blouse back into her floral shorts. Finally she said tonelessly, 'Yes?'

'Is it true?'

She glanced at him through her lashes but said nothing.

'Look—' he stood up and came round the table to her '—you don't have to be embarrassed about it.'

'It's over and done with, Bren,' she said quietly.

He paused, standing so close to her she could see the little golden flecks in his eyes.

'What surprises me,' she went on in what she hoped was a normal voice, 'is that Michelle of all people should have noticed, and—'

'They all did. All except me,' he said sombrely.

Her lips parted. 'How…do you know?'

'We had a reconciliation after you'd gone. Sonia insisted on it. She said she wasn't going to have the first Christmas we'd had together for years ruined. She said that if we didn't make up, *she* would be the one to stay away—or rather go away. That got to Michelle, as well as to me.' He grimaced.

'So?'

'We sat down and had it all out. Michelle now

doesn't believe you and I were doing anything indecorous on the lounge floor.' A glint of rough impatience showed in his eyes. 'And I retracted all the unpleasant things I said. But when I told her that what she'd said to you was ridiculous, she refused to change her standpoint. And Sonia agreed. That's why, apparently, they were all so happy to see you responding to Steve. They thought you must have got over me.'

This is the most embarrassing thing that's ever happened to me, Merryn thought. How did I give myself away?

'Well, they're wrong,' she said coolly. 'Not that I didn't hero-worship you a bit, Bren. In fact it was quite a lot, but—' she swallowed suddenly '—I always knew it was a kid sister—big brother affair.'

There was a moment's silence. Then he said abruptly, 'It needn't be any more, Merryn.'

'Why? Because you suddenly find yourself needing a wife?' she asked with irony.

'Let's get this straight, Merryn—'

'No, let's not, Brendan,' she said swiftly, and went to pass him. But he caught her wrist.

'Why are you so angry?' he asked roughly. 'Because I didn't ever notice? And now you're going to make me pay for it?'

'No,' she said through her teeth. 'I would *scorn* to stoop to anything like that, and to have you think it of me fills me with disgust towards your thought processes, Brendan Grey!' she flashed, and tried to break free.

'Ah, but I wonder how much this disgusts you,' he drawled, and pulled her into his arms.

'Bren—'

'Not this—we know how you like this,' he murmured, just holding her. 'We did quite a bit of it one way or another yesterday, didn't we? But how about this?' His eyes mocked her as he ran his hands down her body. 'And this? You may speak your mind when I've finished, Merryn,' he advised her blandly.

'No, I'll speak it now—don't do this, Bren,' she said hoarsely. 'I—'

'Don't kiss you, Merryn?' He scanned her face and his lips twisted. 'Strangely enough, I don't think I can help myself.'

She gasped, and her eyes flashed furiously. 'Oh, yes, you can—you *agreed* I wasn't the one to do this to.'

'That was before I knew how you felt.'

'You *don't* know how I feel—'

'Well, this is one way to find out,' he drawled, running his hands down her arms, then her waist and hips beneath the thin stuff of her shorts. 'So slim and silken,' he murmured, and a glint of humour touched his eyes. 'So cross. Why don't you tell me to do my worst, Merryn?' But he gave her no chance to answer as he slid one hand through her hair and lowered his mouth to hers.

Was it those last words that spurred her to do the unbelievable? she would wonder later. That made her so angry she decided to do *her* worst? How could you call it your worst, though, when it was your best...?

They broke apart once, both breathing as if they'd been running. She eyed him with utter hostility but moved in his arms, and he bent his head again and they kissed again, with hungry, angry passion—at least it was angry on her side. And their bodies twined and blended and spoke for them both in a way that was electrifying for Merryn.

What ended it was the sound of a car tooting outside.

He held her away from him and looked into her eyes. 'Saved by the bell,' he said barely audibly. 'Dear Merryn, you *have* grown up.'

She tore herself out of his arms just in the nick of time as Rox breezed into the kitchen.

'Anyone home? I'm delivering Mum back but I can't stay to chat.'

'How—?' Merryn swallowed as she tucked her blouse in once again. 'How's Miranda?'

'It's just a touch of colic—she'll be fine. I heard all about the ruckus this morning!' She winked at Brendan. 'Didn't you know that Michelle has taken it upon herself to be the high priestess of all that's good and *proper* in this clan?'

Brendan swore and Rox turned laughingly to Merryn. 'Don't let her get to you, Merry. Remember when she had a crush on, of all people, the married man next door? She used to lie in wait for him where he couldn't help but trip over her, then pop up as if it was all an accident, despite being made-up to the nines and wearing her most seductive clothes.'

'Thanks, I will. Remember that,' Merryn said in a strangled sort of voice. 'I'll go and help Sonia.'

Dinner was a quiet, strained affair, although Sonia appeared not to notice. She was very taken up with putting the final touches to the things she'd made for the play house, and that occupied most of their conversation over the meal.

It came as something of a surprise, although to Merryn it was a relief, when Brendan said casually that he was going out.

'How nice, dear!' Sonia beamed at him. 'Who with?'

'Some of those old friends you threw at me so determinedly—a game of night tennis.' He looked at her wryly and added, 'So it wasn't all in vain.'

Merryn wondered if his mother caught the faintly malicious undertone, but she only said, 'Excellent. Why don't you take Merryn? I'm sure she could do with a break after a day like today.'

Their gazes clashed, Brendan and Merryn's. They hadn't been alone since Rox had interrupted them in the kitchen, but Merryn had had ample time to discover that if the only comment he could make about what had happened was to do with how she'd grown up, not to mention everything that had preceded his kissing her, then she was dangerously close to hating him.

'Certainly,' he said with a shrug. 'If Merryn would like to come—would you?'

She looked straight into his hazel eyes and said coolly and casually, 'Sorry, but Merryn has other plans for this evening.'

'Have you, dear? You didn't mention them,' Sonia said innocently.

Merryn only just stopped herself from grinding her teeth audibly. 'Don't you remember?' She turned to Sonia. 'We're going to put the final icing on the Christmas cake tonight?'

'Oh, that! I can do it.'

'No, you can't. You don't want to be on your feet for that long—'

'Then we could do it tomorrow morning, Merryn.'

'It's much better to do it when it's cooler—'

'Look, I wouldn't dream,' Brendan interrupted, 'of upsetting anyone's plans—particularly Merryn's. And I really think, beloved—' he addressed his mother '—you should take the hint. Merryn doesn't *want* to come out with me.' He glanced at Merryn wickedly.

'You're absolutely right,' Merryn retorted swiftly, and got up to remove their plates. But retreating to the kitchen didn't prevent her from hearing Sonia saying sadly that she had the feeling this Christmas was jinxed somehow. Or from hearing her son replying bracingly that she shouldn't worry, it would all come right.

'There.'

Merryn stood back and regarded the cake that stood

resplendently on the kitchen table. It was iced in white with silver latticework and gold bells, and it had green and red ribbons around it. There was a miniature Father Christmas in his sleigh with tiny reindeer in one corner and a sprig of mistletoe in another, and artistically piped across the centre in green and red was a 'Happy Christmas' message.

'Stunning,' Sonia said. 'Between us we could go into business.' She'd helped make all the fiddly bits.

'It's very bright.'

'The brighter the better as far as the kids are concerned. I wonder how Miranda is?'

Merryn looked at her affectionately. 'I'll give Rox a call if you like.'

'Oh, no, I'm just fussing, probably.' Sonia stretched and yawned, then she put out a hand to touch one of Merryn's. 'I'm so sorry about what happened this morning.'

'That's all right. It wasn't your fault,' Merryn said prosaically.

'No, but I can see that it's made things difficult for you and Brendan.'

'I don't think it's made things difficult for Brendan at all,' Merryn replied ironically.

Sonia grimaced. 'That's what I mean—uh—he really was astounded when Michelle insisted that you…that you…'

'Had had a crush on him? From what he told me

you agreed with her.' Merryn couldn't help the tinge of pain in her voice.

Sonia sighed. But she said with more spirit, 'No, I didn't—not that it was a crush. I just knew that—that Brendan meant more to you than anyone. There's a difference, Merryn,' she added quietly and steadily.

Merryn thought for a moment, then shrugged.

'Has it never changed?'

'Yes, it's changed now,' Merryn said after a long silence. 'He's finally convinced me I—it's a waste of—whatever.'

Sonia's brows rose. 'It didn't strike me as if that's how he feels.'

'Then it should have,' Merryn returned. 'Shall we put this away and go to bed? And would you mind if I spent most of tomorrow out? There are a few friends I want to catch up with before Christmas.'

Sonia looked as if she would like to take issue with this, then she glanced at Merryn's shuttered expression and wisely decided to hold her peace. 'Of course not, dear. I'm coping so much better now, aren't I? I really don't need you dancing attendance on me all the time.'

Merryn left early the next morning and drove to her flat, which she'd locked up for the six weeks she was to spend with Sonia. It was an enormous relief, she discovered, to close her own front door on the world. Nor did she have any intention of socialising—all she wanted was to be on her own, to take stock...

It wasn't large, her flat. One bedroom, lounge-dining area all in one and a small kitchen. But it was right on the river in a modern low-rise block. And it was a pleasure to sit on her small verandah and watch the river traffic go by: barges, ferries and yachts, scullers and rowers.

She spent the first couple of hours airing and dusting, handling some of the treasures that she'd accumulated on her trips, and enjoying the cool blue and grey decor she'd done herself. Slate-blue carpet throughout, a comfortable pale grey leather lounge suite, a silvery grey and lemon bedspread on her double bed, touches of lemon and apple-green and rose in a lovely wall hanging in the lounge, lithographs and etchings, and old brass lamps she'd picked up in faraway places and polished and restored.

When she'd finished dusting and polishing, she could feel that the tension had eased, but she refused to allow herself to think of Brendan. She had a shower and put on a floating, cool, long white dress, then made herself a snack from the few things she'd purchased on the way over. She sat with her bare feet resting on the cool marble of her coffee table as she ate slowly. Then she curled up on the settee and fell asleep.

It was the doorbell that woke her—the last thing she'd expected. She got up with a frown then experienced a pulse of concern—Sonia?

It was Brendan.

'What are you doing here?' She stood with the door

only half open, blinking at him dazedly—and not only
because she was disorientated but because for the first
time since he'd come home, other than for the party,
he was formally dressed in a suit and tie with his
tawny hair sleek and tidy.

'Mending fences,' he said briefly. 'Let me in,
Merryn.'

'No, I don't have to—I mean,' she amended as she
thought she sounded childish, 'there's nothing to say.'

'Yes, there is.' He looked her up and down, taking
in her bare feet, the filmy frock, her disordered hair.
'Unless,' he added sardonically, 'you have someone
with you?'

The implication was plain—someone you've been
sleeping with. Merryn glanced down at herself and
drew a frustrated breath. Because of the heat, after
she'd showered she hadn't put on a bra, and the white
dress did little to conceal the fact. Then she looked
up at him and said arctically, 'Don't class me with
yourself, Brendan. I was hot, that's all. There's no one
here.'

'All the more reason to let me in, Merryn,' he said
brusquely. 'We can't ignore each other for the—'

'I wasn't proposing to.'

'Then let me in.'

She eyed him indignantly, then opened the door
wider and walked away. Walked into her bedroom, in
fact, where she closed the door and took her time
about changing into another dress, dark green with

white spots, brushing her hair and slipping a pair of green leather flat shoes on.

He was standing at the verandah doors when she came out. He'd taken the jacket of his beautiful light-weight grey suit off, as well as his navy tie, and they were both slung over a chair. He'd pushed his sleeves up haphazardly and his hands were shoved into his pockets as he examined the view. There was impatience stamped into every line of his back.

When he swung round, he said nothing for a long moment as they gazed at each, and hostility lay almost tangibly on the air between them.

'What do you want, Brendan?' she asked quietly at last, and sat down composedly. 'I had every intention of coming back tonight, if that's what you were afraid of. You didn't really think I'd desert Sonia this close to Christmas, did you?'

'Perhaps not, but between us we've contrived to dampen the Christmas spirit considerably. She's miserable, in other words,' he said dryly.

Merryn swallowed. 'Then we'll just have to put up a smokescreen until it's over.'

He strolled into the room and sat down opposite her. 'Carry on as if none of this has happened? My dear Merryn, do you think that's possible?'

'Yes,' she said through her teeth. 'Besides, what did happen? Nothing of great, earth-shattering significance.'

A fleeting smile touched his mouth. 'Are you trying

to say I didn't make the earth *move* for you? We didn't quite get to that stage, if you recall.'

Merryn breathed deeply and warned herself against futile expressions of anger. But she did say, 'If it amuses you, be my guest.'

'No, it doesn't amuse me, Merryn,' he retorted swiftly. 'You see, I just happen to be the man you kissed yesterday with extreme passion, and—'

She flew to her feet, all her warnings to herself forgotten. 'What was I supposed to do? Why should it be your prerogative to take the initiative whenever the whim takes you?'

'Do you mean I goaded you into it?' he drawled.

'Yes, you did. You see, as you so rightly remarked at the end of it, I have grown up. And I'm *not* some wet little girl who can be kissed into submission— again, whenever the whim takes you.'

He stood up abruptly and towered over her. 'How experienced are you, Merryn?' he queried softly.

'*Very,*' she spat at him.

A muscle flickered in his jaw and she saw that she'd shocked him. 'So,' he murmured, 'all this family concern that little Miss Merryn might still be nurturing hopeless dreams about me was unnecessary?'

'Yes.'

He stared down at her and said roughly, 'Then Steve makes even less sense.'

'Leave him out of it,' Merryn ordered.

'Because he never entered it?' he said mockingly.

'Because…' Her shoulders slumped suddenly. 'Just go away, will you, Bren? I've had enough.'

'I can't,' he said, but wryly and in a lightning change of mood that bewildered Merryn.

'What do you mean, you can't?'

'I mean that I have no transport, Miss Merryn, and I was hoping that you'd give me a lift home.'

She set her teeth. 'Don't tell me you *walked* here— how did you even know I was here?'

'I didn't, I took a punt—and, no, I didn't walk, I took a taxi. I had a business lunch in town to which I also took a taxi—after dropping the BMW off at a garage for repairs. It won't be ready until tomorrow afternoon.'

'And who—' Merryn put her hands on her hips '—has been with Sonia all day?'

'I dropped her at Rox's. She wanted to be with Miranda. Do you honestly think I would have deserted her all day?' he parodied quizzically.

'I think…' Merryn stopped and counted to ten beneath her breath. 'All right. I'll just lock up.'

'We don't have to rush. Sonia is spending the night with Rox. In fact, if you had something cold to drink to offer me, I'd be most grateful.'

Her lips worked but no sound came. He watched her for a moment, then said gravely, 'Perhaps we could put in a little work on our smokescreen act at the same time, Merryn? How long have you had this place, it's very—you.'

'What's that supposed to mean?'

'If you happen to have a cold beer, I'll tell you.'

'I…' She sighed suddenly, and swung on her heel.

'Here you are.' She put a frosted can of beer and a tall glass down on the marble table, and a glass of fruit juice for herself.

'Thanks.' He pulled the ring tab off the can and poured the beer. 'Sure you wouldn't like something stronger for yourself?'

'It's only three—' She glanced at her watch and amended that with a surprised look. 'It's five o'clock! How could I have slept so long?'

'I don't know.' He sat back and stretched out his long legs. 'Do you live here alone, Merryn? I mean, no flatmates, fellow flight attendants or girlfriends?'

'No. I came into my parents' money when I was twenty-one, so I was able to buy this. Tom approved. He told me it would be a good investment as well as it being my own place. I guess I'm lucky to be— independent.'

He lifted an eyebrow. 'You deserved a bit of luck after losing them like that.'

'Perhaps.' She shrugged. 'You haven't told me why this place is very me.'

'Ah.' He sat back and looked around. 'Well, it's refined and discreet—there's a sort of harmony about it. And it's restful, but it's also…' he paused '…classy.'

She coloured faintly and wished she'd never asked.

'I'm surprised we've never met,' he said then.

'Met?' Her brows drew together.

'On a flight.'

'Oh. We probably will one day.'

His lips twitched. 'And you'll be able to treat me with firm, practised, distant courtesy.'

For some reason Merryn looked amused.

'You find that hard to visualise?' he suggested.

'Yes.' She couldn't resist smiling openly.

'That's better,' he murmured, almost as if to himself. 'Where would you like to have dinner?'

'Dinner? I...' She stared at him, arrested.

'Seeing as Sonia is not home, there's no reason for you to go back to cook is there?'

'No, but—'

'But me no buts, Miss Merryn. How about Riverside? We could take a ferry instead of driving round and having to find parking.'

Merryn paused. Riverside was a complex of restaurants and shops on the opposite bank, adjoining the Botanical Gardens and the Heritage Hotel. There was, as it happened, a ferry station within only minutes of her flat, and the trip upriver under the Story Bridge was short. And the ferries ran regularly.

'Well...'

'Why don't we really treat ourselves?' he suggested, and named a restaurant famed for its fine food that overlooked the river.

'We mightn't get in, and I'm not dressed for it,' Merryn responded.

'We could always give them a ring, and I'm sure you have some other clothes here,' he said gravely.

'But...' Her shoulders slumped.

'Just humour me in this, Merryn,' he said in a different voice after a moment.

Her eyes flew to his and she was shaken to see how serious he was. 'All right,' she said uncertainly.

He relaxed. 'That's my girl. Why don't you go and change? I'll give them a ring and watch the news while you do.'

Merryn closed herself once again into her bedroom and leant against the door bewilderedly. What had she missed? she wondered. Why had he changed moods so thoroughly and so quickly? Why had she told him something about herself that was not true? She bit her lip and pushed herself away from the door to go to her built-in wardrobe. There was not a lot left in it—most of her clothes were at Sonia's—but she examined the dresses remaining and then pulled an outfit out, knowing that it was the only one that would do for the ultra-chic restaurant.

Some time later she walked back into the lounge, and Brendan turned from the television to look at her.

The outfit was camellia-pink—a satin-backed crêpe vest that buttoned down the front and a short, straight skirt. She had patent leather little-heeled shoes to go with it and a matching patent purse with a silver chain shoulder-strap, and she'd pinned her hair back on one side with a white satin flower on a clip.

Brendan said nothing, however, as his hazel gaze roamed up and down her.

'Too dressy?' she asked after a full minute.

'No. Not at all.' He stood up and reached for his tie. 'When does the next ferry go?'

She looked at her watch. 'In ten minutes.'

'Good.' He knotted his tie and shrugged on his jacket. 'Shall we go?'

'Have…have you changed your mind?' Merryn heard herself say.

He looked at her enquiringly. 'What about?'

'Taking me out to dinner,' she said a little impatiently.

'No. Why should I?'

Merryn looked at him exasperatedly. 'I got the feeling the—the situation was no longer pleasing you.'

'Then you got it wrong, Merryn,' he said quietly.

But she stared up at him, unable to shake the conviction that things had changed again—only she couldn't say whether it was for the better or the worse.

CHAPTER SIX

THEY were both quiet on the short trip up the river.

The sun had set but the last of the daylight had turned the water into a mirror for the deepening violet sky. Lights were coming on in the tall buildings on the city side, etching the steel contours of the Story Bridge so that it looked as if it was set in a fairground. There was not a breath of breeze.

As they climbed the stone steps of the Riverside embankment Brendan said, 'Brisbane is looking its best. One forgets the charm of it.'

'I know,' replied Merryn. 'I often think it's just the right size for a city. Not too big, not too crowded.'

'And trimmed for Christmas.' He gestured towards some lights.

'Yes. Only three days to go.'

He took her elbow and ushered her into the restaurant. It seemed he was known as the head waiter sprang to attention and welcomed him by name, assuring them that they had one of the best tables. Because they were early there weren't many other diners, and as Merryn sat at a table by the window it crossed her mind that she was glad it was so—a bit of peace and candlelight mightn't come amiss.

They ordered, and a bottle of wine was brought. Merryn sipped hers, looking out over the river. Brendan seemed content to sit and watch her. And they stayed in that state of almost suspended animation until their first course had come and gone.

Then he said, 'I brought you here for a special reason, Merryn.'

Her eyes widened. 'Why?'

'I thought some neutral territory—and this has to be a particularly nice spot of neutral territory—as well as some fine food might take the tension out of affairs between us.'

'Did you?' she murmured, and picked up her wine glass.

'Yes,' he agreed wryly. 'I also thought it might be a nice spot to ask you to marry me.'

Her hand trembled and she spilt some wine, but fortunately only on the tablecloth. She put the glass down and blotted the wine with her napkin. 'Brendan—'

'Could you let me put my case first, Merryn?'

She stared at him, but he was watching a pulse that was beating rapidly in the glossy hollow at the base of her throat. Then he raised his eyes to hers and they were, if anything, sombre.

'I don't understand,' she said a little helplessly.

'I'm afraid that's my fault. I didn't understand either. You see, it was like knowing two different people—the old you and the new you. It was a while before I could merge them into the same person. And because I had always had a special place in my heart for the old you, my Miss Merryn, it was even more difficult.'

She pleated the damp napkin in her slim fingers and looked at him through her lashes. 'Are you trying to say you preferred the old me?'

'No. I'm saying that for most of the time you were like a beautiful stranger. Except when you offered me your concern. Then I had...' he paused and smiled—almost wearily, she thought '...these flashbacks.'

'When you remembered the mouse?'

'When I remembered the mouse,' he agreed. 'Then the two of you merged together and I was riddled with guilt because I knew then that I—wanted you. But I still didn't know how much.'

Merryn licked her lips.

He went on after a moment. 'I should have understood when the mere thought of you and Steve disturbed me unreasonably. I kept blaming him.' His lips twisted, 'But I would, I now know, have had the same difficulty with any man you may have chosen.'

'You...none of this struck you... I was twenty-one when we last met.' She stopped abruptly.

'If that's the admission I hope it is,' he said quietly, and put his hand over hers as she moved jerkily, 'I can only say that I must have been an incredible fool.'

'But...but...' She discovered that her tongue had a tendency to want to cleave to the roof of her mouth.

'Have a sip of wine,' he suggested.

She did so, and quietened a little.

'But?' he prompted presently.

'You didn't *say* or intimate any of this until after Michelle...' She stopped and gestured futilely.

'I did, as a matter of fact. You see, it was after Michelle's party that I—that things started to come clear to me. When the nameless kind of dissatisfaction with life that I was suffering from was no longer nameless. I found I could put a pretty accurate name to it—and add to it the name of a girl I couldn't get out of my mind or heart.'

'When?' she whispered. 'When did you tell me?'

'I tried to that day at Sanctuary Cove.'

Merryn gasped and her mind ranged back.

'I thought,' he said, and his eyes were compelling but with a touch of bleakness in their hazel depths, 'that if there was any…answering chord in your mind and heart, you would give me some indication.'

'I… I…' Merryn clasped her hands to her mouth.

'There was none,' he said gently. 'Only the kind of concern someone who had once valued me but in an entirely different way would show. Only the concern of a friend, never a lover… And I remembered that at Michelle's bloody party it had been the same.' He looked rueful. 'I thought that as a man who wanted you with an increasing hunger, and who was beginning to see that it would always be there, I might as well not exist for you. It had simply never entered your calculations.'

'Oh…' Merryn breathed incredulously.

'I also thought how well adjusted you were.' He fiddled with the stem of his wine glass with his tawny head bent for a time. 'And how maladjusted I was by comparison,' he said dryly. 'The last thing you needed in your life.'

'Your lobster, sir, madam!' the head waiter said, appearing at their sides with a flourish.

Merryn sat back as their meal was placed in front of them. Lobster Mornay in its pink shell, gleamingly coated in sauce, set on a bed of rice and accompanied by a dish of sautéd vegetables.

'I didn't *know,*' she said huskily, causing the waiter to look at her interrogatively. She closed her eyes and heard Brendan murmur something, and when she opened them they were alone.

'Don't let it get cold, Merryn,' he said quietly.

'I don't think I feel hungry now.'

'Yes, you do. Just try some.'

So she picked up her fork and of course it was delicious, but when she'd finished she pushed the platter away and said abruptly, 'Why are you telling me this now, Brendan?'

He thought for a moment. 'As opposed to yesterday afternoon?'

'Yes…'

'I didn't think you'd believe me. I thought you were embarrassed, furious—'

'I was, but…' She couldn't go on.

'Do you believe me now, Merryn?'

'I…don't you *care* about the things I said this afternoon? I saw—you looked shocked.'

He smiled slightly. 'As a matter of fact I admire you

very much for refusing to be kissed into submission. Admire you and love you for it,' he said very quietly.

'What about——?' She stopped.

'Being very experienced? Yes, it did shock me for a moment, then it dawned on me that I might have—angered you enough to make you toss that at me, or something like that. It...I didn't believe it, Merryn.'

'Because I lack...expertise?' she suggested.

'No.' His eyes softened. 'In fact what you brought to it was something so fresh and lovely it was worth far more than expertise.'

Merryn was silent, staring into his eyes, bemused.

And then he said quietly, 'Was I wrong?'

'About my being experienced? No, but...'

'You find it hard to believe I love you?'

'I—it seems so sudden.'

'Not really...' He hesitated. 'Unless it's a case of you discovering that something you thought you'd wanted for so long had only become a habit with you?'

She felt the colour steal into her cheeks and looked away.

'You can tell me, Merryn. I'm not foolish or egotistical enough to believe that because I've suddenly seen the light it must inevitably be the same for you.'

Her gaze swung back, and it shook her to see the painful query in his eyes.

'But perhaps I haven't put it adequately into words yet. Haven't told you,' he said softly, 'that when the two Merryns I knew merged into one person, it was the only answer that made sense to me.'

'Sense?' she whispered.

'Yes.' He sat back. 'All the turmoil ceased suddenly—all my inner turmoil, that is. Because whatever the outcome is, and however bad it will be to think of you with someone else, I've got my answer to the big question that was plaguing me. There was a woman for me, only I'd been too close, then too preoccupied to see how she grew up and brought all those attributes I'd loved when she was a child to the full flower of womanhood.'

Merryn discovered she was speechless.

'And that's something,' he went on, 'that will give me a kind of peace for the rest of my life. I'll always have you in my heart and on my mind, Merryn.'

They stared at each other, then slow tears brimmed and spilled down her cheeks, and she said, 'Please, could you take me home, Bren? I'm almost unbearably happy.'

The ferry was crowded this time, and they couldn't find seats. But she stood in the circle of his arms. And they walked hand in hand to her flat. Only when the door closed behind them did she say, 'I think I've loved you all my life, but I was so afraid when you knew at last that it was only pity—'

'Pity—no.' He pulled her into his arms. 'But hope, yes—deep, desperate hope. And the complete inability not to rush my fences... Merryn, darling, I've kissed you twice now, both times without your permission—'

'Yes, you may,' she murmured. 'In fact, if you don't, I shall die a little.'

He did.

It was a kiss that got out of hand, and when he stopped, breathing deeply and raggedly and looking at her with so much longing in his eyes, she took him by the hand and led him into her bedroom.

'We could wait until we're married, if you'd rather,' he said softly. 'By the way—will you marry me?'

'Of course. But, no, I don't think I can wait that long. There's just one thing.'

They hadn't turned on the light, but there was moonlight streaming in and laying a path of gold across the river. They were standing with their arms about each other's waists.

'What's that?' he asked.

'I'm not only *not* very experienced, I haven't ever slept with anyone.'

'Haven't you, my darling?' he said, so gently she caught her breath. Then he kissed her again and sat down on the end of the bed, pulling her down in his lap. 'There's nothing to be afraid of.'

'It wasn't because I was afraid of it,' she said. 'It's just that I couldn't imagine it with anyone but you.' She paused, then smiled a bit shakily up at him. 'I kept thinking that some day it would leave me, the way I felt about you, but it never did. Oh,' she said, and looked at him with a sudden glint of mischief in her eye, 'about Steve.'

'My nemesis—it was an invention?' he suggested.

'Yes. You see, I thought I was quite safe, coming home to look after Sonia. Then when you turned up out of the blue and all you could say was that I'd grown up—' she felt him tense, and touched his cheek with her fingertips, '—I decided to manufacture some self-defence. Little to know—'

'Little to know—' he took over '—how you were playing right into the family's hands, let alone Steve's?'

'Well, I did suspect that Steve—' She broke off and looked uncomfortable.

Brendan laughed quietly and laid his chin on her hair. 'He'll get over it—I'm sorry,' he added abruptly.

'What for?'

'How I hammered the "grown-up" bit. It might have been a bit of self-defence on my part—against the sheer shock of coming home to find that what I'd been looking for was right here on my own doorstep. But you didn't even seem to like me at times.'

She chuckled, and he tilted her chin and kissed her again.

'There's one thing I need to tell you,' he murmured when they drew apart. 'This lunch—this business lunch I had today was rather important.'

'Oh?' Merryn frowned.

'Yes. A while back an Australian engineering consultancy firm contacted me with a view to a merger. I knocked back the idea at the time, but I got in touch with them a couple of days ago to see if they were still interested. It seems they are. So—'

'Bren,' she interrupted urgently, 'you don't have to do—'

'Yes, I do. I'm coming home, my love.'

'What about the faraway places?' she asked, wide-eyed.

'They no longer have the appeal they did—although there'll be times when I'll have to go away. But it will be nothing like before. And that's something I wanted to ask you.'

'If *I* can give up the faraway places?'

He nodded.

Her mouth dimpled at the corners and she said, 'Perhaps. You could always take me with you. Until we start a family…'

And those were the last words she was to say for a while.

'When will we tell them?' she murmured, much later.

Their clothes were strewn on the floor and their love-making had been joyous and ardent.

He brushed the midnight swathe of her hair aside and kissed her bare shoulder lingeringly. She moved her naked body closer to his under the sheet and sighed, because it had been so right, so wonderful, and only hours ago she'd been in such despair.

'If I had my way—why the sigh?' he murmured, and ran his hands down her gently. 'All right?'

'Never righter,' she whispered. 'How about you?'

He held her extremely close. 'The same. Do you really believe you've got someone of your own now, Merryn?'

'Yes, Bren, I do.'

'When will we tell them?' he repeated, even later. 'If I had my way I'd spirit you off and dispense with telling them at all.'

'I know what you mean,' she said with a laugh in her voice, 'but we couldn't do that to Sonia.'

'No. She'll be so relieved. I feel as guilty as hell for putting her through— What is it?'

Merryn sat up. 'I've had an idea! You know, Sonia was never really happy about a cold Christmas dinner.'

'She wasn't?'

'No. I—well—I sort of forced it on her.'

'That doesn't sound like you, Merryn,' he murmured. 'Besides, it *is* more practical in this climate, and she is still slightly incapacitated with her hip.'

Merryn paused, then said with decision, 'All the same, I know in my heart she would really love to stick to what is a family tradition—I was the one who wanted to break it.'

Brendan pushed himself up on one elbow and stared into her eyes. 'Why?'

She considered, then said a little painfully, 'I didn't want to spend the day remembering other Christmases, with all the trimmings—and you.'

'Darling Merryn,' he said quietly, then pulled her into his arms. 'I'm *sorry*.'

'Bren,' she whispered, 'this makes up for—everything.'

'You're kinder than I deserve,' he said, after kissing her deeply and then lying back.

A glint of mischief lit her eyes. 'All the same, I'll need your help.'

'Oh?' He observed her pink-tipped breasts, her slender waist, the light in her grey eyes, then closed his eyes briefly and gave silent thanks. Then he said, 'Just tell me, my love—although I must warn you that cooking Christmas dinner is probably beyond me.'

Merryn grinned. 'I'll do the cooking, but I'll need your help with the shopping. And I'll particularly need your help to keep it a secret—I thought we could surprise Sonia. I think, after all we've put her through one way and another lately, she deserves a lovely surprise, and it solves the problem of her getting involved and overtiring herself. I can do a lot of it here anyway—if you'll cover for me.'

'Consider it done,' he said promptly. 'Just don't wear yourself out,' he warned, and drew her back into his arms. After a short, sweet interlude, he said, 'Only one thing remains to be resolved, then—when *will* we tell them?'

Merryn freed a hand and ran it through his hair. 'Why not make it a double surprise?'

The next days flew, and there were times when Merryn was tempted to regret her decision. Organising a large traditional dinner at the last minute entailed frenzied shopping amongst other last-minute frenzied shoppers. It entailed driving miles to track down fresh turkeys and also discovering that simple things like glacé cherries were in such demand they'd disappeared off the shelves, but by Christmas Eve it was all assembled in her flat.

'Are you sure you can do this?' Brendan asked, eyeing her over-laden kitchen counters.

'I'm going to do as much as I can tonight.' Sonia was spending Christmas Eve at Michelle's, where all her grandchildren were gathered.

'Can I stay?'

'Of course. You can even help—can you peel potatoes?'

'Probably—there are some things I'm much better at, though.'

'Oh?' She raised an eyebrow at him. 'I thought you said—'

'Such as this.' He removed the grater she had in her hand, set it down on top of a pile of onions and took her in his arms.

'Ah, this,' Merryn murmured.

'You agree?' he queried gravely, running his hands down her back, then linking them behind her neck.

'That you do it better than peeling potatoes?' She paused thoughtfully. 'Possibly.'

'You do know what you're courting with that temperate response, don't you, Miss Merryn?' he said with further gravity, although there was a wicked little light in the depths of his hazel eyes.

'A full…demonstration of how good you are?' she hazarded.

'Precisely,' he agreed.

'There's only one thing that bothers me about that, Bren.'

'Which is?'

'Just the thought of it may drive everything else, including the potatoes, from my mind.'

'Now that,' he said with deep satisfaction, 'is a very proper response, coming from a wife-to-be.'

'I'm glad you think so,' she responded demurely, and sighed heavily.

'And it never crossed your mind to make me feel very guilty at the same time?' he said softly then. 'Not to say to remind me that you will then have to be slaving away until all hours of the night?'

'Perish the thought.'

He laughed, cupped her face and kissed her lightly. 'Hand me the potato peeler—I can see that I will have to have my wits about me. Married to you, I mean.'

'On the other hand...' Merryn's lips curved '...after tomorrow you could take me away somewhere and— do whatever you like with me.'

'Now *that*,' he said, and kissed her again, 'is an offer too good to refuse!'

Christmas Day dawned bright and clear.

'Merryn, I feel dreadful about leaving you to do everything!' Sonia objected.

'There's not a lot to do,' Merryn replied, and crossed her fingers.

'All the more reason you should come with us!'

Merryn glanced at Brendan and he took over.

'You've got me to go to church with you and to visit less close members of the Grey clan,' he told his mother. 'Why don't you make the best of it? Don't forget Merryn will have to clear up after *this* gathering of the clan—shouldn't we let her have a bit of peace?'

'Oh, all right.' Sonia gave in and kissed Merryn, missing the wry look she and her son exchanged over her head. As soon as she heard the car pull out of the driveway Merryn took a deep breath and set to work again…

At midday Sonia returned, and sniffed the air. But right on cue the rest of the family arrived, and the presence of six excited children and one baby, whose first Christmas it was, distracted her. There was a great tearing open of the presents beneath the tree, then the play house was ceremoniously opened with a champagne wetting of the roof.

By one o'clock all thoughts were turning to food, and Sonia said, 'I thought we were eating outside, Merryn?' She eyed the verandah table, which was bare, and frowned suddenly.

'I had a change of plan,' Merryn said placidly. 'Why don't we all come inside?'

So Rox and Michelle gathered their children, tearing them away in some cases from the play house and pond, and they all trooped inside.

'I also thought we were eating outside,' Michelle said. 'And if you ask me it's much easier with the kids. Why else have a cold Christmas dinner—?'

'Beloved, hold thy tongue,' her brother recommended quietly, and opened the dining-room door with a flourish.

Everyone checked on the threshold, for it was a sight to behold. The big old table was laid with a lace cloth, there was a centrepiece of scarlet poinsettias and gold ribbon, the table was set with crystal and silver and beside each plate there were Christmas crackers and bon-bons. But what caused Sonia to blink and then to have tears in her eyes were two golden steaming turkeys and a magnificent ham, glazed and decorated with pineapple and cherries, beside dishes of roast potatoes and pumpkin, cauliflower, beans and peas. And on the sideboard was a wonderful Australian Christmas cream pudding, topped with glacé cherries and nuts...

'Merryn—oh, my dear!'

'Happy Christmas, darling,' Merryn said, and hugged her, and everyone—even Michelle—clapped.

'But how did you *do* it?' Sonia said as the feast got underway, crackers were pulled, silly hats were donned, trinkets examined and riddles read. 'Are you a magician?'

'No,' Merryn laughed. 'I had a lot of help from Bren—and by the way, all the other stuff I'd got in went to the Salvation Army.'

'Oh, what a brilliant idea—but what made you change your mind?' Sonia asked, still looking bewildered.

Merryn turned to Brendan, sitting on her other side, and he took her hand under the table and squeezed it gently. Then he stood up and clinked his glass with his knife.

'If I could have your attention,' he said as the hubbub subsided slowly, 'it's just occurred to me that I haven't given Merryn, who's worked so hard to achieve this hot, traditional Christmas dinner on such a hot Christmas Day, her present. I—'

'You don't have to make a speech about it, Bren!' Rox objected.

'Yes, I do, as it happens,' he countered. 'So—'

'You didn't make a speech about giving me mine, nice as it was,' Michelle put in with a grin. 'What I'd like to know is, who chose it?' She sipped some more wine and laughed rollickingly.

'Michelle,' Ray said seriously, 'do you think you're setting a good example to the kids? That's your fourth glass today.'

Here we go, Merryn thought, and it appeared as if Brendan felt the same, because he put his hand under her arm and helped her to her feet. Then he pulled a velvet box from his pocket, taking her as much by surprise as everyone else, drew a diamond solitaire from it and slipped it onto her finger. Then he kissed her thoroughly and leisurely to the tune of a stunned silence. Finally he turned to them all and said, 'Ladies and gentlemen, I'd like to drink a toast. To my wife-to-be.'

'I *knew* it. I was right all along!' Michelle was the first to speak, then she surged to her feet, holding her glass aloft, 'To Brendan and Merryn! May they have a long and happy life together.'

'How could we possibly go wrong now?' Brendan said wryly to Merryn.

EXPECTING

She's sexy, she's successful... and she's pregnant!

Relax and enjoy these new stories about spirited women and gorgeous men, whose passion results in pregnancies... sometimes unexpectedly! All the new parents-to-be will discover that the business of making babies brings with it the most special love of all....

Harlequin Presents® brings you one **EXPECTING!** book each month throughout 1999.
Look out for:

The Baby Secret by Helen Brooks
Harlequin Presents #2004, January 1999

Expectant Mistress by Sara Wood
Harlequin Presents #2010, February 1999

Dante's Twins by Catherine Spencer
Harlequin Presents #2016, March 1999

Available at your favorite retail outlet.

HARLEQUIN®
Makes any time special ™

Look us up on-line at: http://www.romance.net   HPEXP1

**Race to the altar—
Maxie, Darcy and Polly are**

The **HUSBAND** *Hunters*

in a fabulous new
Harlequin Presents® miniseries by

LYNNE GRAHAM

These three women have each been left a share of
their late godmother's estate—but only if they marry
withing a year and remain married for six months....

Maxie's story: **Married to a Mistress**
Harlequin Presents #2001, January 1999

Darcy's story: **The Vengeful Husband**
Harlequin Presents #2007, February 1999

Polly's story: **Contract Baby**
Harlequin Presents #2013, March 1999

Will they get to the altar in time?

Available in January, February and March 1999
wherever Harlequin books are sold.

HARLEQUIN®
Makes any time special ™

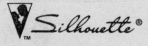